THE INTERLOPER

BY DAVE ZELTSERMAN

To fellow noir fan, Ron Clinton

THE HUNTED
PART ONE

CHAPTER 1

DAN WILLIS WATCHED through a pair of binoculars as his target left his house through a side door to collect the morning newspaper. The target was one Brian Schoefield. Age thirty-seven, average height, and carrying an extra sixty pounds that made him appear soft with fat sausage-like arms and legs. He wore a bathrobe and slippers, both worn and tattered, and Willis could make out that Schoefield also wore a stained tee shirt under his robe. Probably boxers, too, but that was only a guess on Willis's part. Overall, Schoefield had a pasty look about him.

It was nine fifty in the morning. Schoefield stopped to squint at the sun before moving cautiously to where his newspaper had been tossed. It was almost as if he knew he was being watched. Willis doubted that. More likely, Schoefield had just woken up. That was evident not only from his pasty look, but from the way the little hair Schoefield had left on his scalp was sticking up in disarray as if he had just rolled out of bed, which only added to his overall sloppy appearance.

Willis sat in a house three addresses down on the opposite side of the street. The house had been foreclosed four months earlier and still lay vacant. Like most of the houses on the street, it was mostly a dump. A small two-bedroom cape-style house that needed a lot of work, although not as much as Schoefield's house seemed to need, at least from the outside. Willis guessed the bank would probably end up knocking it down and building something bigger. That was probably the fate of most of the houses on the street.

With the blind down and open only a crack, Willis wouldn't be able to be seen in the second floor bedroom where he was camped out. He'd arrived at six AM with only a folding chair, a thermos of coffee, and a bag of donuts. He'd waited patiently since for his target to show. Half of the coffee had been drunk and three of the donuts eaten. He knew he should've brought healthier food, that the donuts would only make him sluggish and slow him down later, although that wouldn't matter. Today was only for surveillance.

If the assignment had been marked as a homicide, Willis would've been done already. From that distance, he would've had no problem putting a bullet through Schoefield's skull. But Schoefield had been marked for an accidental death. Those were trickier, which meant that the assignment was going to take more time and require more surveillance. Suicides were even trickier. Natural causes were the easiest. With the drugs he had access to, Willis could usually get those assignments done within a day. He preferred them and not just because of the four-thousand-dollar bonus he would receive for jobs done in less than a week. With natural deaths, he could usually inject his targets while they slept and they'd never have to know they were being terminated. Even though his targets were enemies of the state, Willis preferred peaceful deaths. He derived no pleasure from the fear and pain he forced some of his targets to suffer.

Schoefield hesitated for a moment to look around before he reached down to pick up the newspaper. The actions of a guilty conscience, Willis thought, his lips pressing into a grim smile. Once Schoefield had his paper, he moved back to his house and disappeared inside. Only then did Willis allow himself the luxury to move from his post so he could stretch out his legs and arms, all of which were stiff from his almost four hours of silent vigil.

Dan Willis was forty-two. Six feet two inches, a hundred ninety pounds, he had a rangy build with long and muscular arms corded with thick veins; his powerful hands even more so. His face was long, rough-hewn; his eyes slate gray and heavily lidded, his nose thick and revealing several bumps and bends as a lifelong reminder from his amateur boxing days when he was a teenager. Willis's hair was still mostly black, peppered only slightly with gray, and was kept short. While he had shaved earlier that morning, he was someone who would never look clean-shaven. Even at that early hour, he already had a pronounced five o'clock shadow. He wasn't what anyone would consider handsome, but he never had any trouble with the ladies, at least before he took the job with The Factory. Since then, he hadn't had much interest. The last time he'd been with a woman was thirteen months ago.

After allowing himself the luxury of stretching for as much as sixty seconds, Willis returned to his chair to continue his surveillance.

CHAPTER 2

DAN WILLIS JOINED the U.S. Army after finishing high school and was assigned to Military Intelligence. While he didn't kill anyone directly, he knew his actions contributed to dozens of Iraqi hostile deaths, if not more, during the first Gulf War. After three tours, he decided the army wasn't for him, and when he left it was with the rank of Sergeant, although he probably would've made Staff Sergeant if he had signed up for another tour. He next tried college, and after two years decided that wasn't for him either. Without too much difficulty, he found a job as a salesman for a liquor distributor in his hometown of Akron, Ohio, and discovered that he was good at it. He easily developed a good rapport with his customers who were buyers for liquor stores, bars, and restaurants, and he did well. The life appealed to him. He made decent money. He met interesting characters as well as plenty of attractive women to flirt with and some to have affairs with, and he made sure none of them ended badly. After fourteen years with his sales still going strong, his supervisor called him in to tell him he was out of a job. The powers that be decided that they were going to automate customer ordering through their website, and so they were going to let their sales force go.

"You're making a mistake," Willis said. "My customers like me, and without me pushing our brands you're going to see orders drop by at least a third, probably more than that."

His supervisor was Tony Manzoni. A thick bull of a man who ignored the smoking ban in the workplace and always kept a lit stogie between his lips. He grunted out in agreement.

"You're preaching to the choir," Manzoni said. "But it ain't my call."

Willis nodded, understanding that Manzoni's hands were tied. "You got anything for me?" he asked. "Delivery, maybe something in the office?"

Manzoni shook his head slowly, ash dropping off the tip of his cigar. "Nothing. I'm sorry, Willis. But I got to let all you guys go. Brass ain't giving me any options here."

At first, Willis wasn't concerned. With his rep, he was mostly convinced he'd get another job with a competing distributor, but it was late 2012 and with the national employment holding steady at ten percent for over four years, he found that wasn't the case. Worse, it seemed to be a growing trend with many of these distributors to axe their sales force in favor of automating orders online. Willis spent his first month contacting distributors throughout the country without any luck. While he would've liked to have stayed in Akron where he had built up solid contacts, what really mattered to him was finding a job. In a way, he was lucky. He had never married, his expenses were low, and he had saved some money. After three months of striking out with other distributors and seeing his funds shrink, he realized he was going to have to get a job in another industry, but still held out hope that he'd be able to transfer his sales experience and line something up. With each successive month of unemployment he felt less sure of that. After eleven months of being out of work and piling up debts that he knew he'd never get out from under, he considered either suicide or robbing banks, and was torn over which one. That was when he got a call. The man calling identified himself as Colonel Jay T. Richardson, and asked whether Willis still considered himself a patriot.

"I see you're an ex-Army guy," Richardson said with a heavy Southern drawl which Willis couldn't quite place. Maybe South Carolina. Maybe West Virginia. "According to your records you served two years in the Gulf where you did a fine job defending your country. My question to you, Mr. Willis, is whether you'd still be willing to do the hard work necessary for your country's sake?"

"Why are you asking me that?"

"'Cause, Mr. Willis, our country needs men like you right now, and if you're willing, we'd sure like to discuss the matter with you."

Richardson refused to talk more about what the job entailed, but Willis agreed to be flown down to Virginia and be interviewed. Richardson transferred the call to his secretary who then filled Willis in on the details. The interview process would be a five-day ordeal and Willis was not allowed to mention the interview to anyone, was not to bring a cell phone with him and, further, was not to bring any device that provided GPS tracking—that he'd be searched and if he violated these terms he'd be sent back home. Willis agreed, and the secretary booked him on a flight leaving the next morning.

When Willis arrived at Norfolk International Airport in Virginia, he was met at the gate, then taken to a room where they searched him as they'd promised. After that, they put him in a van filled with other candidates and whose windows had been blacked out so they couldn't be seen out of. The candidates had been warned not to talk to each other; that if they did they'd be disqualified. And so, for the three-and-a-half-hour van ride, they all sat quietly without a single word being spoken. When they arrived, they were taken for physicals and fitness tests. A few of the candidates washed out. After that, they were separated. Willis was taken for a psychological evaluation.

With the questions they were asking, Willis figured out quickly that what they were really after was knowing how he'd react if he'd have to take a life or see people die, so he lied and gave them the answers that he knew they were after, which were basically making him look like a cold-blooded sociopath. He must've passed their psychological evaluation, because next came the lie detector test. Willis knew that for the most part they didn't care about his answers and were after whether they could get a clear true-false reading from him. If the polygraph results were fuzzy, he'd be eliminated from further consideration. Of course, if he revealed something alarming to them he'd also be eliminated, but what they really wanted to know was whether they'd be able to plug him in at any time in the future and be guaranteed an accurate reading. Willis was able to relax enough to pass the test. Once the polygraph test finished, he was done with his second day of testing.

Starting on day three was what Willis could only figure

was an IQ test. For two days they threw problems and puzzles at him, and put him under severe time pressure to solve them, often with a lot of background noise and other distractions. It was tiring, but Willis held up during the testing, and must've passed because they didn't send him home at the end of day four. It was on day five that he met with Colonel Jay T. Richardson. Up until that point, nobody had told him what the job was that he was interviewing for. He had his ideas, but they were only guesses.

Richardson was in his sixties. Built like a fireplug, he had thick silver hair cut like a bristle brush and a red face that wrinkled like a beagle's when he smiled or scowled. At first, he sat scowling at Willis, and kept that up for a good minute before signaling for Willis to take a seat. The two men were alone with Richardson seated behind his desk. Willis took the chair across from him.

"Son, what I'm about to tell you is highly classified. You know that, don't you?" Richardson said, still scowling deeply.

Willis knew that and confirmed that he knew it. Before the process started, he had to sign disclaimers acknowledging he'd be under the threat of treason if he ever mentioned a word about the place or anything he had learned.

Richardson nodded and leaned forward, his scowl weakening. "What I'm about to tell you will shock you," he said with a sincere gravity. "Our country has been overrun by insurgents. These are everyday people like you and me who have been indoctrinated and are now hell-bent on destroying us. We're at war, son, and like it or not we're fighting for our very lives."

Richardson's lips pressed tightly together, his red face turning a bit redder, his eyes glistening with anger. "The problem is that while we've been able to identify who they are and what their objective is, it would be a severe security breach if this were to leak to the public. Because of that, Congress created a new department, Homeland Protection, of which I'm a part of."

Willis had never heard of a Homeland Protection department, but he didn't doubt that what Richardson was telling him was the truth.

"We need foot soldiers, son," Richardson continued. "This is maybe the most important war this country will ever fight, but it's not going to be easy. It's going to involve great personal sacrifice and you'd be doing assignments that you might find unpleasant. But they're necessary. Are you interested, Willis?"

"How's the pay?"

Richardson smiled at that. "The pay's good," he said. "Better than what you were making peddling liquor. And the job security will be even better."

Richardson explained more about Homeland Protection and the job he was offering Willis, which was to be one of over four thousand new foot soldiers against the new hidden menace, soldiers whose existence would never be able to be acknowledged by the government. The problem was that while they were able to identify the insurgents, they didn't have enough evidence to round them up or prosecute them, so Congress gave Richardson and Homeland Protection extraordinary powers to deal with the insidious and imminent threat to the country's survival. Before getting Richardson's call, Willis had been a coin flip away from either blowing his own brains out or committing crimes that could've resulted in innocent lives being taken. He accepted the job with little hesitation. He needed a paycheck and any kind of steady work, and the signing bonus they were offering would get him out of debt. He decided he'd be able to reconcile the job requirements with knowing that he was protecting his country.

Over the next three months, Willis went through extensive training with a squad of forty-seven other new hires. It was weird and very different than his army training. The rules were no communication among each other, so, while he was part of a squad, everything he did was in isolation with any sense of camaraderie banished. During those three months, Willis learned efficient ways to kill, stage fake suicides, and cover up murders so they'd appear to be accidental deaths. Firearms were his strength, as well as hand-to-hand fighting. Back when he was in the army, Willis could've been a sniper, he was that good with a rifle.

Upon completion of his training, Willis was assigned to the Boston area. His only contact was going to be his immediate handler, a man whom he would know as Barry, and who he would only have a phone number for. Barry would monitor Willis's performance and would provide support as necessary, such as intel and access to weapons and drugs. The Factory, the name of his division of Homeland Protection—which he surmised was short for The Death Factory—had some sway with the local authorities. While Barry couldn't have a murder covered up, he could sometimes arrange for a lower police presence in a certain area and other such things, which could make Willis's job easier if he planned ahead properly.

During the time that Willis had been actively working for The Factory, he had eliminated twenty-three targets. Brian Schoefield was to be number twenty-four.

CHAPTER 3

SCHOEFIELD LEFT HIS house an hour and ten minutes later. He had that same cautious look as he made his way to his car, again seeming as if he knew he was being watched. Willis didn't believe that was the case, but even if Schoefield knew he was under surveillance, Willis didn't much care. After Schoefield drove off, Willis used the opportunity to relieve himself and then slipped out the back entrance so he could walk to where he had left his car three blocks away. He wasn't in any hurry. Since he had planted a tracking device on the undercarriage of Schoefield's car, he'd have no problem finding where Schoefield was heading to.

It turned out Schoefield drove to a nearby coffee shop downtown. Willis was able to spot Schoefield through the window as he sat alone engrossed in his newspaper, a large coffee on the table next to him. Willis could've set up surveillance to see whether Schoefield was meeting anyone, but he guessed it wasn't the case, and instead drove back to Schoefield's house.

He already knew from Barry that Schoefield didn't have an

alarm system. If he did have one, the odds were Barry would've been able to get Willis the security code to disable it. The locks on the house were decent, but it still didn't take Willis much effort to break in using his burglar picks.

Willis was surprised at how clean and well kept up the inside of the house was, especially given the disrepair of the exterior. The house was a small two-bedroom ranch, but it had a pleasant feel inside, and while it seemed decorated by a woman's touch, Willis saw no clear evidence that Schoefield had ever been married; at least there were no photos of children on display, or alimony or child support bills.

Willis started in the kitchen as he searched through any mail or papers he could find, then moved to the living room, and finally Schoefield's two bedrooms, the second of which had been set up as an office. What Willis was doing represented a breach of protocol since he wasn't there to figure out a way to kill his target, but instead to satisfy his own curiosity. It was just hard to believe that the sad sack he'd been observing was an insurgent, but then again he felt that way with almost all his targets. As Richardson told him, these were people who looked and acted like anyone, and in many cases, natural born citizens who had been indoctrinated into the insurgency. Still, the assignments had been nagging at Willis, and with Schoefield he wanted to see the evidence himself. After going through Schoefield's file cabinets, he still hadn't found anything unusual. What did stand out was that Schoefield had his computer password protected. Why would anyone password protect their computer inside their own home? Willis considered making it look like a home burglary so he could take the computer and have someone crack into it and find the evidence that Schoefield was a traitor, but he couldn't think of how he could explain the need to steal Schoefield's computer to Barry. It probably would only put him in deep trouble with The Factory. A beep alerted Willis that Schoefield's car was on the move. He'd been in Schoefield's house for almost two hours with nothing gained. He cleaned up any evidence that he'd been there and left through the back door. After that, he made his way back to his surveillance post. The GPS tracking unit indicated that Schoefield was heading back home. If he ended up going someplace else instead Willis would track him down.

CHAPTER 4

AFTER FIVE DAYS of surveillance Willis had Schoefield's routine mapped out. He'd wake up between nine thirty and nine fifty, pick up the newspaper from his driveway, then leave his house an hour later so he could sit anywhere from an hour and a half to two hours in the coffee shop by himself reading his newspapers while lingering over a large coffee. When he'd return from the coffee shop, he'd stay holed up inside of his house until around seven o'clock when he would head off to a local bar where he'd watch the Red Sox while stretching out two beers so they'd last most of the evening before heading home. By all appearances a loner, although from the time he spent at the coffee shop and the local bar, he wasn't necessarily a loner by choice.

Of course, Schoefield could've been at those locations each day awaiting contact from the insurgency, but Willis couldn't shake the thought that all Schoefield was was a sad little man and not part of any terrorist or revolutionary organization. He had dug as much as he could into Schoefield's background, and what he found was an ordinary, middle-class life. Schoefield had majored in computer science in college, and after graduation worked as a programmer for an insurance company until being laid off four months ago. No arrests, no unusual political activity, nothing to signal Schoefield as a terrorist in the making. Willis had been warned about that—that the insurgents were keeping low profiles until it was time to strike, but still, Willis had a nagging feeling that they had made a mistake with Schoefield, although there were other factors that pointed to something being wrong about him, such as his wariness each morning when leaving his house and his keeping his home computer password protected.

Willis could have gotten the job done in less than a week, but he kept his surveillance going and let his bonus slip away. Something felt very wrong. Almost all the jobs had felt wrong, but this one in particular. Or maybe it felt no more wrong than any of the others, but he'd finally reached a point where he couldn't keep on doing the work on blind faith: he needed to see some evidence of the insurgence. He had two days left in his deadline when Barry—if that was even his supervisor's real name—called to warn him that his deadline was quickly approaching. If Barry was his real name, Willis didn't have a clue whether it was his first name or last. Most likely it was a code name. Whichever it was, that was the first time Barry had called him worried about whether Willis would get his job done on time, but it was also the first time Willis had let himself come so close to a deadline.

"I wouldn't have thought that this assignment would be as challenging as you seem to be making it," Barry opined good-naturedly, but his voice contained a hint of sarcasm. Willis so far hadn't been able to place the accent, but if he had to bet he'd go with upstate New York. It certainly wasn't Boston.

"I'm being cautious with it," Willis said, keeping his own voice flat. "If you had marked him as a homicide, it would've already been done."

"But you will make your deadline?"

"I'll make it."

"Good. Make sure you do."

Willis knew that if he failed to, he'd get a reprimand, and while they had never told him directly, he was pretty sure that The Factory only allowed their field workers one reprimand.

Barry was about to end the call when Willis asked whether Schoefield could be a mistake.

"We don't make mistakes," Barry said, coldly.

"He doesn't seem like he's one of them."

"None of them are going to seem like they're one of them. That's the point. You've been through the training, you should know that, Willis." There was a long pause before Barry asked whether Willis had broken protocol with his latest target, a distinctive chill now in his voice.

"Of course not," Willis said. He knew Barry was recording the conversation so he could run it through voice stress analysis software as a way to perform a crude lie detector test, but Willis had taken the precaution ten months earlier of loading voice stress analysis software on his laptop and training himself to lie effectively, and it turned out to be not nearly as hard as he would've thought.

"See that you get this assignment done on time," Barry said curtly, then ended the call. If Barry's own voice stress analysis software showed that Willis was possibly lying, Willis would be receiving another phone call and there would be more questions.

CHAPTER 5

THURSDAY EVENING AT eight thirty, Schoefield sat alone at the bar watching the Red Sox game. Willis watched from across the street while hidden in the shadows of an empty storefront's doorway. Schoefield had been sitting alone in the bar for almost an hour, still nursing the same beer he bought when he first showed up. It was the last day of Willis's deadline. He checked the time, left the doorway, headed to the bar, and took a barstool so there was one empty one between him and Schoefield. There were seven other people scattered around at tables and a couple sitting at the other end of the bar, but that was it outside of Schoefield, a bored and sullen-looking waitress, and the bartender. While being seen in a public place with a target was frowned upon by The Factory, it was allowed if it was deemed necessary for the job.

Willis ordered a beer and grabbed a handful of peanuts from a bowl. When the Red Sox third baseman booted a ball he should've made a play on, Willis made a wisecrack and with a tight grin etched on his face shook his head with disgust, shooting Schoefield a 'what are you gonna do' kind of look. When Willis was a kid, he was a Cleveland Indians fan, but it had been a long time since he cared about baseball, and he certainly couldn't care less about the Red Sox, but he could play the part of a long-suffering fan. Schoefield murmured out something in agreement, but kept his focus on the TV. After some more well-timed wisecracks and banter on Willis's part, Schoefield loosened up a bit and joined in. Willis held out his hand and introduced himself to Schoefield giving him a fake name while Schoefield gave him his real name.

Willis moved over to the barstool next to Schoefield and bought his new buddy a beer, which was going to be the first of eight beers he was going to be buying Schoefield, and there would also be five shots of whiskey. Willis made sure to keep himself at half the number of drinks he was buying Schoefield. At first, Schoefield nursed the drinks Willis bought him, but as Willis egged him into making drinking bets on the game, Schoefield was soon pouring the booze down. At first, their conversation was kept superficially on the Red Sox and other Boston sports teams, which while Willis had no interest in he could fake well enough, but after an hour or so of free beers and shots of whiskey, Schoefield needed only minor prodding from Willis to recite his life story; the number of times his heart had been broken by different girls, his fifteen years working as a computer programmer, and how recently he'd been laid off when his company decided to transfer the work to an outsourcing firm in Pakistan. At that point, bitterness had crept deep into Schoefield's voice, and his mouth contorted as if he had bit into an overly sour lemon.

"All of us became disposable," he said, somewhat slurring

his words. "They could get the work done for thirty cents on the dollar for what they were paying us." He muttered into his beer, "They just threw us away."

"Bastards," Willis said.

Schoefield nodded dully. "It's the way this country's been going. The rich just keep getting richer while the rest of us keep getting more and more fucked." He paused for a moment before adding, "There's going to have to be a change." Another long pause, then barely a whisper, "If I had a rocket launcher."

"What?"

"If I had a rocket launcher. Some son of a bitch would die."

"What the hell are you talking about?"

Schoefield smiled broadly, the sheen glazing his eyes showing that he was drunk. "Never mind," he said. "Just reciting from an old Bruce Cockburn song. But fuck, a lot of truth in that old song."

That was what Willis needed to hear. It took almost two hours of loosening Schoefield up with booze, but he finally got what he needed. He looked at Schoefield sitting hunched on his barstool feeling sorry for himself as he rolled an empty beer mug between his two chubby hands and stared blankly with eyes that held nothing but contempt.

"You need some cheering up," Willis offered. "Why don't we both get laid? That should cheer me up, and I'm guessing it would sure the fuck cheer you up, too. What do you say?"

A nasty glint broke through Schoefield's glazed eyes as he smiled thinly at Willis. "I don't swing that way," he said. "Sorry if I gave you the wrong impression."

"I don't either, you dummy," Willis said. "I'm talking about leaving this dump and finding us a couple of willing ladies. What do you say?"

Schoefield thought about it, but shook his head. "I'm not exactly the type that any girl wants to have a one-night stand with," he admitted, his smile turning glum.

"Don't worry about it," Willis said with a wink. "The place I'm thinking about, we'll have no problem finding ladies raring to go. And nice ones, too. I'll be able to hook you up. Guaranteed. Come on, let's get out of here."

Willis paid up his tab, then signaled for Schoefield to follow him. Schoefield didn't seem entirely convinced that Willis would be able to follow through as promised and find a girl willing to spend the night with him, but the prospect of it was too enticing for him not to try. He stumbled on after Willis. When they got outside, Willis told Schoefield he'd better drive. Schoefield, smiling dumbly, pointed out that they were standing right in front of his car, which, of course, was no surprise to Willis. He handed his keys to Willis who got behind the wheel while Schoefield plopped himself down into the passenger seat.

Willis drove three towns over to a more industrial area. A darker, seedier area. Schoefield didn't seem to notice, and instead spent the time telling Willis more stories of his failed love life and how badly he always struck out in the past at bars and nightclubs, with the obvious eagerness building in him that that night would be different. Willis didn't bother responding, nor even listening anymore. Schoefield's voice had become little more than a mosquito's hum as far as he was concerned. The time for talking was done. Schoefield had nothing left to say that he cared to hear.

When Willis pulled over, it was an area where he had busted

the streetlights earlier that morning. There was barely enough light from the moon for them to see where they were going. Willis pointed out the steep cement steps they needed to go down to get to the street below them. "The club is down there," he said. "Parking over there is impossible, but easy enough up here."

That made enough sense to Schoefield not to argue the point, and Willis let him lead the way. When they got to the stairs, Willis picked up the brick that he had left there when he had broken the streetlights. He held it in his right hand, but before he used it he asked Schoefield why he sold out his country.

"What the fuck are you talking about?" Schoefield started, his voice surly, argumentative, like every other drunk who wants to pick a fight. Willis didn't need to hear his answer. He had already heard enough earlier to satisfy him. He hit Schoefield with the brick hard enough to cave his skull in, and watched as Schoefield's body crumpled forward and tumbled down the cement steps. There was no reason for Willis to check that his target was dead, not with the way Schoefield's body lay positioned at the bottom of the steps.

Still carrying the brick, Willis went back to Schoefield's car to wipe off any fingerprints and to leave Schoefield's keys in the ignition. He waited until he walked three blocks away before he dumped the brick he'd used into a sewer. Five blocks away he found the car that he earlier had arranged to be there. He waited until he was driving out of that area before calling Barry and leaving a message that Schoefield had gotten drunk and ended up stumbling and falling down a staircase, with cause of death being either a caved in skull or a broken neck. That any autopsy done would confirm that finding. Willis knew from his training at The Factory that a medical examiner would accept that the damage done to Schoefield's skull was caused by the cement steps.

Before Willis arrived back at his apartment, Barry called him to tell him about his next assignment.

"I was hoping to put in for a vacation," Willis said. "I could use some R and R."

"No rest for the weary," Barry said coldly. "It can't be helped. This is a war we're fighting, Willis." His tone turned conspiratorial as he added, "And we both know you took almost two weeks off with this last one." The line appeared to go dead for a long moment, long enough that Willis thought he had lost the connection, but Barry came back and told him he could have his vacation after he finished two more assignments. "But try not to slack on these, okay?"

Barry ended the call without another word or giving Willis any details on his next assignment. He wouldn't have to. The next one would be on a secure message board. The Factory didn't want any paper trails, so Willis would have to memorize the details from the message board. It was against Factory protocols for him to print it out or write any of it down. After Willis disconnected from the message board, the information regarding his assignment would disappear into the ether. The Factory made damn sure nothing could get back to them. Willis couldn't much blame them. If he ever screwed up one of these assignments and was caught by the police, he'd be on his own.

CHAPTER 6

WILLIS TOOK THE next four days off anyway. His next assignment had been marked as a murder. After he checked the satellite photos of the target's home using Google Earth, he felt confident that he'd be able to get the job done in less than a week despite taking an impromptu vacation, so he'd still be able to earn his bonus and keep Barry off his back.

He decided to spend those four days at the beach, but the problem was he couldn't relax, not with the assignment hanging over his head, and also not while expecting Barry to call to break his balls. He knew his badge had a tracking chip implanted in it and that Barry had to have the GPS coordinates of where he was. But if Barry were to call him to complain, he'd be giving away that fact, which he probably wouldn't want to do. Besides, unless he had another field agent watching the target, he'd have to accept Willis's explanation that he had only followed the target to the beach resort as part of his surveillance.

Each of those four days at the ocean turned out to be joyless days. He was too anxious to do something as simple as lie back and enjoy the sun, and his mind raced too much to make sense of the paperback book he tried reading. Even the sight of all the young girls in bikinis did nothing for him. That bothered him more than anything else. Ever since getting involved with The Factory, he'd lost all interest there. His second night playing hooky, he went to a strip club, and again found nothing of interest. Surrounded by naked, gyrating women, and not even a stirring. It worried him for most of his time while at the club until he decided to put it out of his mind.

He felt a sense of relief after ending his unofficial four-day vacation, and he spent the next morning hidden in the woods across from his target's home. He found a spot about a hundred yards away where he could rest the rifle barrel against a log and have a clear view of the target's front door. With a dark blanket underneath him and branches covering him, he was well camouflaged, and as soon as his target stepped outside, Willis would be able to track him through his rifle's scope and explode his target's head the same as if it were a pumpkin. The assignment would be quick and easy. One rifle shot and he would be done.

Willis had been maintaining his vigil since five AM. At six thirty, his target emerged from the house wearing a tee shirt, shorts, and running shoes, and scooting out with him was a mostly white bull terrier with a few smudges of black on his ears. As the dog stepped outside, he sniffed a couple of times in Willis's direction and then scampered off towards him. Probably thinking the dog was running off after an animal, the target shouted at his dog, directing the bull terrier to get back to him. After a few reluctant growls, the dog scampered back to his owner's side.

None of that was why Willis had relaxed the pressure he'd been applying to the trigger. A thought had been gnawing at the back of his mind, something he couldn't quite get a firm grip on, and as he had lined up his target in the rifle scope, he realized what it was. When he had earlier seen his target's photo, the man had seemed vaguely familiar, and now Willis knew why. The target had been one of the candidates that had ridden in the van with Willis when he was driven to The Factory for his interview. He didn't remember seeing him afterwards. The target certainly hadn't been part of Willis's silent training squad. Since talking wasn't allowed among the candidates, Willis hadn't earlier heard the target's name or anything about him.

Willis removed his finger from the rifle trigger. He needed to know which one it was—whether his target was a traitor who had almost infiltrated The Factory, or if he was a field worker, like Willis, who was now tagged for termination. It was possible the man washed out during the interview process, but it was also possible that he had been assigned to another training squad. That Willis hadn't seen him again during his three-month training program didn't mean that the man wasn't currently connected to The Factory.

Willis's target was like a leaner and better-looking version of himself. Two years younger than Willis, same height, and about twenty pounds lighter. His name was Mark Foley and he had the same similar rough features that Willis had. Willis watched as Foley and his bull terrier jogged out of sight, then pushed away the branches that were covering him, grabbed the blanket he'd been using, and fixed the area to erase any evidence that he'd been there. Then he moved further back into the woods so there would be less chance of that bull terrier sniffing him out. He wanted to time Foley's run.

CHAPTER 7

WILLIS RETURNED EARLY the next morning to the woods outside of Foley's house, setting up further back. Like the previous morning, his target left the house at six thirty to go on his morning run with his bull terrier. This time, Willis had set up deep enough into the woods where he had to use binoculars, and while the bull terrier let out a couple of grunting-like barks, he made no attempt to take off in Willis's direction. Once Foley and his dog were out of sight, Willis approached the house. The other day, Willis had tried researching his target's background and found precious little about him online other than a résumé that had been posted four months earlier. All Willis could glean from that was that Foley held his last position for nine months before being laid off four months ago, and that he had been working as an account executive for an advertising agency.

The Factory never included background information on their targets. Only a name, a photo, an address, and whether the target lived alone or not. Most of the time, although not always, they provided security alarm information. According to what they had posted on the bulletin board for Foley, he lived alone, which was inadequate. They should've known about the dog so they could've warned Willis about it. If they missed that, it was possible they could also have missed a new girlfriend or other recent overnight company. Willis was careful not to make any noise as he used his burglar picks to break into Foley's house. He saw that Foley's security alarm had been activated. He used the code that The Factory had provided and that did the trick in disarming it. The fact that the alarm had been set meant no one else was there, but Willis still moved quietly until he verified that. Then he went about looking for evidence that would indicate whether Foley was an insurgent who needed to be eliminated or a Factory field agent that needed retiring. While he found out that Foley was divorced and paying child support to his ex who now lived on the other side of the country and that Foley had served in the Marines, he didn't find anything to answer the big question. It didn't surprise him that Foley was ex-military. He expected that The Factory recruited mostly ex-military. He also found Foley's day planner and noted the time and location of a meeting that Foley had scheduled in two days.

Yesterday, Foley had been gone for an hour and fifteen minutes for his run—if that was what he was really doing. It was possible that he was instead meeting a contact with the insurgency. Whichever it was, Willis was giving himself forty-five minutes to search the house and then he'd get out of there, and when his watch buzzed him that his time had expired, he reset the security alarm and left the house. He didn't bother going back into the woods. If Foley was running the same route as the other day, Willis would be able to watch him from his car.

*

Willis spent the next day watching Foley without learning anything. He could've ended things easily by waiting in the woods with his rifle and blowing Foley's head off as he went for his morning run, but he didn't do it. He gave himself the excuse that he wanted to get the truth out of Foley, find out which it was with him. But if it was just that, Willis could've slipped into Foley's house when the man went on his run, then put the dog down when they returned and have plenty of time to interrogate his target. But he didn't do that either. Instead, he chose a much riskier and more difficult plan, and one where he'd be throwing away his bonus. He didn't understand why he was doing that. He wasn't one for sentiment. So what was it? Why was he so reluctant to kill a man's dog in front of him?

The following day while Willis drove to the location so he could carry out his plan, he cursed himself out for the harebrained scheme he had settled on. He swore to himself that he wasn't going to take any chances. If any glitches showed up, he'd abandon the plan and take care of his assignment the smart way by waiting inside the target's home the next morning for when Foley and his bull terrier would return from their early morning run. Since he knew about Foley's scheduled appointment, both the time and place it would be, he was able to make a good guess on the route that Foley would drive. He had scoped out the area and found a more or less deserted stretch along that route that was made up of abandoned warehouses. Once he got to that deserted area, he pulled over and waited for Foley. If

Foley drove by and there was no other traffic, Willis would go through with his harebrained scheme. If Foley took a different route, then that would be that and Willis would have to take care of the matter the next day.

Willis sat anxiously for twenty minutes, cursing some more for the sentimentality he was showing. Time was running out. If Foley was keeping his appointment and driving along the route Willis expected him to, he should've been there already. Willis was right about how deserted the area was. In the twenty minutes he'd been camped out there, only eight other cars had passed him. He was about to give up when he spotted Foley's car in his rearview mirror.

Willis swung into action then, pulling away from the curb as Foley passed him, then gunning the engine so he could catch up to Foley and force him off the road and onto a side street. The street was even more desolate than the main drag with only boarded up factory buildings with shattered windows, leading to a dead end. Foley had to swing the front end of his car onto a sidewalk littered with garbage and broken glass to keep from being hit. Willis angled his car behind Foley's to keep him boxed in.

They both left their cars at the same moment, Foley's door slamming shut, Willis's closing quietly. Foley was hot under the collar and too angry to realize what was happening and that he was already little more than a dead man. With his right hand clenched into a fist, he took two steps towards Willis, shouting, "What the fuck is your problem?" Then he stopped as he noticed the tire iron Willis held. He started smirking then as if he thought it was only a robbery and the joke would be on Willis when he saw how little money he had, but the smirk died quickly. Just as Willis had recognized him the other day through the end of a rifle scope, Foley must've realized why Willis looked familiar and where he had seen him before. Almost as if a switch had been thrown, his color paled. In a scared, panicky way he looked around and realized he was trapped with buildings on both sides and behind him and Willis in front of him. For an instant, it looked like he was going to try running or fighting, but then his eyes deadened and he stood glumly with his shoulders slumping. Without much to his voice he asked Willis what he was waiting for.

"Are you working for The Factory?" Willis asked.

Foley laughed. It was a weak laugh, not much to it. "I don't get it," he said. "Why me?" His eyes shifted away from Willis and his head lowered as if he were waiting for the executioner's blow.

"Why?" Willis demanded. "Because either you're a traitor or you're one of us and you screwed up badly. Which is it?"

Foley shook his head in response, his eyes cast down toward his feet. Willis moved in to hit Foley with the tire iron. Foley tried blocking the blow with one arm while stepping toward Willis so he could elbow him in the groin, but Willis had been expecting some sort of move from his target, and so he moved quickly and swept Foley's feet out from under him, sending him hard onto the pavement. Then he smashed the tire iron into Foley's right knee, shattering it.

"Which is it?" Willis demanded again.

Foley lay on his back and grabbed his damaged knee, his eyes squeezed shut, his face locked in a rigor of pain. Then in response to Willis's question he started laughing a wheezing, sickly laugh.

Willis hit him several more times with the tire iron breaking more bones with each strike, but all Foley did was laugh his sickly, wheezing laugh that sounded more and more like a broken garbage disposal that was about to die out. He refused to answer Willis's questions. They'd been on that side street for no more than three minutes, and while it seemed unlikely anyone driving by would notice them, especially with the way they were blocked out by their parked cars, Willis decided he'd been there long enough. There was always the risk that some curious cop might drive by. Besides, it was appearing even less likely he'd get anything out of his target. With a couple more blows from the tire iron, he finished Foley off.

After moving his car, he swung Foley's older model Ford around so it was parked properly and the rear of it was left less than a foot from Foley's body. After popping the trunk open, he first wrapped Foley's head with a towel so he wouldn't get any blood on himself, then he dumped Foley's corpse into the trunk and closed it. After that, he pulled the remote for Foley's garage door opener off the sun visor.

When Willis got back in his car and drove away, he started cursing himself for what he was going to do next, which he knew made no sense. Why should he care whether a dog starved to death or died of dehydration? It was stupid to put himself at risk like he was going to be doing. It was only more sentimentality on his part, and he didn't understand it and was disgusted by it, but he still drove back to Foley's house.

As he pulled into Foley's driveway, he used the remote to open the garage door, then drove in and shut the door behind him. He then used Foley's keys to open the door connecting the garage to the house. He knew there was only minimal chance that he had been seen driving into the garage. Foley's house was at the end of a cul-de-sac with woods bordering it, and Willis had watched the area long enough to know that at that time of the day the neighbors would be at work. Still, even though it was only a small chance, it was more than he should've been willing to take.

From the back of the house, a fierce barking and growling started. Willis entered the security code on a panel next to the door to disable the alarm system, then followed the noise to a laundry room where the bull terrier was crated. Even though the dog was seventy-five pounds of solid muscle and had a powerful jaw that could kill, Willis wasn't concerned. Dogs were pack animals and Willis would be the alpha male within any pack of dogs or men. With a steely eye fixed on the dog, he ordered him to stop and the dog submissively obeyed him. Willis opened the crate and the dog came out meekly, his tail between his legs.

Willis originally was going to let the dog out of the house so the animal could find someone to take him in, but instead Willis started doing something even stupider that could put him at an even greater risk. He found a garbage bag in the kitchen and went through the house throwing all evidence of the dog's existence into the bag. Dog food, treats, toys, water bowl, food bowl, leash, photos, anything he could find. As he did that, the dog followed close to his heels. Once he had the bag filled up, he went back to the crate, collapsed it, then carried it and the bag into the garage. He put the bag in his trunk and the collapsed crate into his backseat. He opened the passenger seat, and the dog jumped in. Then using the remote, he opened the garage door, drove out into the driveway, closed the door, and drove away.

It was more than stupid. If the police discovered Foley had a bull terrier, then the dog could end up leading them straight to Willis. If anything about that was reported on the news, Willis would find a place to dump the dog. But the police might hold that information back, and still be looking for the bull terrier as a way to find Foley's murderer. If the police caught Willis with Foley's dog, what could he tell them? That Foley sold the dog to him? Maybe, but it was still stupid and sentimental of him to be doing what he was doing, and if The Factory ever found out about it they'd terminate him on the spot for his stupidity and recklessness.

Willis grimaced severely as he tried to understand why he was taking the chance he was with absolutely nothing to gain from it. He noticed the bull terrier staring at him with an accusatory look, as if he suspected what Willis did to his owner. Willis turned his grimace to the dog, and the dog looked away.

CHAPTER 8

LATER, WILLIS REPORTED to Barry how he handled the assignment and that it might be a few days or longer before the police discovered the corpse. During his report, Barry remained quiet, and he let the silence build for a half a minute after Willis finished before commenting how it seemed as if Willis had chosen an odd way to complete his assignment.

"Interesting," Barry said, as if he were musing over the issue, although at the same time letting some annoyance slip through. "You have your target living alone on the end of a cul-de-sac bordering woods. I would've thought a home invasion gone bad would've been a more natural way to do this job. Or perhaps you could've simply hidden in the woods with a rifle. Very interesting that you would choose this riskier method with potentially more exposure."

"I thought killing him as a result of a road rage incident would be more believable to the police," Willis said flatly. "A home invasion wouldn't have made much sense to the police, nor an execution-style murder."

"Oh, come now. A home invasion could've been looked at by the police as the perps picking the wrong home, possibly mistaking the target's home for that of a drug dealer. And nothing at all wrong either if the police had been led into thinking it was a paid hit."

"I thought a road rage killing made more sense," Willis said stubbornly.

Barry must've been running a stress analysis test on Willis's answers, and was satisfied enough with the apparent truthfulness of them to let the matter drop. He asked instead whether the target had said anything to Willis while Willis was beating him to death. Barry had to be suspicious of that. Maybe he later discovered his screw-up of how Willis and Foley were in the same van together when they were taken to The Factory interview and training center. But he also had to be thinking that if Willis's plan was to torture Foley to extract information from him, it would've made more sense to do a home invasion and have the time and privacy to get whatever information he wanted.

"Nothing consequential," Willis said. "He didn't have much time to say anything. I shattered his jaw with my first strike so he wouldn't be able to shout for help." Willis paused, then added, "I recognized him. I think he might've recognized me also."

"What do you mean?"

"My target was in the same van as me when we were driven from Norfolk International Airport to The Factory headquarters."

There was a pause from Barry before he mentioned that some sort of mistake had been made. While his voice implied the right tone of irritation and surprise, he was lying.

"You shouldn't have been assigned to him," Barry said. "I'll look into how that happened." Another long pause. Then Barry asked, "You weren't interested in questioning your target about that?"

"Not particularly. Should I have been? The way I figured it, he was an insurgent who almost infiltrated The Factory."

"That's true," Barry confided. "He washed out during the interview process for other reasons. We didn't learn about his connection with the insurgency until recently."

"It's a good thing he washed out then."

"Good thing is right." Barry was satisfied enough with Willis's answers to let the matter drop. He told Willis the bulletin board had already been updated with his next target, and when he finished this one he could have three weeks off for vacation. "I'd have to think some extra cash would come in handy for whatever trip you have planned. So let's see that you get your bonus for this assignment, okay, Willis?" He ended the call before Willis could answer him.

The dog was lying on his side by Willis's feet, an eye fixed on Willis. Willis reached down to scratch the dog behind his ear and the dog consented to let him do it. The fur was coarse like a brush bristle, the skull as hard as a brick. From his conversation with Barry, Willis felt certain that The Factory had no idea that Foley had had a dog. The dog let out a little pig-like grunt and rolled over onto his back, offering Willis his chest, and Willis complied by scratching it. He had returned home five hours earlier, and for most of that time the dog had a miserable time adjusting to his new surroundings. He was unable to lie quietly and got up every few minutes so he could whimper or let out some of his pig-like noises, then he'd walk to the door and scratch it. Willis had tried feeding him, but the dog had no appetite. He also tried driving the dog three towns over to a woodsy area to take him for a walk, but the dog only plopped himself down on the ground and moped. When Willis was a liquor salesman in Akron, he lived in a small apartment. Once he was hired by The Factory and he understood what his job was going to be, he decided to rent a house in a rural area where he wouldn't have neighbors snooping around or prying into his business. There wasn't another house within a quarter of a mile of where he was living, but even so, he wasn't going to take the dog for walks near his house, at least not until he knew it was safe and the police weren't broadcasting that they were looking for a man with a white bull terrier. Better to drive to that remote woods area.

While Willis expected the dog to be moping for a while, he was glad to see that he was beginning to accept his situation. When Willis stopped scratching the dog's belly, the dog flipped himself to his feet and scampered over to his food dish. After a couple of snorts, he began eating his food with only a minor reluctance.

"I'm going to have to call you something other than dog," Willis said. He tried to think what name to give the animal. He'd never had any pet before and it always seemed odd to him when pet owners gave their animals human names. "How about Bowser?" Willis asked.

The dog lifted his bullet-shaped head from the now empty dish and made another of his pig-like grunts, which as far as Willis was concerned settled the matter.

Willis thought about turning on the computer and seeing who his next target was going to be, but decided that could wait.

CHAPTER 9

WILLIS FELT A sense of unease as he read about his next target, Melanie Hartman. She was thirty-two and pretty, even though from her driver's license photo she looked like someone who got very uncomfortable in front of a camera. All of Willis's previous targets had been men, and the idea of killing a woman bothered him. He knew it shouldn't matter. A traitor's a traitor regardless of the person's sex. If a woman joined the insurgency and was actively working to destroy the country, then she should pay the same price as any of her male counterparts. But one of the things about the target that made Willis especially uneasy was that while she was divorced, she lived with her ten-year-old son, and there was nothing about her sharing custody. It was possible the boy's father was completely out of the picture and that after the assignment was completed the boy would be left orphaned.

Willis steeled himself as he studied her picture. If the woman was willing to join the insurgency, then her son would be better off orphaned than living with her. So he'd terminate his first female target. Over time he'd get used to the idea just as he'd been able to do with his other targets. He'd better since he doubted that Melanie Hartman would be his only female target. The Factory must do that intentionally. Desensitize male field workers like himself with male targets before giving them a woman. It made sense that there would be an equal number of women in the insurgency. Willis accepted that it was probably bothering him more than it should have thanks to a poor night of sleeping, which left him feeling lousy. He'd already drunk two cups of black coffee loaded with sugar, and it hadn't done much yet to remove the fuzziness wrapping his brain.

His poor night of sleeping had nothing to do with feeling any guilt over killing Foley, although Foley was indirectly the cause of it. Willis had let the bull terrier spend the night in his bedroom. He didn't like the idea of crating the dog as Foley had done; besides, he knew if he did that the dog would've been whimpering all night. So instead, every ten minutes or so, the dog got up groaning like an old man before circling the room and plopping down again. It kept up until four in the morning, and it was only after that that Willis was able to fall into a deep sleep. Forty minutes later, he woke up with Bowser's snout inches from his face, the dog's eyes fixed on him as he lay next to Willis. Willis decided that that would be it for trying to sleep and he rolled out of bed, slipped on some clothes, and then took Bowser three towns over to the woods for a walk.

It was now six in the morning and Willis was back home and working on another cup of black coffee as he stared at the driver's license photo of his next target. Brown eyes, brown hair, a cute slightly upturned nose with freckles dotting it, and an awkwardly shy smile. There were other aspects of the job other than his target's sex that bothered him. The Factory had marked her for suicide, so either he'd have to get to her when the son wasn't home or he'd have to do the job quietly. While The Factory had lax rules about collateral damage, Willis wasn't about to take out a ten-year-old boy.

If the woman was normal, Willis would be able to break into her place late at night and threaten to hurt her son unless she wrote out a suicide note and swallowed the pills he handed her, but if someone was not only willing but actively working to see the country go down in flames, why would she care about her child? The job would have to be done differently, and even the surveillance options for the job were lousy. She lived in a large apartment building with an underground garage, and no building or apartment vacancies nearby for him to use—at least none reported in The Factory's one-page dossier. There wasn't even a nearby diner or coffee shop for him to camp out in.

Willis had enough of staring at the computer screen. He exited The Factory's bulletin board, then turned his frown to Bowser, who was lying by his feet.

"Time to earn the food I've been feeding you," he muttered.

*

He had Bowser on a leash as he walked around Melanie Hartman's neighborhood. He wouldn't be able to do it for long without drawing attention, but he got lucky and spotted her as she drove an older model Honda Civic out from the underground garage. He pulled out a pair of field glasses and memorized the license plate. The Factory's dossier had gotten both the car and license plate wrong. They had her in a newer model Saab.

Hartman had her son in the passenger seat when she left, or at least Willis assumed it was her son since The Factory hadn't provided a photo of the boy. He had no idea how long she'd be gone. Maybe she was driving her kid to school and would be back shortly afterwards, or maybe she'd be heading off to work after she dropped him off. If she returned back to the apartment, the job could become very easy as Willis would have a chance to be with her alone up there. He took Bowser back to his car and left him in the backseat gnawing on a thick rawhide bone. The dog was adapting quicker than Willis could've hoped for. At least one thing was going right.

The apartment building Hartman lived in must've been built in the seventies. Seven floors, concrete, kind of an eyesore of a building, although each unit seemed to have its own balcony. The building didn't have much for security. No surveillance cameras, no concierge or anyone on duty. The back door was easy to break into. Willis moved quickly up the fire stairs and to the third floor where Hartman lived. He didn't pass anyone on the stairs since if they were going down to the garage they would've used the elevator instead.

The lock on Hartman's door was a cheap one, and Willis was able to pick it in seconds and get into her apartment without being seen. Willis had hoped that the balcony could be used for her suicide, but as he looked out the blinds he saw that there were large hedges below that would break her fall. If her balcony was on the other side of the building as half of them were, she would have had a concrete landing. It would raise suspicions if Willis broke her neck before throwing her off of it. The apartment just wasn't high enough, not with the hedges underneath to provide a cushioning. He'd have to check later whether the fire stairs led to the roof. If they did, he could toss her body from there to the concrete side of the building.

Willis moved quickly to search the apartment. If Hartman returned while he was there, he'd have no choice but to try to make her suicide look like she had slashed her wrists, which would be tricky, at best. He'd have to overpower her without leaving any other marks or bruises on her body. And he'd have to shut her up before she'd be able to scream. Damn Factory and their suicides!

He started in the kitchen. His stomach seized up as he looked at a photo of her and her son attached by a magnet to the refrigerator. It was a recent photo, and in it she crouched behind her son, her chin almost resting on his shoulder as she held him around his chest and grinned broadly, all the while looking like every other loving and doting mother. He didn't get why someone like her would join the insurgency. Didn't she have any clue what she'd be doing to her son? Willis forced himself to memorize that photo. He needed to know what her son looked like. Before leaving the kitchen, he found a pay stub which had her work address on it. He searched the rest of her mail, but found nothing incriminating.

The apartment was made up of a room that served as both a living room and dining area, a galley kitchen outfitted with its original appliances and cabinets from the seventies, and two bedrooms, with hers being only a little larger than her son's. Her bedroom was neat and nothing in it to indicate she was an insurgent or had much of a personal life. In the back of a closet that held a surprisingly small number of clothes and shoes, he found a two-drawer file cabinet. He shuffled through the folders quickly, but found nothing other than typical household papers, and nothing about her ex-husband or about her collecting any child support or alimony.

Her son's room was much messier and looked typical for what he'd expect for a ten-year-old's room with comic books scattered about, and the walls decorated with sports and action-movie posters. He gave it a quick search. He checked his watch and saw that he'd been in the apartment a little over twenty minutes. It was time to get out of there. The one thing he noticed that was missing from the apartment was any sort of computer, but that didn't mean much. She could have a smart phone for connecting to the Internet and staying connected to the insurgency that way.

Willis listened by the front door, and when he felt certain that there was no one out in the hallway, he left the apartment and then went quickly to the fire stairs. From there he went up to the top and saw that he'd be able to have access to the roof. The door was locked, but the lock wouldn't be much of a challenge for him. He then knew how Melanie Hartman would die. He'd wait until three in the morning to sneak back into the building, then get into her apartment, break her neck before she ever woke up, carry her up to the roof, then throw her over so she'd land on the concrete. It wouldn't be that hard carrying her dead body to the roof. According to her driver's license, she was only five feet two inches and a hundred and five pounds. He'd be able to put her over his shoulders and climb those four flights easy enough. The police would probably wonder why she committed suicide, but there wouldn't be any forensic evidence to contradict it.

Willis made his way down the fire stairs and out of the building without running into anyone. When he got back to his car, Bowser was still gnawing away at his rawhide bone, but he stopped to give Willis an incriminating look.

"I'm only doing my job," Willis muttered as a way of apology.

CHAPTER 10

WILLIS COULDN'T LEAVE it alone. He had the job figured out so it would be able to be done with little risk, but a thought nagged at him. When he left Melanie Hartman's building he took Bowser for a long walk in a woodsy area, but he couldn't quiet that whisper that was nagging at him. After he brought Bowser back to his house, he drove to the dental office where Melanie Hartman worked as a receptionist. She was sitting up front and as Willis approached her, she smiled cheerfully at him. Up close she was much prettier than she'd been in her photo; her large brown eyes sparkling brightly, her smile anything but awkward, and those freckles dotting her nose gave her a clean-cut, wholesome look like those girls they used to use in those old Ivory Soap commercials. But hell, the former and now deceased porn star, Marilyn Chambers, had once been one of those Ivory Soap girls, so what was the point of putting any importance on that? Willis told her he'd like to make an appointment to get his teeth cleaned, keeping his own voice as friendly and as at ease as if the two of them were long-time acquaintances.

After a few questions, such as whether he was a new patient and if he was experiencing any pain, Hartman consulted a scheduling book. As she flipped through it, her brow furrowed and she bit her bottom lip in a way that made Willis's nagging whisper all that much louder. "Dr. Shulman's schedule is pretty full right now," she said apologetically. "His first opening isn't until a week from next Friday. Eleven o'clock. Would that be okay?"

"I was hoping to get this done sooner."

"I understand. I could call you if we have a cancellation, or I could call one of our other recommended dentists and see if they can fit you in sooner." She winked at him as her smile grew into something sly. "Don't worry, we really do recommend these others dentists. We're not getting kickbacks or anything."

"I don't want to put you out."

"Don't worry about it. I'm happy to do it." She proceeded to busy herself looking through her desk drawers. "Now if I can only find where that list is." She explained to Willis how she'd only been working there for four weeks and she still sometimes forgot where things were.

Willis leaned in, smiled sympathetically. "How do you like it here?"

"Oh, I love it." Hartman looked around the waiting room. A middle-aged woman was reading a fashion magazine while her teenage daughter was plugged into an iPod and skimming through the latest issue of People. The mother was eavesdropping, but trying not to show it. The daughter was oblivious. Hartman lowered her voice to a soft whisper and added, "This job was a lifesaver. I was out of work for four months before Dr. Shulman gave me this opportunity. I am so grateful to him, especially with the job environment we have these days."

"I hear you," Willis said and in equally low voice. "I was out of work for eleven months and it was brutal."

Empathy flooded her eyes and she lay a delicate hand on Willis's arm. The gesture was mostly out of sympathy, and maybe at a subconscious level, some flirting. "You were able to find something too, then?" she asked.

Willis nodded.

Hartman gave a *what-a-dope* smile as if she remembered where the list was kept, and sure enough, dug it out of a file cabinet. She was about to start making calls, but Willis stopped her. "You don't have to do that," he said. "How about making a copy for me instead? I'll make the calls later."

She nodded okay and went to the copy machine. She was dressed conservatively for the office in a skirt and blouse. A petite and slender build, but very attractive. All Willis could think about as he looked at her was what it would be like with her dead weight on his shoulders as he carried her up four flights of stairs to the roof. The moment before she turned back to him, he was again smiling at her. He pointed out the framed photo on her desk and asked whether that was her son, knowing already that it was.

"The love of my life," she said, her smile turning into something very genuine. "That's my son, Jack. I know I was only out of work for four months and a lot of people out there have had it a lot worse, but he's still what kept me going."

Willis nodded as he took the list from her and as he left the office those whispers gnawing at him only grew louder.

*

Willis didn't kill Melanie Hartman that night. Instead, he decided to put her under surveillance and look for any evidence that could convince him that she was an insurgent. Most of the time, he brought the bull terrier with him. The dog provided good cover, especially since there was no empty location near her apartment for him to camp out in. When he was outside trailing her, all eyes of any passerby would go to the dog instead of him. On the fifth day of trailing her, he found a story in the newspaper about Foley's body being found in the trunk of his car. The police spokesman speculated that the murder was most likely the result of a road rage incident, which was what Willis had expected. There was nothing mentioned about a dog taken from Foley's house. It was also somewhat surprising to Willis how little space had been given to the murder. Or maybe not so surprising given how the murder rate had been creeping up in Boston over the last two years, which left Foley competing against a number of other equally violent deaths.

Barry also called him during his fifth day of surveillance to ask why the assignment hadn't been completed yet. Willis explained that it was because The Factory had to mark the death as suicide. "That complicates the matter," he said. "She's got a ten-year-old son living with her so it's got to be done quietly. If her balcony was on the other side of the building, it would be easy. I could toss her off and she'd land on concrete. But with the shrubs underneath her balcony to provide a soft landing, I don't think the medical examiner would buy that her neck was broken by the fall."

Willis was able to go into the details that he did because he knew he was talking over a secured line, and with the level of encryption being used no one would've been able to eavesdrop. When Barry responded, it was only with a minimal effort to hide his exasperation.

"It's precisely because of her ten-year-old son that I thought this would be a trivial assignment for you," he said with a voice that bordered on becoming a whine. "I would have to think that with the right persuasion you'd have her willingly swallowing a handful of pills."

"And what persuasion would that be?"

"Must I be this blunt? That if she doesn't do as you're demanding, you'll cripple her son, or worse."

"That wouldn't work," Willis said. "I thought of that also, but if she's an insurgent hell-bent on seeing this country go down in flames, why would she care one bit about what I might do to her son?"

There was a pause from Barry before he admitted in a stilted voice that that might be true. "A pity that you won't be earning your bonus. That makes three assignments in a row now. Twelve thousand dollars." Another pause, then, "You will be taking care of this by your deadline?"

"Yeah."

Barry ended the call. Over the next week, Willis maintained his surveillance and saw no evidence that Melanie Hartman was anything other than what she appeared to be, which was a very pretty thirty-two-year-old woman whose life revolved around work and her son. During that week, several new violent home invasion murders seemed to occupy the media's attention and there was very little else in the newspapers about Foley, and nothing about him on the TV news. Also, no mention about a stolen dog. Either the police were keeping that to themselves or they just didn't know about it.

On the last day of Willis's deadline, Barry called again to find out why the target hadn't been dealt with yet. There was no exasperation in his voice, only a polite iciness. Willis hesitated before telling Barry that he didn't believe Melanie Hartman was an insurgent.

"Is that so?"

"Yeah," Willis said. "You made a mistake with her."

"We don't make mistakes, Willis."

There was no misunderstanding the threat in Barry's voice. He was giving Willis one last chance to back down and take care of the matter, or there would be severe consequences.

"I've been watching the target almost two weeks," Willis said. "I'm convinced she is what she appears to be. A young woman who puts in ten hours a day at her job, and lives for her son. She's not part of any conspiracy or terrorist organization. You need to double-check her status."

There was dead silence from Barry. Then, "Where is she employed?"

Willis gave him the name and address of the dental office where Melanie Hartman worked. Barry told him that he'd check it out himself.

"Don't do anything until you hear back from me," Barry warned before ending the call.

One day later, Barry called back to tell him that a mistake had been made.

"How the hell did that happen?" Willis demanded.

"It's interesting that you would ask that," Barry said. "We're fighting a war, and as you know, collateral damage happens. If you had answered your psychological profile answers honestly, then this wouldn't matter to you. You fudged on your answers, didn't you, Willis?"

"No. But I take pride in my work, and if I'm spending time and putting myself at risk to take out a target, I want it to be a real target."

"Hmm," Barry mused in a way that made Willis think of a pudgy cat purring as it lay on a satin pillow. "Interesting. To answer your question, Willis, the insurgency has been feeding us misinformation. Most of it we've been able to weed out. This little bit of misdirection slipped through. It's good that you caught it because it would've exposed one of our inside agents if you hadn't. Still, all of us need to accept that collateral damage is inevitable. Any future assignments, just do them and don't waste time investigating the target. We don't have time for that. The war we're fighting is too important. Do we understand each other?"

"Yeah."

"Good. Check the bulletin board. Your next assignment has been added. Get it done quickly, earn your bonus, then take your three weeks off and relax. You're going to be busy when you get back. From the reports I'm getting, this war we're fighting is getting uglier by the day."

CHAPTER 11

AFTER GETTING OFF the phone with Barry, Willis logged onto The Factory's bulletin board so he could get the details for his next assignment. He wasn't planning on doing anything about it yet—he had other things in mind, but he knew The Factory would be monitoring when he checked in.

Willis's next target was his age and looked quite a bit like him. A grim smile compressed his lips as he read through the particulars. He knew the age and physical similarities weren't purely a coincidence—that The Factory picked out the target special for him to send him a not-so-subtle message. That unless Willis got on the ball, he could just as easily be a target himself for another field agent. The target was named Steve Taggert and he was marked for murder. The dossier mentioned a nearby vacant house that was available to use for surveillance purposes. The vacant house was a colonial, and Willis would be able to watch from the second floor and pick off Taggert with a rifle shot when he left his house, just as a field agent would be able to watch for Willis from the woods surrounding his rental house and pick him off when he left one day.

Willis had earlier bought a bag of pig ears, and Bowser was laying on the floor a few feet from Willis busily chewing up one of them. "Boy, what do you think?" Willis asked him. The dog interrupted his chewing for a moment to look at Willis. He let out a satisfied grunt, and then was back to working on that ear.

"Yeah, I agree," Willis said. "They're not out there yet. Might not be a bad idea for us to find a new place, huh?" The dog was too busy tearing apart his pig ear to grunt back an answer.

Willis found a cabin two towns away that he could rent by the week. He paid cash for one week in advance and brought only Bowser, a small suitcase packed with a week's worth of clothing, a 9mm automatic with three extra clips, and a pair of binoculars. He left his Factory badge back in his house.

The next morning, Willis withdrew an amount in cash that wouldn't draw suspicion from anyone expecting him to be going on a three-week vacation. After watching Melanie Hartman for the past two weeks, he was able to bump into her at the small diner several blocks from where she worked and where she had lunch most days—usually a garden salad, although sometimes she'd have a scoop of tuna salad added to it. Hartman recognized him immediately and offered a bright smile while Willis feigned surprise and wrinkled his forehead as he slowly pretended to place where he knew her from. Then snapping his fingers he mentioned that she was the one who helped him out finding a dentist. Flashing an easygoing smile, he asked if he could join her at her table. She hesitated briefly, then told him she'd be happy to have the company.

"So you were able to find someone?" she asked.

"With your help, yeah."

"No cavities?"

"Not a one."

"Even better!"

Willis noted how beautiful her smile was and how it showed just as brightly in her eyes. Completely genuine. He knew there was some interest on her part, and if his situation were different the interest would be mutual. An uneasiness twisted in his stomach as he realized how close he had come to wiping out that smile for all time, but he made sure to keep that hidden and only show a relaxed expression.

"Lunch will be on me, okay?" Willis said. "It's the least I can do for helping me out the way you did. That was very nice of you, by the way."

He could tell she was going to protest, but then probably realized it wouldn't do any good and instead went along with it in a good-natured way. "Who am I to tell a good-looking guy he can't buy me lunch," she said blushing slightly. Willis grinned then. Not a fake one, but the first real one since joining The Factory. He liked the way she looked when she blushed, maybe even more than the way she did when she smiled. Her blush deepened. A waitress came over and Willis ordered a burger and coffee while Melanie Hartman ordered an iced tea and a garden salad, probably skipping the tuna salad to keep the cost down for Willis. After the waitress left, she asked whether he worked nearby.

"Nope. I came here on a business assignment."

"What do you do?"

"Sort of a corporate troubleshooting position." He waved it

away. "Not all that interesting, but it was all I could find after my sales job was eliminated. Those eleven months I spent looking for work were brutal."

"I know. I was only out of work for four months, but those four months were miserable. I was so worried that I wouldn't find a job, especially with all the stories out there about people being out of work for years. If it wasn't for my son, Jack, I don't think I would've made it. Jack was what kept me fighting to find something." Her smile weakened and a moistness showed in her eyes. "I broke down and cried when Dr. Shulman offered me that job."

Willis nodded grimly. "What did you use to do?" he asked. He already had a good idea since he had seen the textbooks when he searched her apartment, but he showed the proper amount of surprise and interest when she told him she used to do something very different.

"My degree is in biotechnology," she said, her smile weakening even more and turning into something bleak. "Four years for my bachelor's degree, another two years for my master's. I was working for a lab in Cambridge doing some advanced research, but they, like a lot of the labs that used to be here, decided it would be cheaper to do their research and development in India or Russia. I'm not complaining, though. You play the cards you're dealt. All I want now is to be able to take care of my son."

The waitress came back with their beverages. Willis watched as the waitress walked away. Anger showed in his eyes as he shook his head.

"I wouldn't blame you one bit if you did complain," Willis said. "People have a right to be angry. Jobs being wiped out left and right and a national unemployment rate of thirteen percent, all while the top one tenth of one percent in this country get wealthier and wealthier. When I was out of work, I had a group contact me. Real revolutionary stuff. Burning down the country so we could start over, stuff like that. I had my moments where I seriously considered joining up." Willis looked away as he took a sip of his coffee, then gazed back to her. He asked whether anything like that had happened to her.

"No, thank God," she said. "Not that I blame you for briefly considering it. I can understand the anger out there, but it doesn't do any good. We need to be constructive and work together and not tear this country apart." Her smile turned apologetic. "I'm sorry, I'm not trying to be preachy. But at least things seem to be turning in the right direction. I read this morning that the unemployment rate has dropped to twelve point six percent, so at least we're seeing some progress."

Willis had wanted to talk with her to find out whether the insurgency had tried contacting her. He wanted to know whether the insurgency had fed The Factory's inside agent Hartman's name as Barry claimed, or whether the assignment had been a major league screw-up on The Factory's part. When Hartman mentioned how the unemployment rate had fallen four tenths of a percent, something clicked in his mind. Something that had been vague suddenly became clear. He understood then why the unemployment rate had fallen and what his role had been. He understood why Hartman had originally been his target, and why she was later removed.

Early on, Willis didn't consciously pay much attention to the targets he was being assigned. They were all loners; either single men or divorced, mostly all of them living in either shabby apartments or rundown houses. It made sense to Willis that these were men whose anger could lead them to joining the insurgency. Later, he started realizing that many of his targets were unemployed, and he assumed that was because that was who the insurgency were actively recruiting. Men who would be angry and depressed and would have little to lose in seeing the country go down in flames. At some point, Willis started to have his doubts and was searching for proof of the insurgency and his target's connection to it. With his last few assignments, all of the detail was at a conscious level, but it must have also been there at a subconscious level for a while now. Maybe even from the beginning.

Willis changed the conversation to a lighter topic, and while he hoped he maintained a pleasant exterior, in his mind's eye he was actively clicking through all twenty-five targets that he had taken out, trying to remember everything he could about their dossiers and his surveillance of them. They all could've been unemployed. He couldn't say for sure since he wasn't paying attention to that early on, and some of his assignments were completed quickly with little surveillance. As he sat talking with Melanie Hartman, his mind flipped through his assignments as if it were a rolodex and he became convinced that not only were they all unemployed, but that they had to have been that way for a while. That was why they all seemed so shabby, except maybe Foley. And that was why they were made his targets.

Their food was brought over. Willis barely tasted his hamburger as he ate it and continued his conversation with Hartman, all the while his mind racing on other issues. When their lunch reached its normal conclusion, Hartman remarked how she needed to head back to work. Willis nodded, exchanged some final pleasantries with her, and acted dense when she hinted about how she wouldn't mind having company on the two-block walk back to her office. Under different circumstances, Willis would've taken her up on it, but with the way things were he was going to need to keep far away from her and her son. It was a shame. He liked her and found himself attracted to her.

After she left, he had a refill on his coffee and drank it while he considered his options. As far as he could see he had three choices. Keep doing his job and collecting a paycheck, go on the run, or do what he could to stop The Factory. He finished his coffee and accepted that he had only been kidding himself. He had no choice about what he was going to do next.

CHAPTER 12

WILLIS DROVE BACK to the shack he was renting so he could pick up Bowser, then drove back to his house. He stopped about a quarter mile away so he could let the dog out. The dog took off, running straight back to the house as if it was a game while Willis crept along behind him. If there was anyone hiding out there with a rifle, the dog would've smelled him out and gone after him. Still, Willis was careful to keep low as he made his way to his side door so he could let himself and Bowser back in.

Once he was inside, he packed up what he was going to need since he wasn't going to be returning. Then he left a message for Barry. Twenty minutes later, Barry called back and Willis told him they needed to talk.

"I believe we're talking now," Barry said coldly.

"Face to face," Willis said. "You're going to have to meet with me in person and explain to me how Melanie Hartman ended up being labeled an insurgent. I'm going to need to see the files and other documentation that led you to that decision."

Barry's tone turned icier as he said, "I already explained to you what happened."

"Yeah, well, the problem is I don't believe you."

"I see. And what do you think happened?"

"Something very different."

Barry went silent for a long moment, then told Willis that what he was asking for was impossible.

"It better not be. In an hour, I'm going to call you from Boston. Someplace crowded where we can both be safe. When I call you I'll give you the location and you'll have fifteen minutes to show up. If you don't, I'll be going to the press and I'll be giving them everything, including copies I made of the dossiers and assignments from The Factory's bulletin board—"

"You were forbidden from making copies of that. You took an oath!"

"Yeah, well, too bad. I'll also be giving them a recording of all of our phone conversations, including this one."

Willis heard Barry exhaling his breath as if he were trying to calm himself down. Then in that same icy tone from earlier, Barry said, "You're not going to get anywhere with what you're doing."

"Possibly."

"It's doubtful that the media will do anything with whatever you give them. Not with our reach and not with the current political environment."

"You could be right."

"The problem, Willis, is that you shouldn't have lied during your psychological profile examination. If you had answered the questions truthfully, we wouldn't be having this issue now."

Willis disconnected the call. It wasn't worth arguing the matter.

What he was going to do next was tricky. He was going to have to bring his Factory badge with him, and they'd be able to track his location with it. It was possible that they'd try to intercept him on his way to Boston. But even with that problem, Willis couldn't help smiling over the way Barry screwed up. Willis had no idea where Barry was located. For all he knew, Barry could've been operating out of Nebraska. Or Texas. Or somewhere in Southeast Asia. Willis was hoping that Barry was located near the field agents he was supervising, and he had further guessed from the hours that Barry kept that he was on the east coast, but it had been only a guess. From the way Barry responded to Willis's demand, he all but confirmed that he was within an hour's drive of the city. Otherwise, he would have tried bargaining that he needed more time for them to meet, whether or not he had any intention of them meeting.

Willis would have liked to have dropped Bowser off at the shack that he was renting, but he couldn't do that since they'd be able to track him driving there. He considered abandoning the dog, but he couldn't do that either. So he let Bowser in the backseat and gave him a thick rawhide bone to work on.

Willis kept to the back roads and avoided any toll highways. Given the little time The Factory had, it was more likely that they would track him to wherever he was going and deal with him there, but if they tracked him to a toll road, they could shut down the toll booths and trap him. With the route he took, he'd keep them off balance as to where he was heading, which was an area in South Boston where he knew it would be easy to park, and more importantly, an area where people tended to look the other way when things went down.

As he expected, there was plenty of available street parking, but he parked illegally down an alley where his car wouldn't be easily visible from the main street. Bowser looked up from his chewed-up bone and offered Willis a quizzical look. Willis got out and pointed a finger at the dog and ordered, "Stay here and be quiet." Bowser grunted out his dissatisfaction over that, and then proceeded to demonstrate his unhappiness by tearing more vigorously at what was left of the bone. If Willis was able to come back later, he expected to see the backseat torn up also. That was okay. He wasn't going to be keeping the car much longer.

Willis cut through the alley, then down a side street and another alley so he could enter the coffee shop from a back entrance. He dropped his Factory badge in a corner of the shop and then kept moving until he was out a side door, keeping himself low and his face hidden. He kept walking until he was positioned in a doorway of a vacant storefront where he'd be able to watch the coffee shop, but still be mostly concealed unless someone flashed a light into the doorway.

It didn't take long for his man to show up. No more than three minutes. The man was about his age, a few inches shorter, stockier, and with the hardness of a killer showing around his mouth and eyes. He wasn't Barry, Willis was certain of that, but then again he still hadn't made his call to Barry, and even if he had, he'd never expect Barry to show.

The man who did show up moved cautiously as he consulted a device that must have been a GPS tracker. He kept close to the buildings so he wouldn't be seen easily from the coffee shop, and he ended up passing within two feet of Willis without realizing it. As the man moved on, he kept consulting his GPS tracker. He stopped three doors away from the coffee shop and flattened himself in another building's doorway. Willis texted Barry providing the coffee shop's name and address, and telling Barry he had fifteen minutes to get there. Barry must've immediately texted the same information to his other man because Willis could hear the buzz of a phone that had been put on vibrate. He watched as the man took a cell phone from his jacket pocket and studied it as if he were reading a text message. The man put the cell phone away, then stepped out from the doorway and continued on. Before he entered the coffee shop, he slipped his hand inside his jacket. Willis knew the man was keeping his fingers inches from a gun that he had holstered. He didn't want to take it out yet, but he wanted quick access to it.

Willis used a pair of field glasses to watch as the man moved quickly into the shop ready to start shooting if necessary. Most likely he would've used the gun to force Willis out of the shop so he could be taken care of someplace less public, but maybe not. Maybe the plan was to end things there and expect the witnesses to be too shocked to give the police an accurate identification of the shooter. Willis could see the man scanning the shop, his eyes narrowing and his mouth pinched. Indecision marred his expression for several heartbeats as he looked for Willis. He noticed the unisex bathroom in the corner of the shop and made his way over to it. When he tried the door handle he must've found it locked. A grimness tightened his mouth. He had to be figuring that Willis was hiding in there. Moving slowly to the counter he bought himself a coffee and then settled down to wait. He again reached inside his jacket as the door opened, then dejection contorted his face as a young woman stepped out of the bathroom. It was only then that the man spotted Willis's Factory badge on the floor.

He got up from his table, walked to where the badge had been left and picked it up. After a quick look at it, he brought it to the girl working behind the counter and showed it to her to see if she had seen the man in the photo. She shook her head. The man waved over the other kid working behind the counter. The kid looked at the badge and also shook his head.

The man left the coffee shop after that. He moved cautiously, not quite sure what to do next. He stood for a moment making a face as if he were caught in the middle of a sneeze, then looked up and down the street searching for Willis. He must've decided that Willis got spooked and bailed on the meeting because his mouth tightened into an angry slash and he moved quickly then to go back to his car. His eyes were little more than dull black dots as he strode past the doorway where Willis was hiding, too sure that Willis was gone and too absorbed in his thoughts to bother looking anywhere but straight ahead.

Like Willis, the man had ignored the available on-street parking and instead chose to park illegally on a side street so that it would've been less likely for his car to be spotted. The man moved with a single-minded purpose. When he reached his car, he used his remote to unlock it and reached for his cell phone, probably so he could call Barry. Up until then he hadn't realized that Willis had been following him. It was only at the last second that he must've heard or sensed something because his body stiffened, but it was too late to help himself. Before he could react otherwise, Willis had a grip of his hair and banged his forehead twice against the car. The first blow dazed him, the second one mostly knocked him out. In a boxing ring he might've been able to remain standing on his feet, but he still would've been counted out by any competent referee. Willis yanked the man's arm behind his back without any resistance, took possession of the car keys, and used duct tape that he had brought with him to secure the man's wrists together. With one hand he grabbed the man by the scruff of the neck and dragged him to the back of the car, popped open the trunk and dumped the man inside of it. While the man lay groaning, Willis grabbed one of Bowser's toys from his pocket—a small hard rubber ball, and he shoved it into the man's mouth and taped it into place. He then wrapped duct tape around the man's ankles securing them together. Before he closed the trunk, he searched through the man's pockets and took his wallet, cell phone, and gun.

Willis drove to a warehouse several miles away that had been destroyed three years earlier in a fire. The building, while little more than a burnt-out shell, still stood. There was a vacant parking lot behind the building where they'd have some privacy. Some winos or drug addicts might be camped out there, but if they were Willis would chase them away. As it turned out, there was no one else there. Just an empty lot littered with trash and broken bottles.

Willis parked, got out of the car, opened the trunk, and slapped the man in the face until his eyes lost their glazed look and were able to focus on Willis. There was some defiance in them, as well as some pain, but also a good amount of fear. Willis left the gag in the man's mouth.

Willis removed the man's driver's license from his wallet and studied it. The man's name was Paul Johnson. He lived in Saugus, which was only about ten miles north of Boston.

"Paul Johnson of Saugus," Willis said, keeping his voice flat. "This is going to go down one of two ways. You're either going to walk away with only the injuries you have now, or it's going to get ugly, and here's how it will get ugly. I will drive you back to your home, carry you inside, and we'll wait for your family. You might not have any family. It's very likely given that you work for The Factory. That's fine. But if you do, I will work on each of them in turn for hours. During this time they'll be begging you to tell me what I want to know, and you might or might not break down and do that. It won't matter. I won't stop until I'm finished with them. After that I'll work on you. You might be able to hold out, you might not. You might beg me to let you tell me what I want to know. It won't change anything. Once I start I'm not stopping until I'm done."

Willis smiled slightly as he studied the man's eyes. All the defiance was gone, and now there was only fear which meant the man did have a family and that he believed what Willis was saying, which made sense since Willis was saying only what he intended to do.

"Paul, it's important that you understand the next part. Not just for yourself, but for any family you might have. If you cooperate fully with me this will go the easy way. If you're evasive, or you lie to me, or I believe you're lying to me, or even if you so much as hesitate in answering me, or try to engage me in any sort of conversation, or simply answer any of my own questions with a question, then this is going to go the hard way. There will be no do-overs, no second chances. If I start down

the path of the hard way, then I'll be playing it out to its conclusion, and nothing you or your family members might say
will stop me. Nod if you understand this."

The man nodded, his eyes showing the weakness of the
defeated.

"Good. I'm going to remove your gag now."

Willis removed the tape from Paul Johnson's face and took
Bowser's rubber ball from his mouth. Johnson's mouth puck-
ered into a grimace over the taste of the bull terrier's toy.

"Are you going to cooperate?" Willis asked.

Johnson nodded glumly.

"No gestures. Words only."

"Yes," Johnson forced out, his voice raspy and weak.

"Good. Do you know where Barry is now?"

Alarm showed in Johnson's eyes, but not from the thought
of giving up Barry. Instead it was because he didn't recognize
the name. Willis could see it plainly and so he believed Johnson
when he claimed he didn't know who Barry was.

"He's my handler at The Factory. He was the one who sent
you to kill me."

"Tom Barron," Johnson said. "That's his name. Yes, he
should be at the office now waiting for me to call him back."

"You're doing well so far. You're almost home free. Don't
screw this up now. Where's the office?"

Johnson gave him the address of a downtown Boston location only a few blocks from Chinatown.

"What type of building is it?"

"A high-rise. Fifteen floors."

"Underground parking?"

"Yes."

"Any armed security there?"

There was a flicker in Johnson's eyes, but that flicker died out almost instantly and he told Willis there was no security personnel maintained there, or any armed personnel.

"I thought I saw a flicker in your eyes where you considered lying to me," Willis said. "Since it might be the lighting around here and I might've only imagined what I thought I saw, and I want to be fair since you've been cooperating so far, I'll flip a coin. Heads we continue the easy way, tails we change course and do it the hard way."

Willis dug a quarter from his pocket, flipped it, and showed Johnson that it was heads. Johnson's face collapsed when he saw that. It was as if he barely escaped suffering a major coronary. Of course, Willis didn't bother telling him that he could flip a coin a hundred times and make it come out heads each time.

Willis stuck the quarter back in his pocket. "That was your one and only break," Willis said. "You understand that, right?"

"Yes," Johnson whispered, his color having turned chalk white.

"How do I get into the garage?"

"My badge will get you in. The gate is automated. You don't have to show it to anyone."

"No voice prints or eye scans?"

"No, just the badge."

"Tell me about the office itself. Any armed security."

"No, it's only midlevel supervisors like Tom Barron. I'm considered support, but I only go in when I'm called, and I think that's true of other support specialists."

"How many others like Barron are working there?"

Willis could see Johnson start to panic as he desperately

tried to count how many there were. "I think eight," he said. "But I'm not sure."

"Give me their names."

There was more panic wetting his eyes as he thought Willis might think he was lying, "Other than Barron I only know two of them. That's the way it's organized. I've been assigned to support three of the supervisors. Barron, Allen Patterson, and Elliot Finder."

"Okay, Paul, we're almost done. There was that one flicker which I still think I might've seen, but I'm giving you the benefit of the doubt on that. You're almost home free."

Willis closed the trunk shut on Johnson and then got back behind the wheel. He was surprised the security would be so lax there. But maybe they needed to keep a low profile, and there would be field offices in every major city. He had no doubt that Johnson believed that only the badge was needed, but it was possible that they had other security measures Johnson wasn't aware of. Possibly they used a face recognition system. As he drove to where Tom Barron worked, he considered the pros and cons of moving Johnson behind the wheel. He decided it would be better to leave things as they were, and it might even be to his benefit if they were using a face recognition system.

When Willis got to the building, he found the underground garage and slid Johnson's badge into a card reader. The gate opened up for him as Johnson had told him it would. He drove to the back where the elevators where located and parked illegally in a fire lane. Then he popped open the trunk, got out, and told Johnson what he was going to say when he called Barron on Johnson's cell phone. Johnson repeated it word for word, and Willis dialed the number that Johnson gave him, which was a different number than he had for the man he knew as Barry. Once he heard Barron pick up, he held the cell phone close to Johnson's mouth.

"Willis overpowered me," Johnson croaked into the phone. "He made me tell him where you are. He's on his way up now to kill you. I lied to him, though. I convinced him that there are armed guards in the lobby, so he's taking the fire stairs instead of the elevator. Get out of there now, Barron. You've only got a minute, if that!"

Willis disconnected the call before Barron could respond. He closed the trunk on Johnson.

Johnson's cell phone rang back seconds later. Willis let it ring. Less than two minutes later a man who must've been Tom Barron emerged from the elevator. He was about fifty. A round man with an overall doughy look about him. His nose was a round knob of flesh and his jowls were thick and heavy and hid any chin he might've had. He wore a dark blue suit that hung poorly on him, and he looked more like he should've been a British TV comic than a man supervising the assassination of hundreds of people.

Barron moved his fat chubby legs quickly as he headed to his car. He kept glancing around, but never saw Willis. He was opening the driver's side door for a newer model Buick Regal when Willis grabbed him from behind with both hands and swung Barron to the ground.

"If you think this is going to do you any good—" Barron started to shout, but before he could get another word out Willis had Bowser's toy rubber ball shoved in his mouth, and then secured it with duct tape.

Barron tried to struggle as he lay flat on his stomach, but

it didn't do him any good. His arms were yanked back and his wrists were secured together with duct tape. When he tried kicking with his legs, Willis punched him hard in the kidneys and that collapsed Barron long enough for Willis to wrap his ankles together with tape. Willis took his car keys, then searched his pockets and pulled out his wallet, cell phone, and Factory badge. He left the badge on the ground, then dragged Barron to the back of the Buick, opened the trunk, and heaved Barron into it. Barron's face had purpled and his eyes were wide as he tried yelling through the gag, but little sound came out. Willis closed the trunk shut on him.

CHAPTER 13

WILLIS USED PAUL Johnson's badge to leave the garage, and once he was outside of it, he tossed the badge out the window. He first drove past where he had left Bowser and his car. He wanted to make sure the location hadn't attracted any police, and once he was sure it was safe, he circled back so he could pick up Bowser and his packed suitcases. As he expected, Bowser had chewed up part of the backseat. When he let the dog out of the car, Bowser let out a few of his angry pig-grunts, but also eyed Willis cautiously as if he were expecting a scolding. Willis didn't bother with that. He understood the dog's frustration at being abandoned there, and besides, he was finished with the car.

Willis next drove to the empty house that The Factory had indicated would be available for surveillance of his most recently assigned target. It took an hour to drive there, and about twenty minutes into it, Barron began banging furiously from within the trunk. All he accomplished was causing Bowser to lift his bullet-shaped head with curiosity and to bring a thin smile to Willis's lips.

When Willis arrived at the abandoned house, he pulled into an attached garage, dumped Barron onto the floor and then dragged him into the house, leaving him in a small foyer. Bowser started barking angrily from inside the car. Willis removed the gag from Barron's mouth, and went back to the garage to warn Bowser to be quiet. He tossed the rubber ball to Bowser so the dog could gnaw on it. "Give me ten minutes," he warned the dog, who stared at him with his head cocked to one side. The dog grunted as if in acknowledgement.

Barron had been left lying on his side. Willis pulled him back so he was against the wall, then lifted him into a sitting position. Willis remained standing, forcing Barron to crane his neck to look up at him.

"You're making a big mistake, Willis," Barron forced out, his pasty face mottled purple with rage and shiny with perspiration. He paused before saying, "It's not too late to rectify this. You were a good worker for us. Better than most, actually. We should be able to figure out a way to get you back on track."

"Shut up."

Barron smiled sickly. "Or what? You'll kill me?"

"Eventually."

"Look, Willis, you were hired for a job. An important one that's needed to keep this country safe."

"Yeah, right. These were never insurgents you were having me kill." Willis made a face as if he'd swallowed something unpleasant. In a disgusted voice he added, "These were only poor saps who had the misfortune of being unemployed."

"They're still insurgents. They're still working to destroy this country. Even if they don't realize it."

Willis felt the muscles around his mouth tighten. "Yeah? How's that?"

"Have you heard the latest figures for the unemployment rate? Twelve point six percent. Do you know what the rate would be without this initiative? At least fourteen percent. Do you have any idea what this high of an unemployment rate for this long a period does to the economy? To investments? Consumer confidence? Simply the morale of this country? It dooms us, Willis. The perception is we're all going down the toilet and that becomes a self-fulfilling prophecy as companies stop investing and people stop spending. The only way to stop this downward spiral to death is to change the perception and get the unemployment rate back to a more manageable seven percent. And we're on track to do this, Willis. Another four years and we'll be there. And the men and women working to achieve that goal are all heroes, just as you were before this nonsense today."

For a long moment, all Willis could do was gape at Barron. Even though he had realized what was going on, hearing the man's logic for the reason of it was like tumbling down a rabbit hole where black was white and up was down. He didn't want to get into that kind of discussion with Barron, but he couldn't keep himself from asking why they couldn't be training these people for new jobs instead of solving the problem by killing them.

"What new jobs would these be? It's not just manufacturing that's been decimated in this country, but corporations have been on a frenzy to outsource any industries and jobs they can, and whatever's left, if it can be automated or moved online, it's eliminated also. So if we train these people to be lawyers or accountants or engineers, what good is it going to do? Hell, Homeland Protection has created more jobs in this country over the last two years than all the Fortune 500 companies combined. Look Willis, studies don't lie. If someone's laid off and they don't find another job within three months, they're not going to. Ever."

"Yeah? What about Melanie Hartman, the target you gave me?"

Barron shook his head sadly at Willis. "She's the exception. You're always going to have exceptions. But goddammit, Willis, you should understand this better than anyone. I saw your folder. You were a top sales rep for your industry when you were laid off. How much luck did you have finding another job? And guess what? Since you've been with us the situation has only gotten worse." Barron forced a toothy smile and in a more chummy manner added, "We all make mistakes, Willis. I can understand you flying off the handle the way you did, but now that you see how things really are, how about we try to fix this? It's not too late."

Willis stood rubbing his jaw with his left hand as he considered what Barron had told him. For a while he forgot that Barron was there. When his gaze shifted to meet Barron's, he shook his head.

Barron sneered in contempt. "Then what the hell is it that you want? To kill me? Are you that pedestrian? Is that what you think you need to do to make everything alright?"

"I want names," Willis said. "Your boss, anyone else above you, any of your fellow supervisors."

Barron's sneer turned into more of a look of self-righteousness. "You're not getting anything from me," he stated.

"You have a family, don't you, Tom?" Willis said. "I could hurt them if I had to to make you talk. I've already killed a lot of people thanks to you. A few more won't matter."

Barron shrugged indifferently. "Do what you have to."

Willis lowered himself so he sat on his heels and was eye level with Barron. "I'm guessing after Johnson called you, you had time to send personnel to your home while you were running out of the office. One or two men aren't going to help. Unless you sent a lot more than that to protect your family, I'll be able to get to them."

"Again, do what you have to." Barron had looked away from Willis, but he turned to meet Willis's gaze, his own eyes every bit as much steel as Willis's. "Unlike you, I'm a patriot. I'll sacrifice whatever I have to for this country, including my family." With defiance burning in his eyes, Barron added, "There's not a damn thing you can do to make me talk."

"We'll see."

Willis went to work. After fifteen minutes, it was obvious that he wasn't going to get anything out Barron, and he stepped away.

Panting, Barron yelled at him in a croaking voice, "You're a coward, Willis! You don't have the stones for a little torture! How the fuck did you ever kill twenty-five men?"

Willis didn't respond. He left Barron yelling at him as he walked back to the attached garage. Bowser sat sulking in the backseat gnawing angrily at the rubber ball. Willis put his hand under the dog's muzzle and ordered him to drop it. The dog complied.

"I'll be back in one minute," Willis told him, and he left the dog again in the car. When he walked back in the foyer, Barron was still yelling at him, his voice more hoarse, a triumphant glee in his eyes.

If he had been in a high-budgeted action movie Willis might've come out with some catchphrase, such as 'I'm laying you off,' and then pump several bullets into Barron's brain. But it wasn't a high-budgeted action film, so instead he ignored Barron's insults and simply walked over and pinched Barron's nostrils closed. When Barron opened his mouth to gasp for air, Willis shoved the rubber ball deep in there while still keeping the nostrils pinched shut. Less than a minute later, Barron slumped to the side dead.

Willis had already made peace with what he was going to do next. He had names for two other supervisors, as well as knowing that Colonel Jay T. Richardson ran The Factory. Maybe he'd be able to get more names too from Barron's cell phone. He was either going to work his way up from the bottom or down from the top, but one way or the other he was going to do what he could to blow up The Factory and put them out of business. He would have to abandon every aspect of his past life, but he was fine with that. It wasn't as if he had any connections to anyone or anything. He would also have to live on the fringes, rob, or commit other criminal activities to survive and fund his war against The Factory. He had decided he was fine with that, too. Besides, it wasn't as if he had any choice. He wasn't going to commit any more murders for The Factory, not after discovering the truth. If he ran they'd hunt him down until they found him. If he fought back he'd have a chance, and if nothing else, Willis was a pragmatist.

He left Barron lying dead on the floor. He didn't bother pulling Bowser's ball out of the dead man's throat figuring he could buy Bowser another one. Instead he walked back to the garage, and got in Barron's Buick Regal. Bowser growled out one of his pig grunts as Willis pulled the car out of the garage and drove away, almost as if he were asking whether Willis was done yet. Willis nodded, although he was far from done. First off, he was going to have to dump the car and get another one under a fake name. It shouldn't be that much of a problem. But that was only the first of many things he was going to have to do.

He felt tired all of a sudden. More so than he'd felt in a long time. He needed to go back to his rented shack and rest for a day or two. He and Bowser had a long road ahead of them.

THE DAME
PART TWO

CHAPTER 1

THE POKER GAME they were going to hit had been underway for two hours in the neighboring hotel suite. Seven men of different shapes and sizes sat around a circular table, all of them intent on their cards and their bets. It was supposed to be a mob game, but one of the men was a major league ballplayer, another a well-known actor. Also hanging around were three other men who were there presumably to provide protection, although they performed other errands as necessary, such as pouring drinks. All three of the muscled thugs were built more like small bulls than men with thick bodies that showed barely any neck and all of them looking stiff and unnatural in their suits. All three were also packing. Two of them sat reading the newspaper, the third stood stone-faced as he watched the game. Dan Willis had earlier broken into their suite when it was empty and strategically hid surveillance cameras, each of them no bigger than a quarter, and he now watched the suite on a computer monitor that was split into three screens. At different times, he'd been able to make out bulges that showed holstered guns on all three of the goons acting as protection. He hadn't yet been able to tell if any of the players were carrying.

In the same room with Willis were three other men: Pruitt, Lowenstein, and Hack, although Willis didn't know whether these were their real names or not, nor did he care. The name they had for him was Burke. Although he had paid a lot of money for a safe cover identity, he was no longer using Willis, even for his criminal activities. The Factory was looking for him. He couldn't afford to risk any crew members he worked with giving up his real name to the authorities if they were picked up. So now he had two cover identities; Jack Connor, which he used as his civilian identity, and Burke, with no first name given, for his criminal associates.

Pruitt sat on a sofa on the opposite side of the room, a hard sneer frozen on his narrow face. He had harsh, bony features and a sallow complexion, and his right knee bounced up and down as if he were aching for violence. He was in his mid-thirties, on the short side at five feet six, and thin and hard as a knife blade. A bundle of raw nervous energy waiting for an opportunity to bust loose. In contrast to him was Lowenstein; a large man of about fifty with an overall softness about him, who sat like a Buddha on the same sofa as Pruitt, his eyes crinkling good-naturedly and his lips pulled up slightly into an amused smile. Rounding out the team was Hack, who stood with his back to the room and an eye pressed against the door's peephole. He was in his late forties, a mostly nondescript man with thinning hair, slight build, and a fair complexion. Just a face in the crowd who, if he entered a room, you'd barely be able to remember later. Hack turned from the peephole to tell them that the room service cart was heading their way.

"About time," Pruitt said, his voice high-pitched and nasally. In a jerky motion, he grabbed the ski mask laying on the sofa next to him and yanked it over his face. As he popped up off the sofa, he grabbed the .40-caliber handgun that he had earlier stuck inside his waistband, and slid the safety off.

Willis shook his head. "Not yet."

Pruitt had taken a step toward the door. He stopped and gave Willis a hard stare. His voice got tighter and more high-pitched as he demanded to know why not. "The plan we agreed to was to follow room service into the room."

"One of the players is in the bathroom."

Pruitt froze for a long moment before turning to Lowenstein, his eyes darkening under his ski mask. He knew as well as Willis that they couldn't hit the game while one of the players was locked away in the bathroom, but he was too hyped up to allow himself to back down.

"Is this joker in charge now?"

Lowenstein only looked more amused than before as he asked Pruitt to sit down. "For Chrissakes, Charlie. You'll get your chance to bust some heads soon enough. Relax for now, okay?"

Pruitt stared bug-eyed at Lowenstein, the other man's humoring and dismissive tone only seeming to infuriate him more. "So you're saying he's in charge," he forced out in a strangled voice.

Lowenstein sighed heavily before telling Pruitt that he wasn't saying anything of the kind.

"That's exactly what it sounds like," Pruitt complained, his tone now more injured than angry. He pulled his ski mask off. "We plan the job, we fund it, and we let him in as a favor to help him get his feet wet, and now you're letting him call all the shots?"

Lowenstein's eyes took on a more glazed look as some of his amusement dried up. "Chrissakes, Charlie, he's not calling the shots, okay? But he's had good ideas and what he's saying now makes sense," he said. "So stop it. We don't have time for this."

What Pruitt said was technically true. They knew the place and location of the game, and that there would be at least a hundred grand for them to take. And they added Willis to the crew at the last moment. But their plan was to hit the game in fake police uniforms, which probably would've ended with everyone getting shot up; the players, the hired muscle, and the crew hitting the game. Willis insisted on checking out the hotel and the suite before agreeing to do the job. It was his idea to break into the suite ahead of time so he could hide surveillance cameras, as well as use the neighboring suite for their operations. If he hadn't planted the cameras and set up surveillance, they wouldn't have known about the armed protection, or the combination to the safe that sat in the hotel suite—the same safe that now held all the money for the game.

If the safe had been one of the ubiquitous electronic room safes that almost all hotels provide these days, it wouldn't be a problem not knowing the combination. One of Willis's souvenirs from his time with The Factory was an electronic gizmo that looked about the same as an iPod and could reset those electronic safes. But the safe was a real one with tumblers that was cemented to the floor, and without the combination the job probably would've been a bust no matter how they did it.

Maybe they could've tortured or scared the combination out of the player that had it, but only if they had enough time and knew which player it was. It was also Willis's idea to skip the cop uniforms and follow room service into the suite, and while that was no longer going to work, they could still get into the suite whenever they wanted thanks to another souvenir of Willis's from The Factory—a device that looked a lot like a credit card and could override the electronic lock on almost any hotel room door. So now the plan had to be to wait until the player left the bathroom and they could catch the muscled thugs off guard enough so that they could take over the suite without shots being fired.

Pruitt sat back down on the sofa, but continued grousing over his perceived injury of letting a nobody like Willis take over their heist. As far as Pruitt knew, Willis had a military background but was completely green as far as heists went. While it would be Willis's first robbery, he was far from green after his time with The Factory. Willis could've corrected Pruitt's misunderstanding concerning his lack of experience, but he didn't bother. For a brief second, he considered getting up and smacking that borderline psycho upside his head and then walking away from the job, but he stayed put. The score was going to be an even split, and he needed the money. His buying a cover identity cost him a good chunk of what he had, and he was finding that living outside of society was far more expensive than he had anticipated. While the lack of professionalism that Pruitt and the rest of the crew showed bothered him, the job was shaping up to be quick and simple regardless. He would have to trust that he could keep these clowns in line once they hit the poker game. After making up his mind to continue on with the robbery, he focused his attention solely on the computer monitor, and Pruitt's complaining became little more than a nasal drone buzzing in his ear.

The room service cart must've reached the neighboring suite. Willis watched the way the room's inhabitants responded as the hotel employee knocked on their door. No reaction from any of the players, nor from the two thugs reading the newspaper, neither of whom bothered to look up. The thug who had earlier been standing as if he were a stone gargoyle watching over the game, showed no change in expression as he moved to the door and glanced out the peephole. Without any hesitation, he opened the door and walked out into the hallway. Willis couldn't tell what was going on there since he hadn't planted any surveillance cameras in the hallway, but guessed that the thug was sending the hotel employee on his way and that he'd be wheeling the cart in himself. Seconds later, the door opened and the thug wheeled the service cart into the suite, and only seconds after that, Hack let them know that the hotel employee had walked past them. Willis told him to get the employee and bring him back, and to keep it quiet. Hack nodded, slipped on his ski mask, and had a Beretta 9mm pistol out of a shoulder holster as he slipped out of the room. When he returned less than a half minute later, Willis, Pruitt, and Lowenstein all had their masks on and their guns out. The surveillance cameras now showed that the two thugs who had been reading the newspaper in the neighboring suite were busy handing out food trays to the poker players. It was time to hit the game. Willis told the hotel employee what he was going to say when he was brought back to the other room and what would happen to him if he screwed things up. The clerk, a young kid with a lean scarecrow-like body, looked terrified but he nodded his understanding. After that, they were all moving out into the hallway with the hotel employee being half-carried by Hack and Pruitt.

Once they got to the other suite, Willis knocked on the door and prompted the hotel employee to repeat what he had earlier told him to say. The same muscle as from before opened the door, his eyes widening slightly on seeing that the hotel employee was no longer alone. Before he could do anything more than reach for his gun, the clerk was shoved hard into him and Pruitt and Willis were moving quickly past him into the suite. While the thug tried to disentangle himself from the hotel employee, Lowenstein zapped him with a stun gun, sending him dropping to the carpeted floor. Lowenstein moved past him, leaving Hack to secure the man and the hotel employee with plastic cuffs.

No more than two seconds elapsed from the moment the hotel suite door was opened to Willis and Pruitt racing into the suite with their guns drawn. None of the players, nor the two remaining muscle, had time to react. One of the thugs dropped the room service tray he was holding. He had started reaching for his gun, but as he caught sight of the 9mm Glock that Willis pointed his way, his hand slowed. In several quick bounds, Pruitt raced over to him and struck him above his ear with the butt end of his gun. That made the thug stumble and wince, and the second blow from Pruitt sent him to the floor. The third thug didn't move until Willis signaled him with his gun to get on his knees. The man did it, all the while holding a room service tray.

"Fingers interlaced behind your head," Willis ordered

softly. "And all of you in the game, same thing. Not a peep from any of you unless you want your skulls cracked opened."

All of them complied. While Willis and Pruitt covered them with their guns, Lowenstein and Hack used plastic cuffs to secure the paid muscle and then the players, each of them being cuffed with their hands behind their back. For a few seconds, the major league ballplayer looked like he wanted to be a hero with the way his eyes were shining, but Lowenstein made a *tsking* noise and the sight of Lowenstein's stun gun kept the ballplayer from making a move. It took less than ninety seconds to secure the room. Once that was done, Hack went to the safe to retrieve the money while Willis went around the room collecting the surveillance cameras he had hidden earlier, and Pruitt and Lowenstein gagged each of the players and muscle. Hack had already gagged the hotel employee after he had cuffed him. Another four minutes and they were done. Hack had the money packed away in an overnight bag, and he told the rest of them in a hushed whisper that a quick count showed over a hundred and ten grand. After that, they left the suite, all of them going their separate ways with Lowenstein taking the bag with the money and the surveillance cameras. The ski masks were also added to the bag. They had all worn leather gloves from the moment they entered the hotel, so there were no fingerprints to clean up, but Willis still had to go back to the neighboring suite to collect the laptop computer.

CHAPTER 2

WILLIS WASN'T HAPPY about the next part of the job where they'd be entrusting the money to Lowenstein until they could meet to divvy it up, especially since the job went smoothly and quickly enough where they could've divided the money before leaving the hotel suite. Although, maybe not. As Lowenstein had told Willis earlier, things can turn sour in a heartbeat if you hang around any longer than you need to. Maybe someone on the hotel staff realizes that it's taking longer than it should for the guy delivering room service to report back, or maybe a guest walks past the suite and hears something that makes them suspicious, or maid service walks in and surprises them, or any number of other things that could complicate the robbery if they don't leave as soon as they can. It didn't matter. Willis had agreed to that part of the job and he knew it was nonnegotiable; he also took the precautions that were available. It was doubtful, anyway, that Lowenstein would try a double-cross. Not only would he have Willis hunting him down if he did, he'd also have to contend with Big

Ed Hanley, who was Willis's agent for the job and was owed ten percent of Willis's take. While Lowenstein might not realize how dangerous it would be to double-cross Willis, he had to know the trouble he'd be buying if he messed with Hanley. In a way, Lowenstein leaving with the money was a good thing. It put more risk on him and less on the rest of the crew. If the police had been tipped off about the job, Lowenstein would be the one to get picked up while the rest of them would have a better chance of slipping past the cops.

Anyway, it was a moot point. Lowenstein had left the hotel minutes ago without incident, and Willis was back in the other suite packing up the laptop computer and other electronic equipment he had brought, and it would be two hours before they were scheduled to meet at an address in Queens. He finished packing up what he needed to, gave the suite one last check to make sure he wasn't leaving behind any evidence that they had been there, then looked out the door's peephole to make sure the hallway was clear. It was and he slipped out and moved quickly to a staircase. As the other members of the crew had already done, he used the stairs so he could take the elevator from a different floor. In his case, he walked up three flights. Once the elevator brought him down to the lobby, he casually made his way past the front desk, then out the building and to the street, all the while a pleasant and casual smile showing on his face. He didn't lose the smile until he was a block away. It was only then that he let his expression harden with the knowledge that he had completed his first heist and that the new criminal chapter to his life was now fully underway.

It was five weeks ago that he broke free from The Factory, leaving his handler, Tom Barron, dead in the process. He knew he wouldn't be able to stay hidden for long, that no matter where he ran, The Factory would eventually catch up to him. But he also knew that regardless of how many foot soldiers they might employ, at its heart, The Factory was a government bureaucracy. If he were able to eliminate the top bureaucrats running the show, it would crumble apart, especially with how the government officials who brought it into existence had to be terrified of its existence and true agenda ever becoming known.

Since leaving The Factory, Willis dyed his hair blond and grew it out longer, as well as growing a goatee and also dying his facial hair the same blond color. Even though he wasn't what anyone would consider good-looking, beautiful women responded when he turned on the charm, his eyes crinkling good-naturedly and his lips flashing an amiable smile. Back when he was a liquor salesman, Willis met many beautiful women in his travels and had many affairs, some lasting only a night, others lasting much longer. The one thing they all had in common was they ended well with never any hurt feelings, and the women only having a warm fondness toward him. He was a rogue, and he never pretended otherwise and none of them ever begrudged him that.

When Willis lost his job as a liquor salesman, his libido took a big hit, and after he was recruited by The Factory, it went missing all together. It bothered him when he thought about it, which wasn't often since The Factory kept him busy, and his two years associated with them was mostly spent in a low level of depression where he was almost machine-like as he carried out his murders as ordered. At some level, he knew that the two were tied together; the loss of his sex drive and working for The Factory.

After his loud resignation from The Factory, Willis left with Bowser to the White Mountains of New Hampshire. He took along with him seventeen thousand dollars that he had been able to save up, a suitcase full of gear from The Factory, names of two other Factory handlers, as well as the name of The Factory's head man, Colonel Jay T. Richardson. Once there, he rented a cabin in the town of Jackson, and spent his first three days in New Hampshire sleeping, thinking, and taking his bull terrier for long walks along hiking trails. His fourth night he drove to North Conway, and that was where he met Jenny Brislow, a dental hygienist on vacation from Iowa. Jenny was thirty-one, petite, with short blonde hair, a slightly upturned but very cute freckled nose, and a dazzling smile. Willis found himself turning on the charm, and before too long he and Jenny were heading back to his rented cabin. Within an hour, they were both out of their clothes and starting what would become a marathon five-day session in bed interrupted only by food, sleep, and taking Bowser for walks. During the time that Bowser was on his own, he mostly behaved himself, either sleeping by the foot of the bed or gnawing on a bone, and only occasionally getting up to walk around the room and let out little pig-like grunts to show his displeasure at being ignored.

As much as Willis was making up for almost three years of lost time, Jenny matched him in intensity and desire. At the end of those five days, they were both worn out and satisfied, although Bowser was in a surly mood. Jenny had to head back to Iowa. After showering, she slipped on a pair of jeans and a tee shirt over her lithe and toned body that had been naked for most of those five days, and was a body that Willis had grown fond of. With her hair wet and an easy smile breaking over her lips, she kissed him on the tip of his nose and suggested with a note of melancholy that he could always look her up if he was ever out in Iowa. After she left, Willis took Bowser on a long four-hour hike in an attempt to make amends with the canine, then packed up and headed off to Ohio. There, he looked up several dodgy individuals he had met during his travels as a liquor salesman, and that led him to a guy who for ten grand was able to manufacture a fake cover identify, including a passport and social security card. Later, another contact led him to Hanley, who set him up with Lowenstein for the heist and his indoctrination into the world of armed robberies, although The Factory had already hardened him more than several lifetimes of knocking off poker games ever could.

CHAPTER 3

LOWENSTEIN ANSWERED THE door at the Queens apartment where they had arranged to meet. His eyes glinted as he both smirked and nodded at Willis. Then he began chuckling softly, a thin wheezing sound escaping from him. Willis didn't bother asking what the joke was since his attention had been diverted elsewhere. Unfamiliar voices were coming from inside the apartment. A man's and a woman's, maybe more than that. Willis raised an eyebrow, his jaw muscles and body tensing. Lowenstein, still chuckling, indicated that it was nothing to worry about. He stepped aside to let Willis in. At that point, Willis realized the noises were coming from a TV and he followed the large man into the apartment. After the door was closed, Lowenstein fished a tiny GPS tracking device from out of his pants pocket and held it up between his thumb and forefinger for Willis to get a better look at. It was, in effect, the punch line to his private joke.

"Guess what I found stitched into your ski mask?" Lowenstein said, shaking his head slowly and exaggeratedly to show his disappointment in Willis. All of them had stashed their ski masks in the same bag with the money before they left the suite. "Chrissakes, Burke, we're not rank amateurs. If we were going to screw you over, we would've dumped the ski masks before taking off with the money."

Willis accepted the GPS tracking device from Lowenstein and dropped it into his coat pocket. He expected Lowenstein to find the device. A quick check with a bug detector would have found it easily. The GPS tracking device Willis counted on not being found was the one that he had hid in one of the surveillance cameras. That one transmitted at a frequency that most bug detectors failed to pick up, but he saw no reason to tell Lowenstein about that. While Lowenstein led Willis through the apartment, he explained why Willis had acted unnecessarily paranoid.

"I understand how this is your first job with a crew and all," Lowenstein said patiently, as if to a child. "But if you're going to do more jobs, you need to trust your crew members. We don't double-cross one another. We can't. We're finished in this business if any of us ever tries a stunt like that." He smiled sadly at Willis. "It's a small industry. Word spreads quickly."

Lowenstein had brought Willis into a small living room where Pruitt and Hack sat on a sofa sipping beer from cans as they stared at a TV across from them. A local news show was on. Hack looked away from it briefly to nod to Willis. Pruitt seemed more absorbed in it, but broke away from it to give Willis a sideways glance. He fished a beer can from a cooler and tossed it to Lowenstein, then tossed another one to Willis.

Lowenstein explained, "We've got a bet, Charlie and I, on whether the heist makes the news."

"No way it does," Pruitt mumbled, his attention back to the TV. "Not with that ballplayer involved. They'll find a way to keep it quiet."

"We'll see," Lowenstein said.

"Yeah, we will."

A commercial came on and Pruitt looked away from the set and fixed his stare on Willis. "You really pissed me off back there," he said. "But I got to admit, you had some smart ideas. The job went smooth as butter thanks to you. Although don't go thinking we wouldn't have gotten the money without you. Twenty minutes with them, and I would've had them begging to give me the combination."

"Unless the guy who had it ends up going into shock or drops dead of a heart attack," Lowenstein said.

"Not likely."

"Not impossible, though."

Pruitt made a face at that possibility. "One in a thousand the guy with the combination croaks before I get it from him. I'd take those odds all day long."

"Very generous odds, Charlie. I'd put it more at one in a hundred."

Pruitt's face reddened. "So one in a hundred jobs go south because of that," he said through tightened lips. "I can live with those odds."

"Yeah, well, it was a lot more than just the possibility of the job busting up on us. We could've gotten shot up by the hired help if we went in blind like we had planned."

"With cop uniforms on? You kidding me?"

"Could have happened," Lowenstein said, barely able to contain his amusement at seeing the annoyed reaction he got from Pruitt. Before Pruitt could continue the argument the news came back. He looked away from Lowenstein and forced out in a tight and strained voice that Lowenstein was full of it. Lowenstein let out an exaggerated sigh to show Pruitt how his statement had injured him, and then grinning widely led Willis to a small kitchen area where a table was arranged with four stacks of money on it.

"Final count was a hundred and twelve grand," Lowenstein said. "Expenses totaled eight thousand four hundred, rounding up to the nearest hundred, and all itemized. Four-way split makes it an even twenty-five thousand nine hundred. Not bad for your first job. Take any of those piles. They're all the same. Count the money if you'd like."

Willis sat down at the table, put down his unopened beer can and looked at a list of itemized expenses. It added up to what Lowenstein said it did and it didn't appear as if any padding had been done. All four stacks looked about the same height, each made up of bundles of bills rubber banded together. Willis picked up one of the stacks. There was nine hundred in the top bundle, a thousand dollars in each of the other bundles he counted, with a total of twenty-six bundles. Willis thumbed through the bundles he didn't count to get a quick estimate, then placed the money in a gym bag he had brought. While he did all that, Lowenstein drank the beer that Pruitt had tossed to him, and after crumpling the empty can, let it drop to the floor. As Willis got up to leave, Lowenstein asked him what his plans were.

"Why?"

Lowenstein pursed his lips, shrugged noncommittally. "Another job could be coming up very soon. I can't promise anything, but this one could be worth you sticking around for a few days. If this job comes through, the take's going to be seven figures."

"What can you tell me about it?"

"Nothing yet."

Willis mulled it over. While Pruitt and Lowenstein appeared like clowns outside of the job, during the heist they bottled up their juvenile behavior and acted like cold-hearted professionals, and a seven-figure take had him interested. "An even split?"

Lowenstein shook his head. "Among the crew, yeah, but the individual bringing it to me will be taking thirty percent off the top, if the job happens. It's not definite yet, nor is the size of the crew needed, but seven figure takes don't happen often."

From the other room, a loud burst of profanity erupted from Pruitt, then what sounded like an empty beer can bouncing off a TV. Over Pruitt's swearing, Willis and Lowenstein could hear the news reporting on a robbery at a swank New York City hotel. Lowenstein's round face lit up and he could barely contain his glee. Almost giddy, he yelled out to Pruitt that he was going to be helping himself to his winnings from Pruitt's take.

"The hell you will! They didn't say nothin' about that ballplayer being involved!" Pruitt yelled back. "You better not be touching my money!"

Lowenstein picked up a packet of bills from one of the piles and thumbed through it for a quick count. "The bet was only that the robbery makes the news today," he said happily, shoving the money into his pants pocket. "Not whether that ballplayer shows up in the story. You want to fixate on that, that's your problem."

"I swear, if you touch my money, I'll be cutting off your fat hands!"

Lowenstein giggled at that. Willis was getting disgusted with these antics, but the temptation of a seven-figure payoff kept him from walking away. He asked Lowenstein more about the job. The large man looked at him distractedly as if he didn't know what Willis was talking about, then remembered, and whatever amusement had been sparkling in his eyes dried up.

"Let me give you a phone number to reach me at," he said. "This will be for a disposable phone, and I'll be changing phones every few days. Make sure you call me only from a disposable phone of your own."

Lowenstein scribbled a phone number on a scrap of paper and handed it to Willis. "Call me each day around ten in the morning," he said. "If a deal comes together as I hope and I can use you, then we'll see. If not, or you get tired of hanging around, then c'est la vie. But if you're interested, stay in the area. And don't worry, it's safe to be here. None of those mob guys in that poker game have a clue who we are. The only ones who know we did the heist are us four."

Willis slipped the scrap of paper into his wallet. "How about you and Pruitt try not to kill each other before I call you, okay?"

Lowenstein smiled thinly at that. "Ah, that's nothing to worry about. Charlie and I are like brothers. We've been doing jobs together for seven years. Pushing each other's buttons is only a hobby for the two of us. Don't worry about it."

Willis didn't bother responding to that. Lowenstein led

him back to the door. As they passed through the living room, Pruitt once again warned Lowenstein that he'd cut off his fat hands if he touched any of his money. To that, Lowenstein dug out the packet of bills that he had shoved into his pocket and waved it at Pruitt, who in turn rifled a half-filled beer can at Lowenstein's head, which Lowenstein barely ducked. If any of the beer had splashed on Willis, he would've dragged Pruitt off the sofa and kicked the hell out of him, but none of it had so he left it alone. Lowenstein seemed to especially enjoy the reaction he had gotten out of Pruitt and he began giggling like a school kid. He was near breathless as he told Willis to call him the next morning. Willis left without saying whether he would or not.

Willis stuck around the next four days. He wasn't happy doing so, and was tempted to leave New York and find a different crew to hook up with, but he was more tempted by a big score. His share from ripping off that poker game wasn't going to go far. First, Hanley would take his ten percent bite, then another bite as he needed to pay rent for his cover identity, and then yet another large bite as he needed to have money funneled back to him as if it were coming from a legitimate job. Hanley, for a fee, helped set that up for him. He needed his cover identity to appear to be gainfully employed; both for tax reasons and so that *Jack Connor* wouldn't show up on any list The Factory might come up with for out-of-work targets. Once all these bites were taken, there wasn't going to be much left over from that twenty-five grand, and he needed money, both for living off the grid and to track down Colonel Jay T. Richardson and other Factory personnel.

The apartment where he met up with Lowenstein and the

rest of the crew was located in Long Island City. Willis first went back to a room he rented in Forest Hills so he could lock his money in the hotel safe, and then he went to Flushing to pick Bowser up from a pet sitter where he'd left him earlier. He could've left Bowser in the flat, but he wanted to make sure that Bowser would be looked after in case the job went badly and he ended up dead or was arrested by the police.

When he arrived at the pet sitter, Bowser at first gave him the cold shoulder to show how hurt he was at being abandoned for the afternoon. He took Bowser to Forest Park where they walked along a wooded path. It was mostly dark out without much light. Bowser had raced ahead of him, and when he passed a couple of ragged-looking guys who were there either to sell drugs or to mug someone, Willis slowed down, hoping it was the latter. He was keyed up and he would've welcomed the opportunity to work off his nervous energy on them, but they wisely kept their distance.

An hour of walking in the woods didn't help him any. He left and found a restaurant where they allowed Bowser to accompany him, and he ordered celebratory steaks for them both, but he was too distracted to enjoy his food, or even taste it much. A skinny Russian woman with tight curly black hair came over to his table to admire Bowser, her voice sultry and her accent thick as she told Bowser how handsome he was. She lingered by the table, making sure Willis knew that she was interested in him more than the dog. Somewhat half-heartedly, Willis ended up buying her dinner and leaving with her. He hadn't noticed back in the restaurant the overly sweet perfume she wore, but he did when she was in the car with him and it made him think of hospital disinfectant. When they got to his flat, he considered asking her to take a shower to scrub some of that perfume off, but he didn't bother and instead they sat on his bed and had a couple of drinks, then proceeded to get naked. As she squirmed her skinny ass out of a pair of skin-tight jeans, she complained in her thick accent that she didn't want to do it in front of the dog, but her complaints were done feebly and mostly for show and Willis didn't take them seriously. Desire flushed her skin a warm pink and he knew she would shed her clothes whether Bowser was in the room or not, or even if there had been a roomful of nuns sitting in attendance for that matter.

Willis soon found he was only going through the motions and couldn't work up the proper enthusiasm, and the Russian woman, Svetlana, shot him a disgusted look.

"Maybe I should leave," she said.

Willis didn't try to persuade her otherwise. He watched as she dressed and then left without saying another word.

The moment Hanley had contacted him about a possible job in New York, Willis's libido had ceased to exist. He didn't realize it at the time, and even when he did notice it it wasn't something that he thought much about. At a subconscious level, he accepted that it was a self-preservation instinct; he needed to focus all his thoughts and energies on the job and not on chasing tail. After leaving the Long Island City apartment with his share of the take, he found himself distracted with all this pent-up energy inside. Maybe if those two ragged-looking guys hanging near the trail in Forest Park had tried jumping him he would've been able to release it on them, but they hadn't so he thought that he needed another outlet for it. When Svetlana came over to his table, it seemed like a good bet that she'd be able to provide the outlet he needed, but that turned out not to be the case. It wasn't her overly sweet perfume smell that distracted him. Once her clothes were off that smell was mostly replaced by a dank muskiness which he didn't mind, and besides, with her slender hips and toned body he found her attractive enough where he should've been able to ignore any smell. It was something else, some vague and troubling thought nagging at him that he couldn't quite dredge out from his mind.

He had a restless night, getting at most two hours of sleep, none of which was satisfying. By five in the morning, he accepted that there was no real chance of any additional sleep, so he got out of bed and took Bowser for a long three-hour walk, hoping the cool morning air would help clear his head. It didn't. There was too much nervous energy inside with some unknown thought pestering him. He almost left New York, but he didn't. A possible share in a seven-figure heist kept him from leaving. At ten, he called Lowenstein and was told that things were still up in the air and for him to call back the next day.

Willis moved to a new flat in the College Point neighborhood of Queens. He didn't want to stay in any one place too long, and he'd already been in that flat in Forest Hills for five days. That afternoon, he went to a boxing gym three blocks from where he was staying and hit a heavy bag for an hour. At the end of it, his arms felt like lead pipes and a good amount of his nervous energy had dissipated. He still felt a sense of disquiet, and he still couldn't quite figure out the source of it. Outside of the time in the gym, taking Bowser for walks, and picking up takeout food, he kept to his rented room. Bowser naturally attracted women, as did his own rough good looks, but he accepted that until the latest job was done and he was out of New York, that part of himself was going to be shut down. The women who tried approaching him, quickly veered off once they caught sight of the deadness that had settled in his eyes.

That night, he slept poorly again, and at ten in the morning he called Lowenstein and was told things were still unsettled. As with the previous day, he spent an hour hitting a heavy bag until his arms felt dead, and spent the rest of the day in his room except when he needed to take Bowser outside or needed food or coffee. That sense of disquiet was still with him, but he had given up trying to figure out the cause of it, hoping that if he left it alone the answer would pop up by itself. As with the other two nights, he slept poorly and had decided that it was the last time he was calling Lowenstein. If the job was still up in the air, he'd be heading back to Ohio. When he called Lowenstein, the large man gave him an address in Brooklyn where they were going to be meeting later that afternoon.

"The job's on," Lowenstein told Willis. "And it's a beauty. We're all very soon going to be making a shitload of money."

CHAPTER 4

WILLIS ARRIVED AT the Brooklyn address forty minutes early so he could settle in half a block away and observe the people coming and leaving, as well as anyone else who might've been watching the address. He wasn't as concerned about any member of the crew trying something as he was about the police being tipped off, and he wanted to make sure the place wasn't under surveillance. He watched as Hack, Lowenstein, and Pruitt all arrived separately and within fifteen minutes of when they were supposed to meet. None of them looked overly concerned that they might've been followed, with Pruitt striding down the sidewalk with his chest puffed out like a strutting rooster, Lowenstein chuckling over something and Hack taking short shuffling steps as other pedestrians passed him without paying any attention. They were going to be meeting in a private room inside a bar, and during the time Willis had the address under surveillance, roughly two dozen other people entered the same bar, with none of them seeming like law enforcement, or any of them appearing more likely than any of the others as being the brains behind the new heist. No vans were parked on the block either, nor anything else suspicious. Willis waited ten more minutes past their scheduled meeting time before convincing himself that no one else was watching the place.

Willis entered the bar and approached the bartender to give him the agreed upon password. The bartender, who at no time acknowledged Willis's presence, used his eyes to indicate where Willis was supposed to go, which led Willis down a narrow and rickety staircase and then to a poorly lit hallway. At the end of the hallway was a single room. Willis knocked once and entered.

Along with Pruitt, Hack, and Lowenstein, a strikingly beautiful woman sat in the room. She was in her mid-thirties and had large dark eyes, high cheek bones, shoulder-length brown hair, and a sultry mouth even though it was set in a frown. From what Willis could tell with her sitting, she was on the small side, probably no taller than five feet two inches, slender build, and dressed conservatively in a tailored gray suit. There was an iciness about her, and nothing but darkness in her eyes as she glanced at Willis, her frown deepening slightly. Still, if Willis had picked her up instead of Svetlana three nights ago, he would've had no problem mustering up the necessary enthusiasm no matter how distracted he might've been. He hadn't seen her enter the bar, and he certainly would've noticed her if she had.

Pruitt, Hack, and Lowenstein were all drinking beers, the woman had a scotch on the rocks, or at least that's what it had been before most of the ice had melted. A snorting noise exploded from Pruitt, and given the way his head was tilted he looked down his thin, sharply angled nose at Willis, his jaw muscles clenching. "You're late," he complained, his voice an angry nasal whine.

"Traffic," Willis said.

"The rest of us had no problem with traffic."

Willis ignored him and took a seat across from Pruitt and Lowenstein. It infuriated Pruitt, his lean, narrow face quickly reddening, and his eyes taking on a beady look, almost like a rat's. He started to rise from his chair, but Lowenstein moved quickly to place a thick, beefy hand on Pruitt's shoulder to keep him from standing. "I'm sure Burke's tardiness was only because he decided to take it upon himself to stake out the place," Lowenstein said. Then to Willis, "So don't keep us in suspense. Did you see anything suspicious?"

"Nothing," Willis said.

The explanation of Willis's lateness appeased Pruitt enough to let himself be guided back down to his seat by Lowenstein's heavy hand, but he continued to glower at Willis as if he'd like nothing more than to get a chance to take Willis on.

Lowenstein smiled thinly at Willis as he shook his head. "Your initiative was admirable in a way, I guess. But Burke, as I told you before, we're not amateurs. If the police were camped outside with a parabolic microphone they wouldn't be able to pick up what was being said in this room. We chose this location for a reason. Because we're professionals. And to further put your mind at ease that this room isn't bugged or none of us are wired, this is a state-of-the-art bug detector. How about you doing the honors?"

Lowenstein had pulled a small device about the size of an iPhone out of his pocket and slid it to Willis. Willis examined it briefly. The bug detector would pick up any wireless transmitter in the room, but wouldn't be of any help if any of them had a recording device attached to them. Still, it was better than nothing. He first waved the device over his own body to show he wasn't wired, then each of the others in turn, and finally he covered the room. No beeps. There was nothing being transmitted from the room. He took his seat and slid the bug detector back to Lowenstein.

"Have we wasted enough time yet?" the woman asked, both bored and annoyed, maybe bristling a bit over how much time Willis had spent using the device on her.

"I don't think so. I'm guessing this joker wants to waste more time," Pruitt said while glaring at Willis.

"No, I'm good," Willis said.

The woman continued without any introductions. She told them that they were going to be stealing a painting. "This is a seventeenth-century oil painting from the Dutch master Pieter de Berge, who has become very much in vogue lately," she said as if that was supposed to mean anything to them. Like her appearance, her voice had both a smoothness and an iciness to it. "The painting is titled *The Dame*, and I have a buyer lined up who'll be paying seven million for it. After my thirty percent cut, that will leave four point nine million for the rest of you. More than enough for all of us to profit nicely from this."

Hack let out a soft whistle. Even Pruitt looked impressed as his jaw dropped slightly and he absently began rubbing his chin. Willis asked, "When do we get paid?"

"A few days to possibly a week after the job's done, but you'll be holding the painting until I deliver your share of the money to offshore accounts for each of you, if that's what you're worried about."

"This is a once in a lifetime score," Lowenstein told Willis, his voice quick and excited.

"And a perfect setup," the woman said. Her lips twisted into a thin and icy smile. "Almost as if they'll be handing us the painting."

Willis settled back to hear how the robbery was going to take place, and he had to agree with the stunningly beautiful mystery woman. If things were as she said, it was going to be easier than he would've imagined to steal a painting worth seven million dollars. They weren't going to be stealing it from a museum or a gallery, but from a private home in Short Hills, New Jersey. A wealthy businessman named Jonah Landistone had recently acquired *The Dame*, and Friday, which was three days away, the painting was going to be delivered to his home by armored car, and then unveiled later at a party that night. The next morning, the painting was to be picked up by an armored vehicle and donated to New York's Museum of Modern Art to great fanfare. What made the robbery such a piece of cake was that the woman, who Willis had begun to think of as the Ice Princess, had the list of security personnel who were scheduled to guard the painting while it was in Landistone's residence. There were four employees assigned, and each of the crew was going to intercept one of them so they could be kept on ice until after the robbery. Each member of the crew would have a uniform, a counterfeit badge, and would show up at the Short Hills residence as expected. After the painting was brought over, the four of them would take control of the house and leave Landistone and anyone else there tied up while they left with *The Dame*. Once they had the painting in their possession, the Ice Princess would arrange payment, and once their share was paid over, they'd transfer the painting to her.

"This is such a sweet deal," Lowenstein added after the Ice Princess had finished. "The holdup was getting the list of security personnel and knowing how many of them were going to be assigned. If there were only three of them, you would've been left out, Burke. And if there were more than four names, we would've been scrambling to add more crew members. But it worked out perfectly."

Lowenstein's smile had turned brittle, a sheen of excitement covering his face. The deal had him nervous. A once in a lifetime score falling in their laps. Pruitt had that same nervous excitement on his face, even Hack showed a little of it. Willis asked the Ice Princess how she got the list of personnel assigned to protect the painting.

"Does it matter?" she asked flatly.

"Yeah, I'd say so. What if the personnel assignments change between now and the robbery?"

"If it does, I'll know about it, and so will all of you. Does that satisfy you?"

Willis thought about it and nodded. She had someone on the inside. There was other information he would've liked to have had, such as a better count of how many people were going to be at the residence at the time of the robbery, but she had already given them a rundown of what she knew. Landistone was working on marriage number three to a twenty-three-year-old blonde trophy wife who was three years younger than Landistone's youngest child. Of Landistone's four children, there was no reason for any of them to be there, but that didn't mean anything. There would, of course, be household staff which the Ice Princess had an estimate of four members, not including any added staff that might be there for the party later that night. Landistone's private secretary would most likely be on hand, and maybe some members of the museum's board. But as the Ice Princess reasoned, the exact number didn't matter since the crew would be there an hour before the delivery of *The Dame*, which would give them plenty of time to account for everyone in the house and figure out how to handle things. Willis couldn't see any reason to disagree with her.

The Ice Princess took envelopes out of a briefcase and distributed an envelope to each of them. In Willis's was a photo, name, and address of the security personnel he was to intercept, one Craig Gunder, as well as some other information. Willis didn't much resemble Gunder, who from his photo was in his late twenties and had the large fleshy face of someone who had once played offensive line in high school. But that didn't matter since he'd have a counterfeit ID with Gunder's name and his own photo on it, and according to the Ice Princess, they were only going to be checking names at Landistone's residence. If they also had copies of the real IDs, then things were going to get messy, but the robbery would still be a possibility. They'd have to take control of the house earlier, and then sweat things out with the armored car personnel when they arrived.

The Ice Princess impatiently raised her right arm and pulled her suit jacket sleeve back enough so she could glance at her watch. She had a delicate wrist to go with the rest of her delicate features. Abruptly, she announced that she needed to leave, and then quickly zipped up her briefcase and pushed her chair back from the table. Standing, her body looked even better in her immaculately tailored suit than when she'd been sitting. Slender, petite, but with just the right amount of curves. Willis could see the hunger in each of the men's faces as she walked towards the door. After she closed the door behind her, Pruitt elbowed Lowenstein, a smart-alecky grin stretching his lips.

"You've been getting a piece of that?" Pruitt asked.

"Only in my dreams," Lowenstein said with a sigh.

"I'd do her in a second," Hack said more to himself than any of the rest of them. None of the others bothered to act as if they'd heard him.

"How do you know her?" Willis asked Lowenstein.

Lowenstein raised an eyebrow quizzically. "Why?"

"I want to know if we can trust her and the information she's giving us."

"We can trust her," Lowenstein said. "I've worked with her before. She's solid. This deal is solid."

"I don't like that she knows our names and other than you we don't know hers."

"What do you need to know her name for? You planning to call her up for a date? I hate to tell you this, Burke, but you're not her type." Lowenstein couldn't help smiling over his own joke while Pruitt let out a loud laugh. Lowenstein added, "And besides, she doesn't know any of our names except mine. That's done for a reason. Any of you get picked up, she doesn't have to worry about it. And if she gets picked up, same deal."

Willis didn't argue the point. Lowenstein was right. It didn't matter, and it wouldn't help any if he pushed Lowenstein for her name since he wasn't going to give it. Still, it bugged him that he didn't have it, and he wasn't sure why that was. It certainly wasn't so he could ask her for a date, although he wouldn't have minded ending up in the sack with her, even if she'd end up giving him a touch of frostbite. But there was a reason he wanted to know it, something he couldn't quite dredge from his subconscious. It was going to be yet another nagging whisper floating around in his head to add to the one that had been present ever since that poker game heist.

Lowenstein handed Pruitt and Hack a white bedsheet so that they could attach it to one of the walls. He had brought a photographer's light with him, and while they got the sheet ready, he set up the light. Once that was done, he took pictures of each of them for their fake security badges and then Pruitt took Lowenstein's photo. Willis hesitated only briefly before letting his picture get taken. It didn't matter. The Factory had his picture on file, and the few cosmetic things he had done to alter his appearance wouldn't fool them or any facial recognition system that he might run across. At some point soon he was going to have to see a plastic surgeon and do something more drastic. The money he got from this job would help with that.

"I need all of you to set up overseas accounts for the money transfers," Lowenstein announced, a bit of weariness showing in his smile and his voice sounding more gravelly. "Get these account numbers to me by tomorrow." He handed out instructions for a bank in the Bahamas, and as Hack stared at it with a perplexed frown, Lowenstein offered to help him if needed. Hack nodded, relief glimmering briefly over his bland face.

"Each of us needs to figure out by tomorrow how we're going to intercept our guys," Lowenstein added. "If you can't do this, call me."

None of them indicated that it would be a problem. There

was a brief discussion about logistics, where they were going to keep the kidnapped security guards on ice, as well as the painting, and a few other details. Once they were done, they separated with Hack leaving first, and the other three discreetly heading up to the bar so they could blend in among the other customers and then stagger the times for when they would leave.

CHAPTER 5

WILLIS SLEPT BETTER that night. He still had those whispers nagging at him, but having the details of the robbery to think over helped to quiet them, at least it helped him to ignore them. Still, while he had the alarm clock set for five fifteen, he was out of bed by five. After a quick three-minute shower and another minute and a half to change into jeans and a tee shirt, he was heading off to Livingston, New Jersey, bringing Bowser along with him.

At that time of morning, traffic was light getting through the city and he was able to arrive in Livingston a little before six. A gray haziness in the air seemed to add to the overall dreariness of the area, which looked to Willis like a blue-collar town that tried hard to masquerade as something more than it was. The houses he passed had a shoddiness to them, as if there hadn't been much done to them over the last fifty years, and the red brick apartment building Craig Gunder lived in looked even more neglected. Even in its heyday it would've been a depressing place to live. Willis found a place to park,

and then took Bowser for a walk around the neighborhood. No one would think twice about a man walking a dog at that early hour, even if they'd never seen the man before, and if anything they'd only remember the dog and not pay much attention to the man walking him. In Bowser's case, that was even more true. With his clownish attitude and thick bullet head, he was a dog that demanded attention.

Willis made sure to circle back to the apartment building by twenty minutes past six. According to the information he had on Gunder, his target worked a part-time job at a local gas station and usually left his apartment between six thirty and quarter to seven when he didn't have a conflicting security guard assignment. Willis walked around the area trying to get a look at the back parking lot, but couldn't from any of the vantage points he tried. At six thirty, he had Bowser by the entrance of the apartment building's driveway, which went down a small hill before circling behind the building. Willis took the leash off Bowser and then slapped the dog's rear, sending Bowser scampering down the driveway. Willis then made a half-hearted attempt to call for the dog and jogged down the driveway after him.

Willis had gotten lucky with his timing. Gunder had left the building only moments before and was now standing only a few feet from the back door with his hands on his hips as he glowered at Bowser, who seemed oblivious while he nosed around by the dumpster. Gunder heard Willis approach and turned his glower to him. He was large and fleshy as his photo had shown, but if he had ever played high school football, he had gone badly to pot since then. Gunder's small eyes turned beady as his glower deepened. Indignant, he demanded to know whether the dog was Willis's.

"Yeah, sorry," Willis said. "He got off the leash. But he's friendly. Don't worry about him." Then to Bowser, "Come here, boy!"

Bowser glanced over at him, but stayed where he was. Willis had trained him to only come when called by his name. Gunder's expression turned surly as he looked back at the dog.

"This is private property," he complained.

"I said I'm sorry," Willis said.

"That's not good enough. We got a leash law in this town!"

Willis shrugged.

"You're lucky I didn't have my gun with me," Gunder said, his fleshy overly pink lips twisting into something remarkably ugly. "If I did I would've put him down. Next time I see him here, I'll do just that."

Willis didn't say anything in response. He slipped the leash back on Bowser and in his mind he played out what would happen in two days when he'd be waiting again for Gunder, and how much rougher he was now going to be after that last comment. The back door opened just then interrupting his thoughts and a middle-aged woman who looked only half-awake stepped from the building. She glanced over at Willis and Bowser, then to Gunder, before continuing on to her car. Willis grimaced inwardly while outwardly displaying nothing. He was going to have to change his plan. No one had left the driveway during the last ten minutes, and he'd been hoping he'd have a fifteen-minute window where he'd be able to deal with Gunder without any witnesses, but he could no longer expect that. He watched as Gunder walked stiffly to a rusted out Honda Civic, almost as if he had rocks in his shoes, and then as Gunder squeezed his large-sized body into the driver's seat. As Gunder pulled his car out of his spot, he shot Willis another angry glare, then drove off. Willis led Bowser out of the parking lot and up the driveway, then back to where he had left his car.

"How about some scrambled eggs and bacon?" Willis said as the bull terrier jumped onto the front passenger seat. Bowser, on hearing the word *bacon,* let out an excited pig grunt in response and his tail thumped the seat in a rapid rhythm.

Willis drove to Summit, New Jersey, which was fifteen minutes away and only a few minutes from Short Hills. He found a diner in Summit where they let him keep Bowser by his booth, and he ordered scrambled eggs and bacon for both of them. The waitress, a white-haired grandmotherly type, softened at the sight of the dog, and crouched in an awkward arthritic stance so that she could scratch behind one of Bowser's ears. When she returned later with the food, it looked like the portions were double what they should've been on both plates. Bowser wolfed his down quickly, looking as happy as a pig in shit, at least until the food was gone. Then he looked miserable, but after a command from Willis, he lay down at Willis's feet. Willis lingered quite a bit longer over his food, and then even more over two refills of coffee. After he left the diner, he drove back to Short Hills. It was a different world. It was a town of money, with nothing shabby or shoddy about the small mansions he drove past. All the properties were meticulously maintained, with tennis courts and swimming pools visible if you were able to peek through the dense plantings of shrubbery and trees that shielded the homes. Willis had to guess that if any of the mansion owners found themselves unemployed for three months or longer, they'd somehow be exempt from ever making their way onto any of The Factory's hit lists.

Willis drove to Landistone's address, which was an impressive stone building with a large circular driveway in front, and all the extensive landscaping of the other properties he had passed. Willis didn't stop at the address, instead he kept driving, using the route he had worked out the night before that would take him to the nearest highway. The path took him through a dozen different small streets, all heavily wooded, all of which could be blocked easily by the police. After he got to the highway, he checked how long it took him, then tried it again using an alternate route he had mapped out. He was able to shave two minutes off his time using the second route, and more importantly, he didn't spot any locations where the police would be able to trap him easily. Still, when he reached the highway, he turned around and did it again using a third route he had mapped out. Both the second and third time he did it, he drove to streets that were parallel to Landistone's so that he only passed Landistone's address once. After he was done with his third trial run, he drove off in the direction of Livingston, stopping in the town of Northfield where he found a baseball park. It was only nine fifteen and he had some time to kill, so he spent the next forty-five minutes throwing Bowser a hard rubber ball. If he had used a baseball, the thing would've been chewed up after the first throw, but the ball he used lasted for the necessary forty-five minutes, although there wasn't much left of it by that point.

Before getting back in his car, Willis dug through his trunk and pulled out a clipboard, work gloves, jacket, and a cap.

Both the jacket and cap had stitched on it *National Pest Control Services*. Willis put these on and then headed back to Gunder's apartment building in Livingston. He had a similar jacket and cap when he worked for The Factory, and he often used them when he needed to break into apartment buildings during the day.

Willis parked a block away from the apartment building and left Bowser in the car to chew on a thick rawhide bone. He had his burglar pick ready, slipped on his work gloves, and then carried the clipboard as he approached the back doorway for Gunder's building. According to the information he was given, Gunder was single, but that didn't mean much. He could've still had a girlfriend living with him, and while that would've been only a minor stumbling block for Willis, he didn't like to be surprised on jobs. Each of his twenty-five hits for The Factory went smoothly because of his preparation and attention to detail.

The back door lock was a cheap one, and Willis had it picked in less than five seconds. He used the back staircase to get to Gunder's apartment, then stood outside of it listening for a shower running or any other noises from inside. After not hearing anything, he tried knocking and after no answer, he used the burglar pick to get inside Gunder's small studio apartment.

The place couldn't have been more than four hundred square feet and the layout had a small galley kitchen on the end of the room closest to the door. The other end of the room had a double bed, a TV, and a stereo. Outside of a small table with two wooden chairs set up near the kitchen, there were only a few other odd pieces of furniture scattered around the room.

Nothing much personal about the apartment. No photos on display or prints hung on the walls. Just a dirty and stuffy room with none of the furnishings matching and all of it looking shabby, as if every piece had been picked up from garage sales. The room also smelled badly—like a mix of onions and cheese.

Willis checked the bathroom and then the two closets to make sure there were no signs of anyone else living there. He quickly searched through a night table next to the bed and found where Gunder kept the gun that he had made a reference to earlier. Where it was kept, it wouldn't be a problem. Willis was able to leave without anyone seeing him. After returning to his car, he drove back to Queens.

He left an hour earlier the next morning and got to the apartment building by five. Once again, he brought Bowser and took him for a walk. They stayed close to the building so he could watch the driveway. From five to six no cars left the building's parking lot. After that, he headed back to Queens.

CHAPTER 6

AT FIVE O'CLOCK in the morning on Friday, Willis was back inside Gunder's studio apartment. From the wheezing noises Gunder made as he lay on his belly, Willis knew he'd been quiet enough with his burglar pick not to have woken him. At that hour there was enough of a murky grayness inside the apartment that Willis had little trouble making out the outline of Gunder's bloated body as he lay on his bed. Willis walked over to him soundlessly, then shoved the business end of a .40-caliber Smith & Wesson pistol with a silencer screwed to it into Gunder's left ear. Gunder reacted to that, letting out a guttural noise and trying to push himself up as he sputtered awake, still too groggy from sleep to be aware of what was happening. Willis hit him hard with the heel of his hand sending Gunder back onto the bed. With that blow, it must have dawned on him that there was a stranger in the room who had stuck something cold and metal in his ear. His body tensed, but he remained still as he lay on his bed.

"You're realizing now that you've got something you don't

want shoved into your ear," Willis said in a voice that was barely a whisper. "Let me explain what it is so you fully understand your situation. The barrel of a .40-caliber pistol, although what you're really feeling is the attached silencer. With a .40-caliber slug, if I pull the trigger I'll be blowing most of your brains out your other ear. Nod very slowly if you understand what I'm telling you."

Gunder's face screwed up into a tight clench as he fought to keep from crying. He nodded once.

"Okay, good," Willis kept his voice that same soft whisper. "This is going to go down one of two ways. If you cooperate fully with me, then you'll be kept on ice for the day and get to continue your life tomorrow no worse for wear than a swollen ear. The other way it goes down is I blow your brains out and leave you to rot. It's your choice which one, but you need to understand that I'm giving you zero chances. You say one word or do one thing that I don't want you to do, and I'm sending your brains all the fuck over the place. Now, very slowly, move your hands together behind your back."

Gunder did as he was ordered, sweating badly with the effort. Willis wrapped Gunder's wrists together using duct tape, then after forcing Gunder's head up, he gagged him and wrapped the duct tape around his eyes to blindfold him. Once that was done, he dragged Gunder's two hundred and fifty pounds off the bed, dumping him onto the floor. He then pulled him up to his feet and poked the gun barrel hard into the base of Gunder's skull. Using the end of the gun barrel, he directed Gunder where to go with the same precision as if he were an expert puppeteer controlling a marionette by its strings. He led Gunder out of the apartment wearing only the same stained tee shirt and boxer shorts that the part-time security guard had worn to bed.

The hallway light showed that Gunder's skin had paled to a milky white, and he shook badly as he stumbled along, but he made it down the back staircase and to a waiting van without dropping dead of a heart attack. Lowenstein had arranged for each of the crew members to have vehicles to use for their abductions; in Willis's case he'd been given a Chevy van, others had older model sedans with trunks large enough to stash a body. All the vehicles had been taken from a used car lot in the Bronx. Lowenstein had paid off the owner to wait until later that afternoon before reporting the vehicles stolen. After the robbery, the plan was to burn the stolen vehicles in the Bronx, and the owner would collect insurance, as well as keep his mouth shut.

It was a cool September morning, and Gunder began shivering seconds after stepping outside. With his hands tied behind his back and with how weak and shaky he had gotten, he had trouble getting into the back of the van by himself. Willis had to shove him into it. Willis then followed him in so he could bind Gunder's ankles together. Before Willis left the van, he covered Gunder with a blanket he had taken off of Gunder's bed. After that, he went around to the front of the vehicle, got into the driver's seat and drove fifteen minutes along a mostly deserted highway to an empty warehouse in East Orange, New Jersey that Lowenstein had located for them to use.

Willis was the first one to show up. He used a crowbar to jimmy open a door by the loading dock. If the building had a silent alarm hooked up to the police, then things were going to get dicey, but Lowenstein promised that wouldn't be the case—that the warehouse had been abandoned several months earlier after a fire and that there was no active alarm system. Still, Willis got back behind the wheel of the van and positioned it so he'd have a chance of escaping if police vehicles arrived. After ten minutes and no police, he got into the back of the van, cut the tape wrapped around Gunder's ankles, and dragged out his captive. Willis took Gunder through the warehouse and to a back office, where he sat him down on the floor and secured his ankles together again. The evidence of a past fire could be seen plainly as the building was mostly gutted with one wall badly charred and part of the roof missing. Even after several months, the place still had a smoky smell to it. But the office where Willis had dragged Gunder was intact, and even had a space heater. There was also a card table and chairs in the room. Maybe Lowenstein had brought them, or maybe they had been left by the previous tenant. Willis tried the space heater and found the electricity was still on for the building. After that, he left to move the van to a side of the warehouse where it wouldn't be seen if someone drove up to it, and then sat outside by the loading dock and waited.

He didn't have to wait long. Lowenstein showed up twenty minutes later driving an older model Buick. Willis helped him get his hostage out of the trunk, who was also blindfolded, gagged, and had his wrists secured together behind his back by a plastic cuff. They brought him to the same office in the back of the warehouse and sat him down beside Gunder. After moving his Buick to where Willis had left his van, Lowenstein came back to the office with a thermos of coffee and a box of donuts. He pulled a deck of cards from a jacket pocket, and he and Willis played gin until Hack showed up with his abducted security guard. After that man was also brought inside the back office and sat down beside the other two abducted guards, Willis, Lowenstein, and Hack switched their card game to hearts.

It was an hour later that Pruitt arrived. He looked hyped up as if he were barely under control; his eyes had a wildness to them. Willis and Lowenstein left to help him get his abducted guard from the trunk of an older model Camry where he'd been stashed. The security guard was a man in his fifties who had been battered and lay unconscious. Lowenstein let out a disappointed sigh and chastised Pruitt about the condition of the man.

"I thought I made it clear that they were to be brought here alive," Lowenstein said.

"He's still breathing, ain't he?"

"But for how much longer?"

"How the hell am I supposed to know? Am I a doctor?" Pruitt's eyes darkened and his lips curled into a fierce grimace. "Look, this clown forced me to do what I did. He could've made things easy, but the damn idiot tried putting up a fight. He's just lucky I didn't blow his damn head off. And any of you would've done the same."

Lowenstein swallowed back a comment regarding that and instead let the matter drop. With Pruitt grabbing the man's feet and Lowenstein taking hold of the man from around his chest, the two of them proceeded to carry him inside while Willis moved the car so it would be with the others. It was a little after eight, and they weren't supposed to be reporting to Landistone's house until eleven, so when Willis joined them in the office, they switched the game to five-card stud and kept it up until ten thirty. Early on, Pruitt had seemed tightly wound, slamming his cards down when he lost a hand and swearing angrily, but by the time they were ready to leave, he had mostly calmed himself down.

They were all already in their guard uniforms and Lowenstein had earlier handed out their fake badges. They staggered their leaving so that they'd be driving away from the warehouse separately instead of in a convoy. Lowenstein left first and three minutes later Willis followed. By the time Willis left, the security guard Pruitt had worked over still hadn't regained consciousness, which had the chance of making the job already a capital felony. Once they were finished with the job they were going to have to come back to check on him. If he was dead or didn't seem likely to make it, they were going to have to dispose of the body in a way so that the police wouldn't be able to find it. Or at least, Lowenstein, Pruitt, and Hack would. It didn't much matter to Willis. If the police ever picked him up he was a dead man regardless.

Back in the van, Willis unscrewed the silencer from his .40-caliber pistol. If he needed to use a gun in Landistone's home, it didn't matter how much noise it made. In fact, the more noise the better to help get the situation under control. He also dug out his 9mm Glock from under the driver's seat, pulled out the magazine, checked that it was fully loaded, then snapped it back in place. He had three extra clips, which would give him more than enough firepower for the job, unless things went completely to hell.

The twenty-minute drive from East Orange to Short Hills was uneventful. A short, stocky and very well-dressed man stood outside the door frowning at Willis as he stopped the van parallel to him. The man, mostly bald with a fringe of gray hair surrounding a very pink scalp, had Willis show him his security badge, and then after scowling at the badge and checking the name on it against a sheet of paper that he had, he directed Willis where to park, which was around the house and next to where Lowenstein had already parked his car. As Willis was walking back to the front entrance, Hack had also arrived and was showing the same man his badge. The man indicated to Willis to wait inside the house by the front door. Willis did so and stood by Lowenstein, neither of them acknowledging each other. A minute later, Hack joined them, and several minutes after that Pruitt and the thick-bodied man who had checked their badges also entered the house. He introduced himself as Colin Haywirth, Landistone's private secretary.

"Let me give you men the layout," he told them. He lifted a thick arm and squinted at a silver Rolex. Willis caught the flash in Pruitt's eyes and knew that Pruitt was already planning to relieve Haywirth of his watch sometime before the completion of their planned heist for *The Dame*. "It's now two minutes to eleven," Haywirth continued after clearing his throat. "At noon, a priceless oil painting will be delivered to this residence. At seven tonight, there will be an invitation-only dinner party here where the painting will be showcased. The party is scheduled to end by eleven o'clock. Shortly after that, the painting will be picked up by an armored vehicle service, and once the painting is secured in this vehicle, your assignment here will be completed."

"Do you have a list of people attending the party?" Willis asked, playing the part of a genuine security guard. "Also a list of who's in the house now?"

Before Haywirth could answer him, he was interrupted by the arrival of another man. He was in his fifties and even more smartly and expensively dressed than Haywirth. With his full head of salt and pepper hair, bronzed tan, carefully manicured features, thick shoulders, and narrow waist, he reminded Willis of the typical moneyed candidate who'd been bred for high political office. Willis knew the man had to be Jonah Landistone, especially with the way the man clapped Haywirth on the shoulder, then winked at all of them and smiled in a manner that only the privileged are capable of, as if they'd all been close friends since childhood. "So," the man said, "these are the security experts who will be protecting my latest acquisition?"

"Yes, Jonah," Haywirth said, his expression turning dour. "I'm going over today's schedule with them now."

"Good, good." Landistone's interest in them faded quickly. He had put in his fifteen seconds with the hired help and that was enough. With a false smile in place and his attention diverted elsewhere, he added, "This is an important piece of art. Really, an important piece of history. I'll be counting on all of you."

Landistone gave them all a serious look before wandering off. Haywirth waited until his boss was out of sight before telling them that the guest list for that night had forty-eight names on it. "I'll be handling greeting each guest myself," he said. "If someone shows up who shouldn't be here, I'll give a signal for one or more of you to intervene."

"We also need a list of who's in the house now," Willis said, reminding him of his earlier request.

Haywirth looked pained, as if he didn't want to bother

answering the question. Grudgingly, he told them that outside of himself and Landistone, there were four household staff members, three associates of Landistone's, and Landistone's wife. "Several members of the museum board will be coming over later this afternoon," Haywirth added. "Also the caterers will be arriving at three o'clock. That should pretty much be it."

"We'll search the house now," Lowenstein said.

Haywirth turned to face him, puzzled. "What for?"

"What for? We need to make sure that no suspicious characters have already snuck into the house, waiting for the arrival of that painting."

CHAPTER 7

HAYWIRTH GAVE LOWENSTEIN a look as if what he was asking was preposterous. "That won't be necessary," he said bluntly.

"It's standard procedure," Lowenstein said, "If you want I can have you speak to our boss, but there are certain precautions that we are required to take, and one of them is verifying the residence has not already been compromised." Lowenstein turned to Willis and told him to search the upstairs, and that he'd take the basement.

"I said that won't be necessary," Haywirth insisted curtly. "Mr. Landistone would like you to stay on this level and not be wandering his house."

"If you want to accompany us, we can do it that way," Willis said. "But it needs to be done, otherwise we'll be packing up."

Haywirth wasn't happy about it, but he gave in and told Willis he'd go with him first. He said to Lowenstein, "You stay put until I come back down."

"Fine with me," Lowenstein said.

Haywirth led the way from the foyer where they were standing, through a living room that could've been a small wing to a modern art museum all by itself, and then up a curved staircase framed by rich mahogany hand railings. Once on the second level, Haywirth kept close tabs on Willis as he searched through five bedrooms, an office, and three bathrooms. Willis made a show of checking the closets of each room and other possible hiding areas, but all he cared about was knowing how many people were up there and where they were, and all he encountered was a maid who was cleaning one of the bathrooms. The last room he checked turned out to be a yoga studio, and that was where he found Landistone's wife and a private yoga instructor. The yoga instructor was in his early thirties and was lean and muscular and very wholesome looking with his long blond hair pulled into a pony tail. Willis made a mental note that they were going to have to be careful with him. Not only did he look athletic, but he also seemed the type who'd try to play the hero and get his head blown off in the process. He also had interest in Landistone's wife as more than simply a student. That was evident from the way he was looking at her when Willis and Haywirth walked in on them, and also in the way he was holding her hips as he adjusted her position. Willis couldn't blame him. While the instructor was dressed appropriately in a tee shirt and long gym pants, the woman was naked and was an absolute knockout, and her own long, golden hair was also pulled into a pony tail. Her body was slender and nicely toned, and while on the thin side, still had the perfect amount of curves. All of her features seemed almost too perfect, as if she must've had plastic surgery to give her just the right nose, cheekbones, and chin, but Willis guessed it was only that she'd been blessed with exceptional genes. The only thing Willis was surprised about was her breasts. They were nice breasts with a perkiness to them, but they were small, and Willis would've guessed that Landistone would've wanted his shiny, trophy wife to have had much bigger ones.

If she was embarrassed or upset about having strangers walk in on her naked yoga session, she didn't show it. She made no attempt to cover up, but instead remained in her yoga posture, her concentration remaining fully intact on what she was doing. Willis didn't know anything about yoga, but the position she was in looked difficult as she stood on one leg with the other leg straight up in the air. One hand held the raised ankle while the other arm pointed straight out. As she did that, the instructor stood behind her with his hands holding her hips. When they first entered the room, Willis caught a glimpse of hunger in the instructor's eyes, and then a flash of embarrassment as he realized they were being intruded on. The two of them remained like that for several minutes, all the while Landistone's wife appearing to be oblivious to Willis and Haywirth. Finally, she got out of the pose and gave Haywirth a disdainful look. She made no attempt to reach for a nearby towel to cover herself.

"Colin," she said, her tone as icy and withering as the look she gave him, "have you enjoyed standing there gawking at me?"

Haywirth's face reddened. "I'm sorry for barging in like this, Alicia, but it couldn't be helped."

"Of course not. Not when you have an excuse to walk in on me. Go ahead, explain to me why you're bothering me and who this man is." Her expression turned wicked. "Or is it simply that Jonah sent you up here to get a cheap thrill?"

Haywirth's face reddened even more. He explained that Willis was part of a security detail brought in to protect the painting and that he needed to search each room. She smirked at that, but didn't respond otherwise. Now that she was standing facing them instead of twisted on one leg with the other straight up like an arrow, Willis could see from the carefully groomed patch of hair between her legs that her natural hair color was the same golden yellow, and that it wasn't a dye job. Haywirth had begun to stammer and Willis cut him off and told her that he needed to secure the premises before the painting was brought to the house. "You didn't tell me about this person," Willis said to Haywirth, referring to the yoga instructor.

"Sorry," Haywirth croaked out, badly showing his discomfort. "I had no idea he was here." He tried to force an apologetic smile that didn't quite stick. "Or Alicia, for that matter."

Willis pointed to a gym bag lying in the corner of the room and asked the yoga instructor if it was his. The man nodded, confused.

"I need to search it for weapons," Willis said.

"Be my guest."

Willis continued to play the role of an anal retentive security guard, and went through the motions of searching the gym bag, all the while Landistone's wife looked on with a mix of annoyance and amusement, maybe even a touch of desire when her eyes caught his. From the way she looked at him, he felt almost as naked as she was. Once he was done, he and Haywirth left the room and Landistone's wife and her instructor continued on with their private yoga session.

"An attractive woman," Willis commented.

Haywirth nodded, his face still a deep red. He cleared his throat and muttered out that she was quite a free spirit.

Willis wouldn't have put it that way, but he was too busy thinking of the complications those two were going to cause. He'd bet even money that the instructor would try playing the hero later to rescue his very naked and drop-dead gorgeous client who he badly wanted to bed. Willis had to hope they would finish their session before the robbery, and that she'd put on some clothes by then. The type of distraction she could cause certainly wouldn't help the job. On their way down the stairs, Willis told Haywirth that they would need a full accounting of all weapons on the premises, and Haywirth agreed, and told him he'd get that from Landistone.

Later, when Willis was able to catch up with Lowenstein, he gave him the situation upstairs which only caused the large man to chuckle. "Damn, I knew I should've taken the upstairs instead," Lowenstein said, his voice guarded in case anyone walked in on them. "They've got a security system downstairs that's taking feeds from surveillance cameras throughout the house. I had one of the household staff show it to me, but my lousy luck, we didn't pick that room to spy on. From what I can tell, the video goes to a hard drive, so we'll take the computer with us. Hopefully the video is not going offsite. If it is, it is. Nothing we can do about it, and probably won't matter since we're leaving all of them alive which will leave plenty of witnesses to try to identify us. But we'll still shut it down before the robbery. I'll get Hack to take care of it." He started chuckling some more, his belly bouncing under his security guard outfit. "I wonder if the wife knows about the surveillance cameras? She better be damn careful where she bangs her yoga boyfriend."

Pruitt wandered over a short time later to give them the count that he'd come up with, his voice tight with the anticipation of violence and a touch of craziness shining in his eyes. "None of them should be giving us any trouble," he said with almost a note of dejection over that prospect. After that, they took their posts as if they were genuinely working security with Hack downstairs by the security monitor, Pruitt standing guard by a back doorway, Lowenstein doing the same at the front entrance, and Willis standing outside the room where the painting was going to be unveiled. Haywirth came over to Willis shortly afterward to let him know that there was one weapon on the premises—a .38-caliber pistol that Landistone kept locked up in his master suite. Haywirth hemmed and hawed for a moment, then asked Willis whether he'd back him up later that nothing improper happened upstairs if the issue came up.

"I wouldn't worry about it," Willis said.

Haywirth looked like he could've used some additional reassurance, but he nodded grimly and walked off. At a quarter to noon, three additional people from the museum arrived, and then precisely at noon an armored vehicle arrived with *The Dame*. Two armed guards brought the painting to the house, delivered it to Landistone, waited first until two of the museum people removed the painting from the crate it had been packed in, and then for Landistone to examine it before leaving. From the glimpse Willis was able to catch of it, he couldn't tell what the big deal was, and certainly had no idea why it would be worth millions, but then again, he knew less about art than he did about yoga. The dame in the painting wasn't particularly attractive. A chubby, very pale woman with long flowing red hair decked out in an expensive silk dress and lots of jewelry. But while it didn't impress Willis very much, Landistone and the museum people all made a fuss over it. A couple of Landistone's household staff members were in the process of positioning it in its place of honor for that night's unveiling when Lowenstein came into view to let Willis know that the armored vehicle had left. That was Willis's signal to head upstairs. They needed to neutralize whoever was upstairs before they rounded up and took control of the rest of the house. Hack would be watching over the surveillance monitor and once the second floor was taken care of, he'd be joining the other crew members to finish the job.

Before Willis could move from his post, Haywirth wandered over to ostensibly talk about the guest list that night and whether or not they should set up metal detectors in case anyone tried bringing guns into the house, but his real reason was to make sure Willis would back him up in case Landistone's wife leveled accusations against him. That left Willis stuck where he was, which meant either Lowenstein or Pruitt had to take care of Landistone's wife and whoever was still up on the second floor with her. From his vantage point, Willis wouldn't have known whether the yoga instructor had left or not. He hoped he had. He also hoped Lowenstein would take care of it and not send Pruitt upstairs.

Three minutes later, there was a loud thumping noise from above—the type of noise that a body would make if it hit a wood floor hard enough—followed by a short burst of a woman screaming. The upstairs hallways, bedrooms, and office were all covered with enough thick and plush carpeting that you could've dropped a bowling ball without hearing anything. The yoga studio, though, had a polished wood floor. Haywirth looked startled as he turned toward the source of the noise, as did the crowd around the painting. Before Haywirth could move any further, Willis grabbed him by his suit jacket with both hands and swung him into the room with the painting so that the stocky man landed on his back. With one hand, Willis grabbed his ski mask out of an inside jacket pocket and with his other pulled his 9mm Glock from a holster, training the gun on Landistone as he slipped the ski mask on. While he'd been showing his face for the past hour, he'd done so as a menial worker. Most of them, including Haywirth, probably hadn't made the effort earlier to pay close attention to what he looked like. Now they would.

"All of you, on your stomachs now," Willis ordered. A few of them started moving slowly to their knees, a couple of them, including Landistone, didn't move at all. They looked at him as if it was some sort of prank and not real. Willis ran to the closest of them that was still staring at him with a bemused expression, which was one of Landistone's business associates, and hit the man hard across the jaw with the gun barrel, both knocking him to the floor and opening up a large gash. That caused the rest of them to move faster. Moments later, Hack brought two members of the household staff into the room from a different doorway, then Lowenstein followed behind him pushing another member of the household staff into the room. Lowenstein and Hack also wore ski masks.

"Okay, folks," Lowenstein announced after all the hostages were lying face down on the floor, "the easiest way for me and my associates to handle this would be to shoot each and every one of you. We're going to tie you all up instead. So I'd think long and hard before giving us any excuses to go the easy way. Now, put your hands behind your back and don't move as much as a muscle."

One of the household staff began weeping, but all of them did as they were ordered. While Willis trained his Glock on the hostages, Lowenstein and Hack bound their wrists with plastic cuffs and wrapped their ankles together with duct tape. About half of them had been taken care of when Pruitt burst into the room dragging the maid that Willis had seen earlier. He threw her onto the floor and the woman curled up with her knees to her chest crying hysterically. Pruitt was breathing hard under his ski mask, and started to raise his .38-caliber pistol toward the maid, but Hack wisely moved to her and rolled her onto her stomach, then bound her wrists and ankles, and Pruitt reluctantly lowered his gun. Like the rest of the crew, Pruitt had put on a ski mask, but even with that on it was obvious that he was near exploding. Lowenstein asked him about the wife, but Pruitt seemed incapable of answering him. For a good minute he stood fuming, his breathing ragged, a demented burning in his eyes. He walked slowly over to Landistone, as if it took every ounce of strength he had to keep himself under control.

"You know your bitch wife was upstairs nude as a fucking jaybird with another man?" Pruitt demanded, and then he reared back and kicked Landistone hard in the side, who let out a dull *oomph* sound, but otherwise was smart enough not to say anything.

Lowenstein had been moving toward Pruitt, and after that kick he moved quickly to grab Pruitt and pull him away. It was almost like a steam valve had been opened and that act of violence released just enough pressure from Pruitt to allow himself to get under control. He let himself be pulled away by Lowenstein, only putting up a token resistance.

"Not now, for Chrissakes," Lowenstein implored Pruitt.

"His idiot wife and her hero lover tried jumping me," Pruitt said incredulously. "I should've shot them both in their fucking heads."

"Are they both still breathing?" Lowenstein asked Pruitt as he pulled him further away from the hostages.

"She is. He might be. I don't know. I cracked him good a couple of times, and might've split his head open. But the moron asked for it. If he's still breathing, he won't be waking up for a while."

"You can't cry over spilt milk," Lowenstein offered philosophically.

Hack had finished securing the last of the hostages, and Willis and the rest of the crew approached *The Dame*. They stood before it for a long moment. Outside of two of the hostages sobbing, the room was quiet. Pruitt remarked that the painting didn't look like much to him. "Fucking rich people," he added.

Hack had left the room to get the laptop computer that the surveillance system had been running on, and Pruitt and Lowenstein worked to carefully remove the painting from the wall, then to wrap it in some of the material it had been packed in. When they left the room, Willis led the way with Pruitt and Lowenstein carrying *The Dame*. Willis was the first to see Alicia Landistone lying near the front doorway. She was still naked, her hands and feet bound, her eyes red and puffy. She was fighting hard to keep from crying, instead struggling to give them a defiant look but failing miserably.

"What she's doing down here?" Willis asked.

"I'm taking the bitch with us," Pruitt stated.

"I don't think so."

"You don't, huh? Too bad."

"Be reasonable," Lowenstein pleaded. "We can't take her with us. If we do this turns into a kidnapping or worse."

"Yeah? Take a look at what she did to me with her claws" Pruitt let go of his end of the painting with one hand so he could lift up his ski mask to reveal ugly and deep scratches that ran down the side of his neck. "You better believe I'm going to pay her back for these. Don't worry. I won't be a hog about it. The rest of you can take your turns if you want." Pruitt pulled his ski mask back down, his tone taking on a defeatist note. "Besides, I probably killed that guy upstairs, so it's not going to much change anything if we take her or not."

Willis had moved to Pruitt's side and in one quick motion pressed the barrel of his Glock hard against Pruitt's skull.

"I'll make this simple," Willis said. "If you try taking her, I'm leaving another body here."

Pruitt froze where he stood. Hack was joining up with them, carrying a laptop computer under an arm, and he slowed to a stop, first staring at Willis with a gun against Pruitt, then at the naked woman lying on the floor.

"I think you're overreacting," Lowenstein said.

"I'm done trying to placate this psycho," Willis said.

Pruitt's body had gone rigid. He had gone back to holding his end of the painting with both hands, and he remained that way, probably knowing if he let go to reach for his gun he'd be dead.

"You're making a mistake there, pal," Pruitt forced out.

"What? In not shooting you already? Maybe."

"Guys," Lowenstein said, "let's be reasonable. Now is not the time for this. Can we agree to leave the girl here?"

"Fine," Pruitt spat out. "But first take that gun out of my face. And get me a fucking knife. I'm cutting off her fingers. I'm not leaving behind any DNA."

Willis laughed at that. "If they catch up with any of us, it won't matter whether or not they have our DNA."

"He's right, you know," Lowenstein said.

"I don't care. I'm not leaving my DNA under that bitch's fingernails. And I said get that gun out of my face!"

"I'll scrub under her fingernails," Hack offered.

Willis lowered the gun and took a step back. He wanted to get the hell out of there and leave those clowns far behind, but he didn't want to walk away from Pruitt and give him any sort of opening to shoot him in the back. He also didn't trust what Pruitt would do if he left him alone with Landistone's wife. So he stayed where he was while Hack went running to get what he needed. Pruitt and Lowenstein both lowered the painting to the floor, but Pruitt didn't make any move for his gun, content instead to glare hotly at Willis.

"If you ever pull a gun on me again I'll make you eat it," Pruitt spat out. Even with the ski mask on, Willis could make out that the muscles were clenched around Pruitt's jaw.

Hack came back a minute later with a pan that from the smell of it must've been filled with vinegar. "This will get rid of any trace of DNA," Hack promised. He kneeled next to

Landistone's wife, forced her hands into the pan, and scrubbed at her nails with a small brush.

"Are you satisfied?" Lowenstein asked.

Pruitt picked up his side of the painting, "Let's just get out of here," he said in a near strangled voice.

They left the house then. After opening the door, Willis stood back and let the others leave first, and then they all moved in a half jog to the side of the house where their cars had been parked. As they approached the van Willis drove, which was the best vehicle they had for transporting the painting, Lowenstein cried out and dropped his end of the painting. He fell to one knee and grasped his ankle which was now covered with blood. There had been no sound of gunfire, so a silencer had to have been used. Willis dropped into a crouch and searched for where the shot came from. From the corner of his eye he saw the top of Hack's head fly off, and then Pruitt's throat explode into a bloody mess. He realized then how many shots had actually been fired and the source of the gunfire, but before he could turn his gun on Lowenstein, he took two bullets to the chest.

CHAPTER 8

LOWENSTEIN PULLED ONTO a dirt road within the South Mountain Reservation area and ten minutes later found himself giggling like a crazy person. He still couldn't believe he'd pulled it off. It seemed more like a strange dream than anything real, as if it couldn't be possible that only twenty-five minutes ago he had killed all three of them. His giggling stopped and a hardness settled over his features. He held out his hand and studied it. No tremors, nothing. Perfectly level. He might've been bouncing around in his stolen Buick, but his nerves were holding steady. He breathed in deeply and let the air out in a slow exhalation as he thought about the sleight of hand he pulled off. Seconds before he had fallen to one knee, he had palmed a theatrical blood packet, and that was what he smashed against his ankle to make it look as if he'd been shot. That was the distraction he needed. While they searched wildly for the shooter that didn't exist, he slid a .32-caliber pistol with an attached silencer from where it had been secured to his lower leg and got off a perfect shot that blew Hack's head into pieces, then a less than perfect shot where he hit Pruitt in the throat, and back to a better shot as he drilled Burke twice dead center in the chest.

He screwed up with how he shot Pruitt. He still couldn't believe he hit the little prick in the throat. He had the shot lined up to nail him square between the eyes, but the son of a bitch had been in a crouch and must've straightened up at the last moment. If the shot had killed him instantly it wouldn't have mattered. But it didn't.

A harsh, rigid grin formed over Lowenstein's mouth as he thought about what happened afterward. The plan had been to load the bodies into the stolen van that Burke had been driving, but that vengeful *pisher* Pruitt had to still be alive. Lowenstein had walked over to where Burke lay to deliver a *coup de grace* when a loud blast almost made him jump out of his shoes and he damn near felt a bullet whiz by his ear. That was when he saw that Pruitt had pushed himself up to one elbow. The little *pisher* was grasping his throat with one hand while he used the other to take potshots at him, his gun barrel waving wildly in front of Lowenstein as if Pruitt was in a boat that was listing badly and he was having trouble steadying himself. Even though blood was spurting past Pruitt's splayed fingers and his eyes were glazed enough to show that he was seconds from death, the vindictive little prick still had to try to shoot him, and it was just dumb luck on Lowenstein's part that Pruitt missed, especially with Lowenstein standing only five feet away from him. Of course he wouldn't have missed if his hand wasn't shaking as much as it was, and it couldn't have helped that he couldn't have been seeing straight. From all accounts, Lowenstein should've been hit from that distance, but somehow he wasn't. After that first shot, Lowenstein moved fast for cover while Pruitt fired off two more rounds.

If they had been in Newark or Jersey City or any other number of nearby towns, Lowenstein could've waited for Pruitt to bleed out or maybe even shoot it out with him, but he couldn't do that in toney Short Hills. If any neighbors heard the gunfire and called the police, the cops would be swarming Landistone's address in minutes. So Lowenstein had to change his plans and leave the bodies behind while he got the hell out of there. But it probably didn't matter. Hack was dead. Pruitt must've been dead within minutes of Lowenstein driving off—he'd have to be with that hole in his throat and a nicked carotid artery. And Burke should damn well be dead too after taking two rounds point blank in the chest. The odds were the police weren't going to be able to connect him to either Hack or Pruitt, and certainly not to Burke. He had exaggerated to Burke how often he and Pruitt had worked together, and while he might've done some jobs with that psycho nut bag over the last few years, the police wouldn't have any reason to think of them as known associates. And even if the police eventually made the connection, it wouldn't matter. Very soon, Lowenstein would be having a new face, new identity, and twenty million dollars so he could live out his life in comfort in the Bahamas. In a couple of months, he'd even have a new body. He was determined to lose the weight he had packed on since his thirties, and without the stress of having to worry about planning heists and other jobs, he'd be able to concentrate on a diet and exercise program.

Lowenstein turned the Buick down what was little more than a dirt path and drove another three hundred yards before stopping. He was in a dense enough wooded area to give him privacy for what he was going to do next—even given the remote chance that someone drove down the dirt road that he'd been on. He got out of the car and took from the trunk *The Dame* still wrapped in a protective cloth. He removed the cloth and dropped the painting on the ground, then stood over it for a moment to study it. To him it was just a chunky, unattractive chick, and he couldn't see what the fuss was about, or why the painting was supposed to be worth a hundred and twenty million dollars. The seven million price Tania threw at them the other day was only a smokescreen for his now-dead crew. Lowenstein decided that you'd have to be fucked in the head to put that kind of value on a painting like that. Hell, if he was going to hang a picture of a dame on his wall, he'd rather it be a nude shot of Tania. Now that would be a dame worth looking at!

Lowenstein went back to the car for the laptop computer used by Landistone's security system, also for a shovel and a can of gasoline. He dumped the laptop and the gasoline can on top of the painting, and then set about digging a hole. It was going to have to be wide enough and long enough to drop the painting into it, but since he no longer had three bodies to bury, he'd only have to make it about two feet deep. As he dug into the ground, he thought about the killings he had done and tried to decide how he felt about it. He had never killed anyone before. He never had to. Most of the jobs he'd been on had gone smoothly, although the ones he'd been on with Pruitt usually had at least one poor sap getting his head cracked open. But still, nobody ever ended up dead. Right then he was running on pure adrenaline, but later he'd have to live with what he had done, and he wondered how it was going to affect him. As the size of the hole grew larger and his physical efforts made him sweat to where his shirt became drenched, he decided it wasn't going to be something he'd lose sleep over. Hack was already forgotten. Even when the guy was alive he barely registered to Lowenstein. As far as Pruitt went, if Lowenstein was going to be completely honest about it, he enjoyed shooting him and if he had a chance to do it over again, he'd do it gladly. The guy was a borderline psycho and a pain in the ass, and Lowenstein often had to tiptoe around the guy's fragile ego. Over the past year, as he planned the job with Tania he found himself looking forward to when he'd be able to put a bullet in Pruitt's head. With Burke, he knew the guy was a dead man from the very beginning so he never let himself think of Burke as anything but a guy walking his last mile. If anything, Pruitt keeping him from putting a final bullet in Burke's head only made him nervous. Burke turned out to be smarter and more resourceful than Lowenstein would've expected. From what Big Ed Hanley had told him, he thought he was getting someone dependable, but green. After seeing the way Burke handled himself during that poker game heist, Lowenstein would've made the job a three-person one if he could've, but that wasn't an option. The logistics for the job called for four people, but even if that wasn't the case he would've needed a fourth person anyway— Tania insisted on it, something about the insurance company demanding a four-person security team. Finding a last-minute replacement for Burke wasn't an option either—he didn't have time to find someone else, and even if he did, it would've been too risky as it would've made both Pruitt and Hack suspicious. Fuck it, the guy took two shots to the chest. He had to be dead, but the thought of Burke somehow surviving those gunshots made him nervous. If Burke were still alive and the police didn't have him, Lowenstein wouldn't put it past Burke to track him down regardless of how many new faces and identities he bought himself.

Lowenstein stopped his digging to wipe his brow and to catch his breath. A little physical activity and he was soaked through with sweat! Christ, he really *was* in rotten shape. As soon as he got down to the Bahamas that was going to change. Maybe he'd even try running a mile or two every day. As he tried to imagine what his new life in the Bahamas would be like, his thoughts kept drifting back to Burke. He found himself playing back in his head the moment he shot Burke, and he tried hard to picture whether he saw any blood. It was a bang-bang shooting with Burke hitting the ground fast. But was there any blood? Lowenstein couldn't say for sure. There was so much blood from both Hack and Pruitt, and that confused the issue with Burke. Lowenstein struggled to visualize the exact moment Burke was shot, but he couldn't get that detail straight about the blood. After a minute or so, he gave up, deciding that it wasn't worth giving himself an aneurysm over and went back to his digging.

Once the hole became big enough and deep enough, Lowenstein pushed *The Dame* into the hole with his foot. A groan escaped as he picked up the cloth material that the painting had been wrapped in, and he used that to wipe off his perspiration, but it didn't help much as the sweat kept pouring off him. He dug his cell phone out of his pocket and took several pictures of the painting and sent those to Tania, then he poured gasoline into the hole and set what was supposed to be a hundred and twenty million dollar rare painting on fire. He took several more pictures, sent those also to Tania, then tossed the laptop computer into the flames, also the cloth. Once the painting had been reduced to ashes and the laptop computer into a smoldering mess, he filled the hole up with dirt. When he was done he stopped to rest for a moment, and then something hard cracked him on the back of the head and his world went black.

CHAPTER 9

AT LEAST WILLIS understood what that nagging voice had been trying to warn him about ever since the poker game heist. That Lowenstein had been trying too hard to play the goofball, and that his reason for doing it had been so that it would be easier to catch him off guard. Even the crack Lowenstein had made about how thieves like him don't double-cross one another was part of the setup. While Lowenstein had probably been telling the truth about that, he conveniently left out the caveat being that if it was a heist of a lifetime—the type that you could retire from—then all bets were off.

Lowenstein was still out cold from when Willis cracked him on the back of the head with the butt end of his .40-caliber pistol. Willis had suffered three cracked ribs when he was shot, and it felt like a knife jabbing into his chest every time he breathed, but he forced himself to ignore the pain so he could concentrate on what his best options were. He had looked through Lowenstein's call logs and text messages, and he now knew the identity of the Ice Princess. He also saw the photos that Lowenstein had sent to her, and because of Lowenstein doing that, Willis kept coming back to the idea that his best play involved keeping Lowenstein alive. He thought about it for several more minutes and accepted that that was the way it needed to be. Moving slowly to where Lowenstein lay on the ground, Willis pushed the large man over onto his back with his foot, then poured a bottle of water onto Lowenstein's face until the man sputtered awake. If the water hadn't worked, Willis would've poured gasoline next. At first, Lowenstein's eyes held a glazed, dull look, but after a ten count he seemed to make sense of who he was seeing. He nodded grimly at Willis.

"You were wearing a Kevlar vest," Lowenstein croaked out, his voice hoarse. Willis didn't bother answering the obvious. Lowenstein smiled glumly and added in that same gravelly voice, "I should've expected that you'd attach a tracking device to the Buick."

Willis ignored the comment. "Why'd you email the Ice Princess those photos?" he asked.

Lowenstein stared dumbly at Willis for a long moment. "So you've gone through my cell phone," he said with a defeated sigh, his voice beginning to sound more normal. "Ice Princess, huh? Not a bad nickname for Tania Martin. I sent her those photos as an insurance policy."

"Why? Those photos won't help you prove that the painting was a forgery, and they do nothing to hurt their insurance scam."

Lowenstein winced for a moment and touched the back of his head where he'd been hit. He looked at his fingers, saw that he wasn't bleeding, and let out another tired sigh. "That's true. But there's nothing I could do to prove that a forgery was stolen in the first place." He shrugged, then added, "If I brought back what we stole, they'd claim I was bringing back a forgery that I had commissioned to be painted and not what we had taken from Landistone originally. But here's how sending those photos are going to help me. Tania can't give them to the police now. If she did, she'd have to explain why someone would be sending her those photos a half hour after the painting was stolen. Also it would all but convince the insurance company involved that the painting was a forgery and worthless. So if she and Landistone try reneging on what they owe me, and it gets out that I sent these photos to her when I did—which won't be hard since I'd be able to get a record from my phone company of when they were sent—she'll have to explain why she didn't report those photos when she first got them. Tania might not realize it right now—she might think I sent them only to show that I did what we agreed I'd do—but down the road they'll eliminate any possibility of a double-cross. As I said, my insurance policy."

Willis didn't think those photos would help Lowenstein collect a dime. He was pretty sure that once Jonah Landistone had gotten his millions from the insurance company he'd disappear. Maybe with that ice princess, Tania Martin, maybe not, but in any case Lowenstein would've been left with a bunch of photos that wouldn't have helped him do squat. Willis didn't bother mentioning any of that to Lowenstein.

"What's Tania's connection with Landistone?" Willis asked.

Lowenstein smiled apologetically and shook his head gingerly. "At this point, we need to do some bargaining if I'm going to tell you anything further," he said.

Willis smiled thinly, "We do, huh?"

"I'm afraid so. You're a smart man, Burke. A careful man, also. You've kept me alive so far because you feel it's to your advantage to do so. If you want to be able to trust the information you get from me, then we're going to need a deal."

Willis stared at Lowenstein, and after a minute the large man began to sweat. That was enough, Willis didn't need to play it out any further. He had anticipated Lowenstein trying a bluff of some kind, and while he knew that with enough persuasion he could've gotten whatever information he wanted out of him, he had already decided it would be easier to play along. In the end, it wasn't going to help Lowenstein, unless Willis had badly misjudged the situation. He nodded quickly, decisively, as if he had just come to a decision.

"You're either going to cooperate with me," Willis said. "Or I put a bullet in your head and leave you here dead. Make up your mind which it's going to be."

"If I cooperate, what happens when you're done with me?"

"Nothing. I'm after the four point nine million that your dame claimed would be our cut, and once I get it I have no reason to care about you. I'm guessing the cut you worked out with her is a lot more than the number that she fed us. That's your business. If you can squeeze money out of her later, I don't care. I only want my piece of it, and then I'm gone."

Lowenstein chewed on his bottom lip as he considered what Willis had told him and made whatever mental calculations he felt he needed to, all the while his eyes having a faraway look to them. He stopped his lip chewing and his eyes slid sideways to lock onto Willis's.

"Tania Martin is Landistone's lawyer," Lowenstein said.

"Did Big Ed Hanley know you were setting me up to be killed?"

"No. All he knew was about the poker game heist, and he thought that was legit."

"What's the real payoff for this painting? Yours and Landistone's?"

Lowenstein only hesitated briefly before telling Willis that *The Dame* was insured for a hundred and twenty million. "My cut is twenty million. I'm sure Tania is getting a nice cut also. Also the joker from the museum who verified the painting as legit, and I'm sure there are others needing to be paid off. Figure Landistone is walking away from this with at least sixty million."

"When were you going to meet up with that dame next?"

Lowenstein's eyes lowered from Willis's. "Tonight."

"What's she giving you?"

Somewhat dispirited, Lowenstein said, "Papers, new passport, half a million cash."

Willis tossed Lowenstein back his cell phone. "Call her up," Willis said. "We've got a change in plans."

CHAPTER 10

WILLIS HAD CHANGED the time of their meeting to seven o'clock that evening and the location to a remote part of Forest Park in Queens that he had taken Bowser to a week earlier. He had Lowenstein sitting alone on a bench, and it didn't surprise him any when Tania Martin—the same dame he had earlier thought of as the Ice Princess—emerged from some dense shrubs and shot Lowenstein in the back of the head. She was supposed to sit down next to Lowenstein and deliver the half million in cash as a down payment and the necessary papers so that Lowenstein could start a new life with a different identity, but Willis had expected her to do what she did. Lowenstein should've expected it also. At least she used a silencer, so the gunfire wouldn't be attracting company.

Tania Martin had been holding a briefcase. She put it down after she shot Lowenstein and moved quickly over to him and started searching his pockets. If there had been others in the area, she would've lured him someplace else before killing him, but she would've needed to show him the briefcase so that she could convince him that she had what she promised him. Willis waited until she removed Lowenstein's cell phone from his body before he stepped out from where he was hiding and took both her gun and cell phone away from her. Her body stiffened for a second, then relaxed.

"That's what this job has turned into," he growled to her. "Trapping one murderous double-crossing rat after the next."

Almost as if she cared, she asked, "Was he already dead?"

"Nah. He was knocked out by a dose of ketamine, but otherwise he was fine."

"At least he didn't feel anything then," she said.

"Yeah, at least there's that. Go pick up your briefcase."

He walked her over to it, all the while keeping her gun pressed hard into the small of her back. After she picked it up, he took her to where he had left Lowenstein's stolen Buick, and after binding her hands behind her back, he opened the trunk for her to get into it.

"Is this really necessary?" she asked.

He answered her by lifting her and dumping her into it, then slamming the trunk shut. Earlier, he had taken pain killers for his cracked ribs, but it still hurt like hell, and when he lifted her it felt like something ripped inside of him. He had to stand for several minutes for the pain to subside before he could get into the driver's seat.

*

Willis drove to a nearby boarded up elementary school that was slated to be converted to senior housing. The area was deserted and it was easy to break into the building and bring Tania Martin with him. He dragged her to the basement and tied her to a chair, then dumped the contents of her briefcase by her feet.

"In case you had any of your close blood relatives hidden away in the bag. You know, deadly vipers or other poisonous snakes," Willis said.

There were no snakes or anything else poisonous in the briefcase, but there wasn't much money either. Just bundles of paper cut to the size of money. Some of the packets were sandwiched between fifty dollar bills to make it look at first glance as if they were legit, but most of the packets were completely bogus. Willis rifled through them picking out the genuine fifty dollar bills, and tossed the rest of it to the floor.

"You didn't think much of Lowenstein, did you?" he asked with a bitter smile.

Her icy demeanor from before was gone, as was the coolness she had exhibited earlier after shooting Lowenstein. Now she was only scared. Badly. At least he thought so until a single tear rolled down her cheek. That caused him to laugh even though it hurt like hell for him to do so. He had to hand it to her. She had done a damn good job of transforming herself into the damsel in distress, especially given that only minutes earlier she had shown that she was little more than a cold-blooded killer.

"What do you want?" she demanded angrily. In the blink of an eye, her façade of playing the scared, helpless girl was gone, replaced by her earlier coolness.

"The money that was promised. Four point nine million."

She smirked at that. "That was supposed to be divided four ways. Your share would've been one million two hundred and twenty-five thousand."

"The other members of the crew are no longer among us, thanks in no small part to yourself. So I'll take their share. I could instead be asking for the twenty million that you promised Lowenstein, but I'll be content with the amount you sold us on."

"You'll get your money," she insisted. "After the insurance money is paid, you'll get your cut."

"How long will that take?"

"Most likely six months. They'll first want to wait for a ransom demand, and after they don't get one, they'll want to try to recover the painting on their own before paying up."

"Uh uh," Willis said. "I want my money tonight."

"That was never the deal! The deal was for each of you to get your money wired to offshore accounts after I sold the painting!"

"Yeah, well, that deal was bogus from the start since your plan was for all of us to end up dead. So excuse me for no longer wishing to honor it."

"That's not true. That was Phil's idea, not mine."

Willis looked at her blankly.

"Phil Lowenstein," she explained.

"Right. And just a coincidence that you ambushed him tonight."

"I wouldn't have if he hadn't sent me those photos. Once I saw them I knew I had to get that camera away from him. Why else would he take those photos if he wasn't planning to use them to force a bigger cut for himself?"

She said it all innocently as if there was a chance of it being true. Willis was quickly getting tired of her act. "Sorry, lady,

I'm not buying. And since only a damn fool would trust you, I want to be paid tonight."

She kept up her wide-eyed innocent look as she frowned severely. "I can't pay you that type of money until the insurance pays off."

"What can you get for me tonight?"

Her frown deepened. "There's the thousand dollars you just took," she said. "And I might be able to gather up another five thousand, but that would be it."

She could've been lying, she could've been on the level. Willis had a hard time reading her. He had taken her cell phone from her earlier and he found Landistone's cell phone number in her list of contacts. He told her what she was going to say after he called Landistone, and she agreed without any argument. Willis put the cell phone on speaker, then dialed Landistone's number and held the phone close to her mouth. When Landistone answered, he swore in a whisper that she should've known better than to have called him then. "Dammit, Tania, I still have Feds and local police all over the house. This better be important."

"Oh, it is."

"Then I'll call you back when I can."

Seven minutes later Jonah Landistone called back. "So what's so damn important?" he demanded.

"One of them is still alive—"

"Dammit! How did that happen?"

"It's not important. He wants to see you tonight. If he doesn't get what he wants he promises to make this blow up on all of us. And I believe him."

It got very quiet from Landistone's end. Then, "Send him to my home midnight tonight."

"That won't work. He has specific demands and he's not willing to budge from them." She gave Landistone the time and place that Willis had given her, and the amount of money Willis wanted Landistone to bring.

"I'm not doing that," Landistone said. "None of it."

"Then we'll be going to jail. If you meet with him and arrange to give him what he's owed, we'll still be splitting millions later."

There was more silence from Landistone, then he told her that he'd handle things and hung up. Willis pocketed her cell phone.

"And the plan wasn't to kill all of us," Willis said.

She shrugged. "You can't blame a girl for trying."

She was a piece of work, no question about that. A murderous piece of work. Willis had to admire how blatantly she had lied to him and the way she worded what he had her tell Landistone. *Give him what he's owed.* Code for just kill the sonofabitch. Also, how she was careful not to mention the amount of money they would be collecting themselves for the insurance scam; simply leaving it at millions.

It was time for him to leave. He considered gagging her, but it wouldn't matter whether he did or not. She could scream her head off in that basement and nobody would hear her. As he turned from her, her voice snapped at him, demanding that he untie her. He didn't bother responding to that. If Landistone delivered the money he was owed, then it wouldn't matter whether she was alive or dead. If Landistone didn't deliver, Willis would figure out which scenario would be more to his advantage and act accordingly. For the time being, he'd keep her on ice. When he reached the door, her voice had a pleading quality as she asked him to set her free.

"I did what you asked," she implored. "What's the point of leaving me like this? You can't squeeze blood from a stone!"

Now she was genuinely scared. She'd have to be. If Landistone killed him, she'd be left there to starve to death. Willis smiled inwardly as he thought about what she'd said. While you might not be able to squeeze blood from a stone, you should be able to get a few drops from a reptile, but he kept the thought to himself and walked out of there without saying a word to her.

CHAPTER 11

L ANDISTONE ARRIVED TWENTY minutes early. It was at the same burnt out warehouse in East Orange where the security guards were being kept tied up in a back room. Willis had checked earlier, and the guards were all still alive. Even the one that Pruitt had roughed up pretty bad had woken up. Willis was going to have to get the police there soon before any of them expired from dehydration or other problems. He watched as Landistone parked his car behind the warehouse, and then as Landistone crept in the shadows by the side of the warehouse before dropping into a crouch and holding a gun in front of him. Landistone never knew Willis was there and when Willis took the gun from his hand, all Landistone could do was look over his shoulder and stare dumbly at him, too startled to speak.

"That's all I've been doing today," Willis growled at him. "Dealing with one bigger double-crossing rat after the next."

Landistone's complexion had grayed badly, but he found his voice. "I was just being cautious," he got out in a false bravado. "You can't blame me. How was I supposed to know what I was walking into?"

"That's right. You were just being cautious. Hiding in the shadows with a gun drawn." Willis made a disgusted face. "Get moving."

Willis brought Landistone to the front of the warehouse and to the door he had jimmied open earlier. Once inside, he turned on the overhead lights, and was glad to see they still worked. Landistone squinted against the light. While the clothes he was wearing were expensive, he no longer looked like the carefully manicured captain of industry as he did earlier that day, but instead had a shabbier look about him. It was partly the dark circles that were beginning to show under his eyes, partly his grayer complexion and partly the fear flooding his face.

"Is it smart turning on those lights?" Landistone asked. "You could be drawing attention here."

"Keep your voice low," Willis said softly. "There are some people back there. You don't want them recognizing your voice. And we won't be here long enough for it to matter if anyone sees those lights. Where's my money?"

"How am I supposed to raise that kind of money tonight?"

"That's the thing," Willis said. "You have us do a job, but you're not prepared to pay for it. Not very smart, if you ask me. What can you get me tonight?"

Landistone was beginning to recover some of his bluster. "Possibly a few thousand. No more than that. It would take me a week to raise the money you're asking for."

"So I keep you on ice for a week. If your associates don't

send me the money you owe me, then I leave you dead, and take the loss as a busted deal. We can play it that way."

Landistone flinched at that. He opened his mouth to feed Willis another lie, but Willis shook his head to stop him.

"You're broke," Willis said.

"Mostly," Landistone admitted with a slight, sheepish smile. "The damn economy and this damn stock market have nearly wiped me out. As it is, I'm heavily margined and my real estate holdings are all underwater with second and third mortgages. That's why I'm resorting to this." He rubbed a hand through his thick hair and managed a weak smile. "Look, if you give me a week, I might be able to raise twenty-five thousand for you, but that's about it. The rest of it will be paid after the insurance money comes in."

"Sure it will. You have such a great track record of being trustworthy. First you arrange for all of us who did the heavy lifting to end up dead, then you lie to me just two minutes ago. But it's all been pretty much what I've expected."

"Don't worry, I know when I'm beat," Landistone said graciously while flashing Willis a smile that was every bit as false as it was toothy. He held out his hand to Willis, as if they were going to shake and seal the deal. In response, Willis, in a quick and fluid motion, took out the 9mm Glock that he had tucked in his waistband and had been hidden by his jacket, and without hesitation shot Landistone in his right knee. Landistone hit the floor like a sack of bricks and grasped his injured leg. At first he was in too much shock and pain to speak, or even scream, his mouth twisting into a rigid circle. Willis lowered himself so he sat on his heels and could look more directly into Landistone's face.

"The plan was always to disappear once you got the money," Willis said. "You and Tania both."

Landistone's eyes widened as he stared at Willis. Through sobs, he asked Willis how he was going to be able to explain the bullet wound to the police.

"You'll figure out a way," Willis said. "Just like you'll find a way to explain this." He then shot Landistone in the other knee. Landistone's face contorted in agony as if he wanted to howl in pain. No sound escaped from him, though. Willis dug Landistone's wallet out of a back pocket and slipped a piece of paper into it before returning the wallet.

"You also better figure out a way to get back to your car and drive away from here," Willis said. "Those shots are going to be bringing the police here, and I don't think you want to be explaining to them why there are four men tied up in that back room who were supposed to be working for you earlier today. There's a slip of paper in your wallet that has information for an offshore bank account. When your insurance pays up, I expect my money wired to that account right afterwards. If that doesn't happen I'll track you down wherever you're hiding. I won't kill you, but I will shoot out both your knees again. And as painful as it is now, it will be a lot worse the second time around."

Willis turned to leave. He left the overhead lights on and stopped at the door to listen to a scraping noise that Landistone made as he dragged himself along the floor. He left the door open so that Landistone would have a chance of getting out of the building before the police arrived. It would be to his advantage for Landistone to do that, although he had no doubt that Landistone would be able to sell the police a convincing story about why he was there with both knees shot out if they ended up finding him there.

Willis had little doubt that if he hadn't shot Landistone in the knees he would've had no chance of collecting any of the insurance money. Landistone and Tania would've been disappearing to parts unknown once the money was paid. It could still happen, but there was a better chance that Willis would get his money now—maybe as high as fifty percent. Landistone wouldn't be running anywhere anytime soon, not with all the surgeries he was going to require, and if complications set in he'd be hospital-bound for well after the insurance money came in. And there would also be real fear now. No one would want to risk being shot in the knee after already living through it once. And if Landistone did disappear with the money and Willis wasn't able to track him down, at least now Landistone would have to pay a dear price by living the rest of his life with ruined knees and having to always look over his shoulder.

The pain medication was wearing off. Once again, Willis's cracked ribs were making it feel as if a knife were ripping into his chest every time he breathed. He swallowed down some more pills and then headed back to the deserted elementary school in Queens where he had left Tania. He had nothing to gain by keeping her any longer, and since she could be connected to Landistone it wouldn't be any good if she were discovered weeks later tied up and dead in that school. Something like that would ruin their insurance scam.

As Willis drove, he heard news reports about the brazen robbery of *The Dame*. The reports had the yoga instructor alive but with a fractured skull, and greatly exaggerated what was done to Landistone's wife. They mentioned the two members of the robbery who were found dead on the property, but so far the authorities hadn't been able to identify them, which was partly because Willis took their wallets off them before going after Lowenstein.

When Willis got back to the abandoned elementary school building, he found that Tania was gone. He had tied her up pretty good, and had no idea how she escaped, but somehow it didn't surprise him.

He dumped the stolen Buick and switched back to his own car. He had already checked out of his hotel. Days earlier he had wired Big Ed Hanley his cut, and after keeping fifteen hundred in cash, he distributed the rest of his share of the poker game heist into three different bank accounts. He also had an additional forty-two hundred that he had taken off the three dead members of the crew, the thousand dollars he took from Tania, and four guns that he needed to dispose of—the Glock he used in shooting Landistone, and the guns he took off Lowenstein, Tania, and Landistone. He also had their cell phones, and needed to dump those as well. First, he had to pick up Bowser from an eighteen-year-old girl who was holding him for the day. He had met her in a coffee shop and she had taken an immediate shine to Bowser, and Bowser to her. When he arrived at her apartment, she answered the door with Bowser leaning heavily against her leg, wanting all the physical contact with her that he could get, while barely even giving Willis the time of day.

"I loved taking care of this little guy," she said, and she kneeled down so she could hug Bowser and kiss him on top of his head. The dog's tail started beating the door when she did that. She gave Willis a hopeful look. "If you'd like to leave him with me longer, that would be okay."

It struck Willis how much better off Bowser would be with her than with him, and he knew if he made the suggestion the girl would've taken the dog gladly. He almost did. He started to make the offer, but a certain weakness inside made him back down. Instead, he paid the girl the hundred dollars that he had promised her, which she took reluctantly, and he led Bowser away.

"Sorry, buddy," he said. "I don't blame you for being mad at me. She was a real sweetheart, huh? Nice looking, too."

Bowser let out an angry pig-like grunt to let Willis know he wasn't happy about the matter, but once they were inside of Willis's car, Bowser settled down and was pretty much back to normal.

Willis wasn't sure where he was going next. He needed more money before he could go after The Factory, which meant more heists, but the next ones would have to be with a crew he could trust or he'd do them alone. The trip wasn't a total bust. He did get a nice cut from the poker game heist and he learned a valuable lesson about honor among thieves—that there was none. And he still had a shot of getting a multimillion dollar payday out of the painting deal, but that was going to be months away and wasn't anything he could count on. On the other hand, he was played for a fool, almost got killed, and was left with three cracked ribs that hurt like hell. All in all, a mixed bag. All he knew for sure was he wanted to get as far away from New York as he could.

THE INTERLOPER
PART THREE

CHAPTER 1

AT ONE FIFTY-FOUR in the morning, Dan Willis had a ski mask pulled over his face as he sat patiently in a stolen pickup truck, the engine idling softly in the darkness, the lights off. The pickup truck had been backed into an alley off of a desolate city block in East Boston made up almost entirely of abandoned factories and burnt out warehouses. There was still one operational warehouse on the block, and if things went right, the crew Willis was working with would be stealing one point five million dollars worth of pharmaceutical drugs within the hour.

Four minutes later, the car Willis expected drove past him. While he didn't know what car it would be or who would be driving it, he and the rest of the crew were still expecting someone to be driving toward the warehouse at that time. It turned out to be a badly dented older model Ford Escort. Willis waited where he was until one of the other crew members turned on the brights of the stolen car he was in and accelerated directly at the Escort, forcing the other car to slam on its brakes. Willis then gunned the engine and swung his pickup truck out of the alley and pulled up behind the Escort, blocking the vehicle. Willis got out of the vehicle and moved fast to the driver's side door of the Escort, then tapped the window with the barrel of the .40-caliber pistol he was holding. The driver of the Escort looked like a college kid. His eyes grew large and his skin paled to the color of milk as he focused on the gun. Willis tapped the window again and signaled for the kid to lower the window. The kid was scared to death, but he did as he was directed.

"I've got about forty dollars on me," the kid forced out in a faltering voice. "You can take my money, the car, the pizzas, please, just don't hurt me."

"If you shut up and act smart, you won't get hurt. Get out of the car now, and leave the keys where they are."

The kid did as he was told. Willis had him take off a grease-stained jacket and an even greasier-looking baseball cap, both of which had the name of the pizza shop the kid worked for stitched on them. Willis tossed these to Charlie Hendrick, who was the driver of the other stolen car and was standing off to the side. If the kid driving the Escort was closer to Willis's size, Willis would've put on the jacket and cap, but the kid was six inches shorter than Willis and was closer to Hendrick's height, although around twenty pounds chunkier. Hendrick was the one who had put the heist together, and like the rest of the crew except for Willis, was in his late twenties, and with his ski mask off looked like the typical slacker who maybe shaved once every couple of weeks and hung out all day playing video games and smoking weed. Big Ed Hanley, Willis's agent for the job, had told Willis that Hendrick and the rest of his crew might not look like much at first, but that they were smart and professional, and so far that turned out to be accurate.

As Hendrick slipped on the jacket and cap, Willis used duct tape to bind the kid's wrists together behind his back, then after hitting the Escort's trunk release latch and dumping out the garbage filling up the trunk, Willis had the kid get into it. It was a tight squeeze, but Willis was able to position the kid so he could close the trunk on him. The kid was shaking badly and looked like he might pass out or start vomiting at any moment.

"Relax, kid," Willis told him. "I'm not going to gag you or bind your ankles together. In thirty minutes the police will be here. Just kick the inside of the trunk and they'll find you. You'll be fine."

He closed the trunk on the kid. Hendrick was on his cell phone finishing up his call with one of the other crew members. He nodded to Willis and got into the car the kid had been driving. Willis first moved the stolen car Hendrick had been using so that Hendrick could continue on to the warehouse, then he got into the pickup truck and followed him, all the while keeping the lights off. Willis pulled over far away enough from the entrance so that security guard working the front desk wouldn't be able to look out the glass vestibule door and see the pickup truck in the dark. Hendrick had pulled up to the main entrance as if he were only delivering pizzas.

From Willis's vantage point he could see the events that played out next, and it was exactly what Hendrick had told him would happen, not that he thought it would be otherwise. Hendrick brought the pizzas to the vestibule door, was buzzed in, and then as he was handing the pizzas to the security guard at the front desk, he pulled the pizza boxes back just enough to make the guard lean forward to reach for them, which got the guard's hands away from the security alarm button on the side of his desk. As the guard awkwardly took hold of the two large pizza boxes, Hendrick, in a quick and fluid motion, slipped from his back waistband a 9mm Glock and brought it out in front of him, pointing it at the security guard, who just stood dumbly for a moment before putting two and two together. Willis didn't wait any longer. He hit the gas and brought the pickup truck up to the front warehouse entrance. Hendrick buzzed him in, and at that point the security guard was sitting on the floor behind the desk, his wrists and ankles bound with duct tape, a gag stuffed in his mouth. The guard peered up at Willis with a hurt, sullen look, probably mostly angry at himself for allowing himself to get taken the way he did.

Hendrick had his ski mask back on. There were no security cameras in that part of the building, only out back by the loading dock and in the warehouse area. It was also doubtful the security guard would be able to provide the police a useful description of Hendrick as he would've first been focused on the pizza boxes, then on the Glock. Even if the guard had paid attention to Hendrick's face during the two or three seconds he might've looked at him, any sketch he helped the police come up with wouldn't do any good since Hendrick had such a nondescript and common look to him. Willis asked Hendrick if everything was all set in back, and Hendrick nodded, letting him know that the security guard patrolling the back of the building had been taken care of by the rest of the crew. It was then up to Willis to do his job.

A four-man crew could normally have handled the robbery. It was stretched to five men because the original crew was stuck for months on how to open the security door that led from the vestibule area to the warehouse. The lock required swiping a card with a magnetic-encoded strip through a card reader and entering a password on a keypad. The problem was not only would a wrong password trigger a silent alarm to the police, but the lock had a failsafe code built in that would open the door while also triggering the police. If the crew used the front security guard's badge and forced him to provide the password, he would most likely give them the failsafe code and they wouldn't know it until they tried driving away from the warehouse and found themselves surrounded by cops. Cutting the power to the door wouldn't do any good since that would also trigger the silent alarm. Same if they tried blasting through the door or any part of the walls. The system in place was near foolproof, and it had stymied Hendrick and the rest of his team.

All other parts of the job had fallen into place. They had the floor plan for the warehouse, they knew how many personnel would be employed and where they'd be, and they had the delivery schedule for when oxycotin was brought to the warehouse before being distributed to local hospitals and pharmacies. When they found out about the guards' nightly routine of having food delivered each night around two in the morning, they had their entry through the vestibule, as well as how they'd take care of the front security guard. But the one thing they couldn't figure out was how to get through the security door without alerting the police. When Big Ed Hanley was brought in by the crew to find a specialist, he knew that Willis was a whiz with locks, and asked Willis if he'd be able to get through that particular model. Willis told him he could without providing any details, and Hanley set up the meeting between Willis and the team.

Willis signaled to Hendrick to buzz the security guards inside the warehouse, which was what the guards expected at that time each night as the guard working the front desk would always buzz them before bringing them their food. Hendrick did so, then joined Willis by the security door, his gun hand by his side, the barrel of the Glock pointing straight ahead. Willis took from his jacket pocket a souvenir from when he was a hit man for The Factory—an electronic gizmo about the size of a credit card except a little thicker—and swiped it through the card reader. A click sounded as the device overrode the electronics within the lock. When Willis pulled the door open, two security guards stood on the other side of it, both of them showing goofy grins. As they realized that two men with ski masks had opened the door instead of their buddy working up front, their expressions froze. Then as their gaze drifted down to the guns that were pointed at them, their grins faded completely. One of the guards simply looked defeated, the other, though, seemed as if he was trying to decide whether or not to reach for his firearm and play the hero. Hendrick helped him make up his mind by stepping forward and smacking him in the face with his gun. Not hard enough to knock him out, but hard enough to stun him and leave him bleeding.

"Both of you, back of up slowly three steps and then lower yourselves to your knees and get on your stomachs," Hendrick said softly, his voice making Willis think of a snake hiss.

Both guards did as they were told, although the one who was hit in the face did so reluctantly. He had a nasty cut alongside his eye, and he shot Hendrick an angry glare as if he badly wanted to say something. Whatever it was, though, he had the good sense to swallow it back. Willis walked past them while Hendrick wrapped their wrists and ankles with duct tape. He didn't bother gagging them since there would be no one around to hear them yell. He warned them both, though, to keep their mouths shut. "Either of you say a word and I'm shutting you up for good," he told them in that same soft, ominous voice from earlier.

Willis made his way to the back of the warehouse. Once there, he slid the same electronic device through another card reader and opened the doors to the loading dock. If the doors were opened from the outside, it would've also triggered the silent alarm to the police. With the doors opened, two of the crew members—Bud McCoy and Jared Gannier—carried into the warehouse the security guard who had earlier been patrolling the back of the building. The guard had his wrists and ankles bound with duct tape, his eyes closed, his head rolling to one side. As McCoy made his way past Willis, he told him that the guard was only napping, but otherwise was fine. "A little bump on his head, that's all," McCoy said. The fifth member of the team, Cam Howlitz, had backed a van up to the loading dock and sat in the driver's seat with the engine idling. The van was one of those indistinctive cleaning service vans that are seen all over the place, but rarely noticed. Like many of those others, it was painted white, smudged with dirt, dinged with dents, and had a generic sounding business name stenciled on it. Howlitz stayed behind the wheel in case the cops showed up. There was no reason for them to, but if they did, the crew would hightail it into the back of the van, and Howlitz would try a getaway. Increasing their odds for escape were two AK47 semi automatic rifles that were stored in the van, each with magazines holding thirty rounds, as well as four fully loaded additional magazines.

While Willis waited for McCoy and Gannier to come back with the drugs they were going to be stealing, Hendrick walked over to him to ask how he got the security door opened so easily.

"Burke, you cheated," Hendrick said with a forced laugh. Hendrick called him Burke, because as far as he and the rest of the crew knew, that was Willis's name. "If I knew it was going to be that easy, no way I would've included you to be part of an even split. A half share at most. But you can make it up to me by telling me about that gizmo you used."

Willis glanced briefly at Hendrick, and said with little interest, "Not much to tell."

A hard smiled showed through the mouth slit in Hendrick's ski mask. "How do I get my hands on one of those?" he asked.

"Can't tell you."

"You can't or you don't want to?"

"Either one," Willis said.

"How about I pay you ten grand for yours?"

"Sorry, not for sale." Willis added in a somewhat conciliatory tone, "But anytime you need use of it, just bring me onto the job. If you're making it an even split, of course."

"Of course," Hendrick said, his voice drifting into the same soft, singsong type voice he had used earlier with the security guards.

Willis could just about read the thoughts running through Hendrick's mind. That if he were to kill Willis, not only would he be saving a full share for the job, but he could grab the device Willis had used, which he coveted. And if he left Willis's body in the warehouse, it would only throw the police off track as there was nothing in Willis's background to lead the police back to Hendrick and his crew. The problem was, though, if he tried that he'd have Big Hanley to contend with even if he offered to pay Hanley the same agent fee that he would've gotten from Willis. Hanley wasn't someone you wanted to piss off, and killing a man that Hanley sent out to you on a job would certainly piss him off.

The moment of danger passed as Willis could see Hendrick give up the idea of double-crossing him, most likely accepting that it couldn't be done without incurring Hanley's wrath. Willis was glad Hendrick came to that decision. While Hendrick and his crew all looked like goofballs to Willis when he first met them, they proved to be hard men and efficient at what they did, and Willis would like the opportunity to do more jobs with them in the future. If Hendrick had tried a double-cross, Willis would've had to kill him, and that would've been a shame. Hendrick, his crew, Hanley, none of them had any idea about Willis. About who he was, the training he had gone through with The Factory, everything he had done, and how quickly and ruthlessly he could kill. After he killed Hendrick, he would've had no choice but to kill the rest of the crew and drive off with the drugs. It would've been a slaughter, both with Hendrick and the other crew members. And if all that had happened, there would be no guarantee that he'd be able to safely find a fence for the stolen oxycotin. There would be a chance that he'd have to ditch the drugs, making the job a complete waste.

A mechanical rumbling noise came from within the

warehouse. Hendrick glanced at a text message on his cell phone, and told Willis that McCoy and Gannier had found a forklift and would be bringing the oxycotin to the loading dock within five minutes. Hendrick's voice was normal again, with all hints of violence gone. Willis didn't bother saying anything in response.

Five minutes later, Gannier drove a forklift into sight, which carried a pallet loaded with cartons, as well as McCoy who sat on the edge of it with his feet dangling in the air. Once the forklift reached Willis and Hendrick, it stopped, and McCoy jumped off. All four of them then started loading the cartons into the back of the van. It took only minutes for them to stack one point five million dollars worth of oxycotin into it, and once they were done and the van was closed up, Hendrick signaled Howlitz to drive away.

The van pulled out of sight and Willis closed the doors to the loading dock. Hendrick handed Willis a disposable cell phone. The plan was for Howlitz to drive straight through to Virginia to trade the drugs for money, which meant he'd be on the road for at least sixteen hours. "Cam should be back by midnight tonight," Hendrick said. "If there aren't any hiccups, we should be splitting the money sometime the next morning, but I'll call you with a time and place once Cam's back."

All of them then walked through the warehouse to the front part of the building, passing all four of the security guards that were left bound with duct tape. The one that McCoy and Gannier had knocked out had since woken up, and had a queasy look on his face, his eyes somewhat unfocused. The pizza boxes were still sitting on the front desk. Hendrick opened one of them and studied it. "Sausage and mushroom," he told Willis. "Smells good. You want one of these?"

Willis shook his head. "You three take them." As the remaining members of the crew dug in and grabbed pizza slices, Willis left the building, got into his stolen pickup truck, and drove off.

CHAPTER 2

WILLIS DUMPED THE stolen pickup truck a mile from where he had left his car. It was a cold October night, and he could've safely left it so he'd have less of a hike, but he felt unsettled and wanted to walk off some of the uneasiness flitting around in his chest.

It was only two twenty-eight. The job took less than a half hour, and went as smoothly as Willis could've expected, even with the fifteen seconds or so where Hendrick considered double-crossing him before dismissing the idea. By then, one of Hendrick's crew would have called the police anonymously to tip them off about the robbery so that the hostages left behind would be taken care of. There was no reason to risk any of them dying from dehydration or other reasons and turning the crime into a felony murder case. Also by then, there was no chance of the police catching up to any of them. Security video taken from the loading dock that showed the van Howlitz had driven wouldn't help them since Howlitz by now had already moved the drugs to another vehicle and had ditched the stolen van. By all accounts, the job went off without a hitch, and all that was left was getting the money and splitting it. Still, though, until the split happened, the job wasn't finished. The last job Willis worked on was stealing what turned out to be a forged painting for a backstabbing sonofabitch named Jonah Landistone. That heist also appeared to go off without a hitch until everything blew up in their faces. Even still, after shooting out both of Landistone's knees, Willis thought he'd be able to collect the four point nine million dollars that Landistone owed him, at least until Landistone died three days later due to complications from his surgeries.

Willis considered briefly trying to strong-arm Landistone's nymphet third wife and widow for the money he was owed once the insurance paid off, but he gave up that idea. He had no way of proving the painting they stole was a forgery, so he wouldn't be able extort his payment from her, and besides, she didn't know what her late husband had been up to, so it was more likely she'd bring the FBI into the matter than to pay Willis. The four point nine million Willis was owed was gone. Once he accepted that, he didn't give the matter any further thought.

The one-mile walk to his car didn't help with the uneasiness he was feeling. He knew part of it was that the current job would remain unsettled until he collected his split, but part of it was also being back in Massachusetts where he had been assigned when he was employed by The Factory. He had planned to stay away from Massachusetts until he was ready to resume his war against his old employer, and that wasn't going to be until he had a plastic surgeon construct him a new face.

*

After the business with Landistone, he spent two weeks recovering from his cracked ribs in the Florida Keys, and that left him with a new urgency on the matter. That was because while down in the Keys, a Factory assassin tried sneaking into the beach house he was renting. Willis was able to overpower the man, and after a long and brutal interrogation extracted from him that The Factory had put a half a million dollar bounty on his head, and that the assassin had kept to himself that he had spotted Willis earlier in Miami before tracking him down to the Keys so that he wouldn't risk losing the bounty to any other Factory employee. Before ending the interrogation, Willis also learned from the assassin the contact information for his handler, which Willis planned to make use of later. Willis tried to get more from the man, but there was nothing more to get. Right before the end, the man's eyes weakened and grew watery as all of his imagined hurt and betrayal broke through. His voice a raspy croak, he demanded from Willis how he could sleep nights knowing what he had done to his country. So the man believed the lie that The Factory had fed him. That they were only killing insurgents hell-bent on the destruction of the United States. Willis saw no reason to correct him on that and make his death even more futile. Four days later, Hanley contacted Willis about the job, and while Willis had felt calm during the days leading up to the heist and while the robbery was underway, he was sure that that incident in Florida, along with the way his previous job blew up so spectacularly, contributed to the overall uneasiness he felt.

Willis was renting a small ocean-front cottage in Cohasset, which was roughly twenty-five miles from Boston. He chose to stay in Cohasset since it was close proximity to Scituate where he had arranged to meet Hendrick and his crew. He chose the ocean-front cottage because of its location. With it being off-season, the other summer cottages were empty, and Willis would have privacy. On his way back to the cottage, he took a detour through the city of Quincy and found an all-night diner. He wasn't particularly hungry, but he had too much restless energy to go back to the cottage then with the idea of sleeping.

Willis sat at a booth and ordered a cup of coffee and scrambled eggs and bacon. The waitress working the late night shift was in her thirties and was thin, small breasted, and had long, frizzy red hair. Her nose was slightly upturned, but it looked cute on her, as did her slight overbite. She also displayed an infectious smile. When Willis started flirting with her, she flirted back, her body language soon letting Willis know that she wasn't just bored or aiming for a nicer tip, but had genuine interest. His time with The Factory had left Willis at times scarier-looking than handsome, especially when his eyes held a deadness to them. When he made an effort, though, and turned on the charm with his eyes crinkling good-naturedly and his lips flashing an amiable smile, women usually responded, and the waitress who introduced herself as Kate was certainly responding. Outside of the two of them and the short-order cook, there was no one else in the diner, and she stood near Willis after his food was brought over, and they continued flirting while he ate. Once he was done, she informed the short-order cook that she had a migraine and would be leaving early. The cook made a face at that, but otherwise kept his annoyance to himself.

Kate owned a Chevy Nova that had to be almost as old as she was, and she followed Willis back to his cottage. Bowser must've heard the cars pull up because he was waiting for them by the door, yawning in an exaggerated way with his tail wagging furiously, all the while trying to look as if he hadn't just been sleeping. When he saw that Willis had company and realized that that meant he was going to be ignored for hours, his tail wagging slowed to a sluggish beat and he let out a few angry pig grunts to demonstrate how unhappy he was over the matter. Kate dropped to the floor and hugged him tightly around his thick neck and told him what a handsome fellow he was, all of which appeased him somewhat. It appeased him a bit more when Willis and Kate took him for a walk along the desolate beach near the cottage. And finally, all was forgiven when Willis filled his bowl with food, which was three hours earlier than he'd normally be given breakfast.

Willis led Kate to the bedroom where they took off their clothes without saying a word to each other. Without her waitress uniform, Kate's body looked more slender and toned than thin, her waist narrow, her stomach showing only a slight bulge, her legs long. Her breasts, while small, had an attractive perkiness to them, and her pubic area was covered by a thick bush of red hair, which Willis appreciated. He had been with several women of late who had been shaving and waxing that area and leaving it completely hairless. There was a hunger in her eyes as Willis lifted her onto the bed. He was near insatiable with her, but she was even more so. They both ignored Bowser when he would occasionally push himself to his feet and let out several unhappy grunts to show how annoyed he was over the situation before plopping himself back down by the foot of the bed. After a four-hour session, Willis and Kate took a break where Willis made coffee and fried up eggs and bacon for all of them, and when he gave Bowser his portion, all was again forgiven. After breakfast, they slipped on their clothes and Kate joined Willis once more as they took Bowser for a walk along the ocean, with this one being much longer than their late night one. When they returned, Willis gave Bowser a rawhide bone to keep him occupied, then he and Kate slipped off their clothes again and started another four-hour marathon session, although they were more leisurely this time. When they were done, they were both spent. Kate squirmed her body closer to Willis so that she lay nestled against him. Up until then, they hadn't talked much, but she then started asking him the typical questions: what he did for a living, where he lived, stuff like that. He found that he liked her too much to simply ignore her. She was also looking at him right then in a funny way that made him think of an injured sparrow, almost like she was desperately needing some kindness from him, but was instead expecting only an excuse for why he needed her to leave. It wasn't so much a neediness as she must've been down this road too many times before. He told her he bought and managed rental storage properties and that he was visiting the area from Akron, Ohio. It was a harmless enough lie, and Akron was a safe place for him to use. He had lived there before joining The Factory, so if she had ever been to Akron and started commenting about the area he wouldn't be caught in a lie. Before she could ask him anything else, the disposable cell phone that Hendrick had given him rang. He got off the bed, dug the phone out of his jacket pocket and took it to the bathroom so he'd have some privacy. He turned on the water in the sink before answering the phone, and Hendrick told him that the exchange went off as planned, that they should be able to meet the next day for their split, and that he'd call him again the next morning to give him a time and place. Willis went back to the bedroom and found Kate putting on her waitress uniform. She gave him a hesitant, uncertain look and told him he probably had work to do.

"Nothing until later," Willis told her. "Why don't you take a shower and I'll buy you lunch someplace nice."

A look of gratitude washed over her face, and another of her infectious smiles broke out. "I am hungry," she said.

After they showered, Willis took her to an Italian restaurant she recommended. It was two thirty then, and since Kate knew people there and it was an off-time for lunch on a weekday, the restaurant manager was okay with them keeping Bowser by the booth they were seated in. They ended up ordering a large sausage pizza, a third of which Bowser happily wolfed down. Willis had a couple of beers with lunch while Kate stuck with coffee. While they ate she told him how she was going to school at night to become a nurse, figuring that even though the economy was awful there would always be a need for nurses, especially with baby boomers growing older.

"I saw on the news just yesterday that the unemployment rate has crept up to thirteen point two percent," she said, a haggardness showing momentarily in her expression.

"It's rough," Willis said, not bothering to point out how much of an understatement that was given The Factory's efforts to reduce unemployment.

Kate sighed, nodding. "I guess I'm lucky to have my waitress job until I can graduate school. So that's my life now. During the week I'm in school each evening from six to nine, then working a ten to six in the morning graveyard shift at the diner." She grinned wickedly. "Normally I'd be dead asleep right now, and I'm certainly going to be dragging tonight. But it was worth it. That was quite a cardio workout you gave me earlier!"

"Me?" Willis asked, raising an eyebrow dubiously, otherwise holding his poker face intact. "You're the one who ran me near ragged."

When they were finished with lunch, Willis drove her back to the cottage so she could get her car. During the ride, she asked the inevitable question about when he was heading back to Akron. In other words, was it only a one-time meaningless hookup or something else? He told her his business was finishing up over the next day. She nodded as her stare fixed straight ahead, a brittleness weakening her mouth.

After he let her out by her car and she was fumbling with her keys, he found himself mentioning that maybe he'd extend his stay and spend an extra week in the area. He wasn't sure exactly why he said that, but he didn't see the harm in it. He had no place else he needed to be for several weeks, at least not until he arranged for plastic surgery to have a new face constructed, which he'd have the money for once he collected his stake in the robbery. Both the cottage and the general area were remote enough that he didn't have to worry about any Factory employees stumbling on him, and the desolate feel of the New England ocean in October appealed to him. He also found himself wanting to see more of Kate, and it wasn't just that he liked the way she looked without her clothes or how active and imaginative she was in bed. He was surprised at how good he felt around her. It was partly her infectious smile, and partly the freshness and kindness about her that reminded him of how life was, or at least how it could've been, before he got entangled with The Factory. His time as a hit man had left him with a heart that was little more than stone. Having Bowser around these past months had opened a thin crack to the stone, and Kate held the promise of something more. Of course, if he looked at it logically it didn't make sense. He couldn't settle down with her even if he wanted to. Or at least he couldn't until he had a new face. But for the time being, he couldn't see the harm of spending another week or two with her.

Kate brightened up over hearing that he was considering extending his stay. The smile that broke over her face forced a trace of a smile over Willis's own lips, and he could count on one hand the number of times he had smiled over the past three years. After she gave him her cell phone number, she stepped forward and embraced him passionately, pushing her body hard into his and kissing him almost hard enough to loosen teeth, then she let go and hugged Bowser just as tightly, which brought an embarrassed expression to the bull terrier that was betrayed by how hard his tail whipped back and forth. After she drove off, Willis sat on a weather-beaten Adirondack chair that the cottage provided on its porch, and stared out into the blue-gray of the ocean, blanking all thoughts from his mind. Bowser plopped down by his feet, his expression soon turning as cryptic as Willis's.

CHAPTER 3

AT TWO-FORTY-ONE IN the morning, Bowser lifted his head, his ears straight up and rigid in attention. Even though the bull terrier was lying by the foot of the bed in the near pitch-black room and his movement was silent, it woke Willis. Immediately he sat up, fully alert and listening as intently as Bowser for any noises from outside. From the way Bowser's head shot toward the front door and then to the back, he must've heard the soft scraping sounds of door locks being picked several seconds before Willis. The dog got to his feet and padded quickly toward the back of the cottage. Willis reached into a space between the mattress and the bed's headboard for a .40-caliber pistol he had wedged in there. He transferred the gun to his left hand, then squeezed his hand into the same space for a folded nightstick he had kept from his time with The Factory. Willis left the bed holding the nightstick in his right hand and the gun in his left. As he made his way toward the front door, he flicked his wrist to unfold the nightstick.

The back door opened first. Willis heard a soft click, a door being swung open, then a man shouting out in surprise, followed by a loud thump and the types of grunts Bowser would make if he were playing a heated game of tug of war. No more than a second after that the front door opened and two men burst into the cottage. Enough moonlight filtered in from outside so that Willis could make out their forms. He had his back flush against the wall and waited until the two men moved further in front of him before he stepped out and hit the closest of the two in the back of the knees with the nightstick. The man let out a dull *oomph* noise and his legs crumpled, and Willis hit him hard enough in the back of the head with his pistol to knock the man out. His partner began to turn around, trying to get his gun into the action, but Willis chopped down on his gun hand with the nightstick, sending a 9mm Glock clattering to the wood floor and the man grasping his injured hand. Before the man could do much else, Willis transferred the nightstick to his left hand so that his right hand was free, and he grabbed the intruder by his jacket collar, first swinging the man head first into the hallway wall hard enough to put a hole through the plaster, then half-dragging and half-running the man to the other end of the cottage.

Bowser was by the open back door, wrestling furiously with the third intruder. He had knocked the man to the floor and had the man's right arm gripped in his jaw, while the man desperately reached with his left hand for a gun that had dropped within inches of his fingertips. Willis kicked the gun away and turned on the back lights to see that the intruder Bowser was struggling with was Jared Gannier, not that that surprised him. Nor did it surprise him that the man he had by the collar was Charlie Hendrick. He was pretty sure, from the moment that he had smacked him with a gun, that the guy he knocked out was Bud McCoy. He listened for a moment for the fourth member of their team, Cam Howlitz, and when he didn't hear anything he had a good idea why these three had come storming into his cottage when they did and what they were after, since it was the only thing that made sense. He hadn't given them his address, but he knew how they found him. The disposable cell phone that Hendrick had given him must've had a tracking chip hidden in it. He swung Hendrick so he went head first into the wall, landing a foot from where Gannier was still trying to fight off Bowser. Willis pointed his pistol at Gannier and told him that if he hurt his dog he'd kill him. Gannier stopped his struggling. Willis commanded sharply for the bull terrier to come over to him, and Bowser let go of Gannier's arm and did as he was told, which surprised Willis, since he had no idea how Bowser would react.

Gannier, now free of the bull terrier, rubbed his arm while giving Willis a sullen, angry look. "Your damn dog might've broken my arm," he complained bitterly. "And who the fuck brings a dog with him when he's traveling for a job?"

Willis didn't bother responding. He grabbed Bowser by the collar and moved him so he was facing toward the front of the cottage, then slapped him on the rear, sending Bowser scampering away. Seconds later, a growl could be heard that came deep from within Bowser's throat as he stood guard over an unconscious Bud McCoy. Again, Willis was pleasantly surprised since he didn't know how the dog would respond, but he must've been well-trained by his previous owner. By then, Hendrick had gotten off his stomach and was sitting on the floor. He grabbed his head and glared hotly at Willis.

"'That was a dumb move breaking in here the way you did," Willis said. "I thought all of you were smarter than that. You're lucky I didn't kill any of you."

A wildness burned in Hendrick's eyes. His lips tightened into a vicious smile, and he couldn't help himself from laughing at what Willis had said. "You're a liar, Burke," Hendrick spat out. "You didn't kill any of us? What about Cam?"

That confirmed that it was the way Willis had been thinking. Cam Howlitz must've been killed after he returned home and the money had to be missing. If these three came here only to kill him, they would've set fire to the cottage and shot him dead as he fled, but they wanted the five hundred and fifty grand before they killed him, and they believed he had the money in the cottage with him. Willis couldn't blame them for that, and he might've tried the same in their situation, although he would've gotten more intelligence before breaking into the cottage and would've known better what he was up against. Still, he wanted to cut the socializing short, so he pointed his pistol at Hendrick's right knee.

"This is a .40-caliber," he said. "There won't be much of your knee left if I shoot you, and I will shoot you if you don't tell me what you know. And only what you know, not what you think you know."

Hendrick's eyes glistened with malice for a moment. He lowered his stare to Willis's gun. When he looked back at Willis, his smile had faded and his eyes had darkened to the color of coal.

"Cam called me around midnight to tell me he had gotten home. I dropped over around one so we could have a few beers while I helped him split up the money into five piles, and when

I got there I found Cam dead and the money gone. So I called Jared and Bud and we came over here to get our money back."

Willis gave him a hard look while also watching how Gannier reacted. It was possible that some unknown interloper had killed Howlitz and taken the money, but it was also possible it was either Hendrick or one of the two other crew members—that one of them might've gotten the idea that they could grab the whole five hundred and fifty grand for themselves while putting the blame on Willis. If either Hendrick or Gannier had done it, Willis couldn't tell, but it would be a dumb thing for any of them to have tried since a search of his cottage would come up empty. If it was one of them, then the person would've had to make sure that Willis ended up dead when they invaded his cottage so the rest of the crew wouldn't be able to interrogate him, and would have to accept that he had hidden the money someplace where they couldn't find it.

"And you were convinced I did it," Willis said.

Hendrick's eyes glazed and he showed a thin smile, but otherwise didn't say anything. Willis waved the gun he was holding as a signal he wanted answers for his questions.

"Yeah," Hendrick said, shifting his eyes away from Willis.

"You hid a tracking chip in the disposable phone you gave me. That's how you found me?"

"Yeah."

"How was I supposed to know where your buddy, Howlitz, lived?"

Hendrick shrugged. "Maybe you followed him home after our first meeting. Or you could've attached a tracking device to his car. Or slipped one in his pocket. Those are my guesses."

Willis shook his head.

"Then you had someone in the government track him for you." Hendrick shifted his gaze back to Willis, his eyes showing some life again. "That device you used to open the security door came from some spook agency. You must've worked for the government. Some nasty spook branch of it, and that's why you had it. So you had one of your old buddies find where Cam lived."

Willis scratched his jaw as he considered Hendrick. If one of the crew was behind the rip-off, it wasn't him. He was having too hard a time controlling himself.

"I had no idea where Howlitz lived," Willis said. "You're right, I spent time working for a government agency that's about as nasty as it gets, but I didn't leave on good terms, and there's no one there who would help me. If I was going to rip all of you off, I wouldn't have stayed here tonight. I would've put a couple of hundreds of miles between us by now."

"Maybe," Hendrick conceded, a flicker of doubt in his eye.

"No maybes. And I would've killed all three of you also. I wouldn't have wasted any time talking to you."

More doubt showed in Hendrick's expression as he chewed on his lip and thought over what Willis had said. There was no doubt, though, with Gannier as he accepted that Willis was telling the truth.

"He didn't do it, Charlie," Gannier said. "We wouldn't be alive now if he did."

"Then who killed Cam? The guy who did it knew he was coming back tonight with the money."

"I want you to convince me that it's not one of you three," Willis said.

Gannier smiled while Hendrick stared at Willis dumbly

for a long moment before realizing what he was suggesting. "It wasn't something like that," Hendrick said. "All of us grew up together. We're closer than brothers. It wouldn't matter how big the score was, we wouldn't do something like that, at least not to each other. Besides, none of us would've had any idea how to kill Cam the way he was killed." He paused and added, "It was done to make it look like he died of a heart attack or something."

"Could he have died naturally?"

"No. The money's gone. Someone killed him. Someone who knows how to make it look like a heart attack or aneurysm or whatever it was that was done to Cam."

Willis saw another possibility. An accidental drug overdose. Hendrick could've met up with Howlitz to snort some lines of coke instead of going over there for a few beers like he said. Maybe they were like brothers as Hendrick said, but if Howlitz expired because of the coke, Hendrick still could've come up with the idea of grabbing all the money. Willis wasn't completely sure anymore about Hendrick, but he decided to wait until he examined the body before bringing the possibility up.

"If I didn't take the money, and none of you did, then who killed your buddy and ripped us off?" Willis asked.

Hendrick started to shake his head, but grimaced from the pain of doing so. "No one else knew about the job," he insisted. "Cam wouldn't have talked to anyone. None of us talked. It doesn't make sense that anyone would've been waiting for him tonight knowing he'd be bringing home that kind of money."

"Any chance he was an addict? Drugs? Gambling? Anyone he could've owed a lot of money to who might've been leaning on him?"

"No way, that's not Cam," Hendrick said. "That's not any of us. We keep our noses clean. A little weed, a few beers during the day, but that's about it for any of us."

Willis thought about it and didn't like at all where it was pointing. If Hendrick knew his friend like he thought he did, it either had to be one of those three, or it was a setup by whoever they sold the oxycotin to. One of them could've followed Howlitz from Virginia and gotten back the money that they had paid. Willis mentioned the last idea to Hendrick, who shook his head and told him there wasn't a chance that that had happened.

"First off, Cam was a pro. If someone tried tailing him, he would've known. If they tried slipping a tracking device in the money, Cam would've found it with a bug detector. If someone planted a bug in the van he drove down there, it wouldn't have helped. He ditched the van in New Jersey, and drove up a different car. Besides, I've done business with these guys before. They wouldn't have the guts to try something like this, and they're happy enough making what they do with the oxycotin."

"If these guys are into pharmaceutical drugs, they must have what it takes to induce a heart attack."

"I'm telling you it's not them."

Willis let it drop. He could revisit it later. "The police know about this yet?" he asked.

"No, I don't think so."

"I don't want to walk away from my share of the money," Willis said. "I'm guessing you guys don't either."

Hendrick said, "Understatement of the year."

Gannier nodded, said, "What he said."

"Okay, so do we have an agreement? We'll work together to track the money down, and we'll stop trying to kill each other?"

Both of them nodded. Willis lowered his gun and signaled for the two of them to get up. A groaning noise came then from where Bud McCoy had been left, followed by a deeper growling from Bowser. The groaning quickly stopped, but the growling continued. Willis helped Hendrick to his feet, then did the same for Gannier. The three of them followed the growling noise to the front hallway where Bowser stood on Bud McCoy, his fangs barred, while McCoy lay on his stomach, his eyes wide open to show he was awake, and perspiration dripping from his face to show he was scared out of his mind. Willis lowered himself so he sat on his heels and could look more directly at McCoy.

"Hendrick and Gannier both understand now that I had nothing to do with what happened with Howlitz, and that I want the money back as much as all of you do. We have an understanding that we'll work together to recover it. Are you okay with that?"

His voice raspy and barely above a whisper, McCoy said, "Yeah, just get that dog off me."

Willis snapped his fingers and ordered Bowser to his side, and once again the dog surprised him by doing exactly what he asked. As Bowser moved over to him, all his ferocity disappeared, replaced by his typical clownish appearance. He sat on the floor, his body bumping against Willis's leg, all the while panting happily as if the past ten minutes had never happened.

Gannier no longer thought his arm was broken. "Probably just badly bruised. But it's bleeding, although not as bad as it could be. That beast of yours could've ripped it out of the socket if he wanted to, but Burke, you got him well-trained, I'll give you credit for that. He mostly did what he had to to keep me on the floor. But I still got to take care of this."

Gannier headed off to the bathroom to fix up his arm. Willis walked out of the room also with his dog following him. Now that Bowser was up, Willis needed to take him for a walk and give him his breakfast. After that, Willis had a dead man to see.

CHAPTER 4

W ILLIS RODE IN the backseat of a four-year-old Chevy
Malibu, with Hendrick driving, Gannier up front
with him, and McCoy occupying the other backseat. Among
the items Willis brought with him was a laptop computer that
had voice stress analysis software loaded on it, and during the
car ride Willis questioned them, asking where they all were
that night and whether they told anyone about the warehouse
robbery. Hendrick bristled at being questioned further, but he
passed the lie detector. Gannier passed also. McCoy seemed
mostly amused by the questioning until the software indicated
he was lying about whether he talked to anyone about the
robbery.

"Okay, I told my girlfriend I was going to have a hundred
grand score soon, but I didn't give any details about any of it,"
he insisted.

That answer checked out. McCoy could be right that his
girlfriend had no knowledge of the robbery, other than there
was going to be one, but that would have to be checked out

later. Before Willis could close up his laptop, Hendrick offered somewhat indignantly that one of them should be questioning Willis with the voice stress lie detector.

"It would be a waste of time," Willis said. "You already know I'm not involved, but even if I was, the software wouldn't show it. It can be fooled with enough practice, and I've had enough practice."

"I believe you that you don't have the money, but maybe you still talked to someone about it," Hendrick argued.

"There's no one that I could've talked to about it. The only person who knew I was going out on this job is Hanley, and he didn't know any specifics except the size of the job and that you needed someone to open a security door of a specific model. Unless you think Hanley had every member of the team under surveillance so he could rip us off?"

Willis had mentioned Hanley rhetorically. While the cut from Willis's take that Hanley would collect would be dwarfed by the whole five hundred and fifty thousand dollar score, Hanley wouldn't risk a lucrative business to pull a stunt like trying to rip them off. Hendrick begrudgingly agreed that Hanley wouldn't be the one behind it, and he let the matter drop.

Howlitz had had a small ranch-style house at the end of a heavily wooded cul-de-sac. Hendrick cut his car lights before he entered the street, but he mentioned that he could've kept the lights on and it wouldn't matter. "An old lady who's mostly blind lives on one side of Cam, the other house was foreclosed months ago and is still empty." He made a face. "And even if anyone on this street saw my car tonight, they wouldn't talk to the cops."

Hendrick pulled into the ranch's driveway, then Gannier

jumped out of the car and opened the garage door. Gannier had bandaged the arm that Bowser had grabbed, but if he had any ill-effects from his wrestling match with the dog, he didn't show it.

The garage could hold two cars. Hendrick pulled into an empty space, and Gannier followed the Malibu into the garage, silently closing the garage door after him. Hendrick and McCoy exited the car. Willis left his laptop computer on the backseat, but grabbed his small gym bag. All of them were wearing gloves, and Hendrick used a key to gain access from a door in the garage to a room that was set up as a den. Curtains covered the windows, but they still kept the lights off. Using a penlight, Willis located Howlitz slumped over in a recliner, his feet up.

"Any chance the money's still here?" Willis asked.

"The money's not here," Hendrick said, his voice tight, angry. "I searched the place thoroughly. Besides, Cam had no reason to hide it. And no fucking way he keeled over like this."

Willis lifted Howlitz's head and shined the penlight at the dead man's nostrils. There was crusted blood, but if he had snorted any cocaine it had been cleaned up. The eyelids were closed and Willis lifted them open and flashed the penlight into them. Blood vessels had broken leaving the eyes bloody. Willis shone the penlight over more of Howlitz's face. The waxen, unnaturalness of the corpse made him think of victims of his when he worked for The Factory, the ones who had been marked for natural deaths, all of which Willis killed by injecting with a fatal dose of digoxin to induce heart failure. Willis took a magnifying glass from his bag and exchanged the leather gloves he was wearing for a pair of latex ones. While Hendrick and the rest of the crew didn't ask what he was doing, they watched with rapt attention as Willis opened Howlitz's mouth and searched his gums for any needle marks. After that, Willis checked behind Howlitz's ears. The Factory had trained him to inject a victim either in the gums or a soft spot behind the ear. The chances of an autopsy discovering the needle mark, or the digoxin in the blood, was slim, and as far as Willis knew, it never happened with any of the victims he terminated that way.

Willis found a needle mark behind Howlitz's left ear. He took a step back and stood silently for a moment as if he were brooding, then walked over to a built-in desk in a corner of the room and began searching through its drawers. The other crew members watched with interest for several minutes before Hendrick asked him what he was looking for. Willis had pulled a stack of papers from one of the drawers and was thumbing through it. "What I just found," Willis said with a disheartened grunt. "This stack of unemployment check stubs."

"What has that got to do with anything?"

Willis ignored the question, and instead searched through the stubs until he found one that showed Howlitz had been collecting unemployment for four months, which fit with his death being a Factory hit. Grim-faced, Willis told Hendrick and the others he needed to break into the house next door that had been foreclosed on. "You can wait here or you can join me," he said.

"Why the hell do you have to do that?" Hendrick demanded.

Willis stared at him blankly and told him to do what he wanted, but not to bother him with any more questions. He turned to leave the house then. Gannier and McCoy stayed with the body, while Hendrick, not bothering to hide his exasperation, joined Willis.

Willis used a lock pick and had little trouble breaking into the empty house. When he was with The Factory, they'd often give him information about a foreclosed upon house in the neighborhood that he'd be able to use for surveillance of his target, and a house right next door would've been ideal. As Hendrick followed Willis through the empty house, he complained about what they were doing.

"No more of this bullshit," Hendrick demanded, his voice showing the strain of the situation. "I'm sick of this secretive act of yours. What the fuck are you trying to find here?"

Willis had brought Hendrick to the same room that he would've used if he had been assigned Howlitz as a target and needed to observe him. A bleak smile tightened his lips as he pointed out a folding chair that had been set up in front of a window that had the blinds closed. Hendrick walked over to the window and lifted up one of the slats in the blinds so he could look out and see a side view of the front of Howlitz's house.

"This chair could've been left behind when the house was foreclosed on," Hendrick offered without much enthusiasm.

"It wasn't. That chair was used by the killer."

"You're saying someone was sitting here, spying on Cam."

"Yeah, that's what I'm saying."

Hendrick thought about it and shook his head. "It doesn't make any sense," he insisted. "No one should've known about this job."

"Our killer probably didn't," Willis said. "At least not at first when he started the surveillance. Maybe he overheard a phone call. Most likely it was simply dumb luck that he killed Howlitz when he did and was able to walk away with the money."

Hendrick eyed Willis suspiciously. "You're talking like you know who did it," he said.

"Not exactly. I don't know the who, but I have a good idea on the why. And it's going to be a bitch getting our money back. But not impossible."

*

Willis told them about The Factory and what he used to do for them, and why he was sure that Howlitz's murder was a Factory hit. Gannier and McCoy both showed dumb grins while they listened to what he told them. Hendrick's face, though, settled into a look of deadly seriousness.

"Tell me again why they would think Cam was a terrorist?" Gannier asked, his tone indicating this was all a big joke.

"They wouldn't. That's the story they fed us. That we were killing insurgents."

"This sounds like a fairy tale," McCoy argued, his lips pushed into a thick scowl. "You're trying to tell us that the government is bumping off guys who are unemployed to make the unemployment numbers look better? That sounds like total bullshit."

Willis didn't bother arguing, or explaining that what The Factory was doing was targeting people they considered unemployable. That it was all part of an Orwellian plan to fix the economy in the cruelest possible fashion.

"Believe it's all a fairy tale," Willis said. "I don't care. But if you want that five hundred and fifty grand back, you better believe me enough to do what I need you to do."

"I don't get it," McCoy continued arguing. "Let's say this bullshit you're telling us is true, which I don't believe for a second. What makes you so sure it was one of those hit men who killed Cam?"

"When we needed to make a death look like natural causes, we used digoxin, which won't be picked up by a toxicology screen and when given in a fatal dose will cause heart failure. We were trained to inject our target in either the gums or behind an ear. The needle mark I found was behind his left ear in the same place that I would've used. The surveillance was set up the same as I would've done it. Whoever did this used the same methods I was trained to use and had knowledge of digoxin and access to it. If it wasn't The Factory, who else would've put your friend under surveillance?"

"You're guessing that that drug you keep talking about was used," McCoy grumbled stubbornly. "And I still think this Factory story is bullshit."

"It's not bullshit," Hendrick said. "Look at the way Burke took us down when we broke into his house—"

"That was because of that damn dog."

"No, it wasn't. He would've taken us all down just the same without that dog. And I know he worked for some spook agency. He wouldn't have that gizmo he used to open that security door if he didn't." Hendrick scowled at Willis. "That was sloppy of that guy to leave a folding chair by the window. Why do you think he did it?"

"He must've been planning to retrieve it after the hit, but got distracted when he found a suitcase full of money."

"Maybe he'll go back for it? Because if he does, we could wait for him."

"He won't," Willis said. "He was wearing gloves. There won't be any fingerprints or DNA evidence on it. While his handler wouldn't be too happy if he found out about it, our killer is not going to care that he left that chair behind."

"How are we going to get our money back?"

Willis couldn't keep from grimacing as he thought about it. "By finding out which hit man was assigned."

CHAPTER 5

MARTIN LUCE ALMOST took Howlitz out two days earlier than he did. The set up seemed good for a quick hit, even with The Factory marking it to look like natural causes. When they were marked to be a simple murder it was always the easiest, especially when you had an empty house nearby that you could camp out in with a sniper rifle, but this one looked like it should be almost as easy. Luce had earlier broken the lone street light in the vicinity of his target's house, which would leave it more than dark enough for him to enter unseen through a back door of Howlitz's ranch-style home at three in the morning as he planned, not that that even mattered. The cul-de-sac had a broken-down, forsaken feel to it. The houses were all small and in disrepair, the lawns mostly weeds. Luce had observed little traffic there, which was partly explained by a neighboring house, where he had set up his surveillance, being empty, and Howlitz's neighbor on his other side being an elderly woman who kept her lights off and her shades drawn at all times, but there also seemed to be a general lack of interest in the neighborhood. He probably could've broken into Howlitz's home in the middle of the day without worrying about being seen. What kept him from doing that was the cleaning service van that Howlitz drove into his garage during Luce's second day of surveillance. It set something off within his internal radar and made him think he should wait and see what plans his target had for the van.

Finishing the job the following night turned out not to be an option. While Luce maintained his surveillance, he watched as Howlitz drove the van out of his garage at eleven ten that night. Luce had earlier attached a GPS tracking device to the undercarriage of the van and used an app on his smart phone to see that the van first drove to South Boston, then at two eighteen drove to Charlestown where it stayed unmoved for ten hours and seven minutes in the same spot before ending up next in a police impound lot. All that time, Luce watched Howlitz's home without the target returning. He had two gallon jugs of water with him, which he drank sparingly, another jug that had been emptied earlier which he used to relieve himself in, and three ham and cheese sandwiches which he took small bites of every time hunger pangs hit him. If he was still in his twenties, he could've sat immobile for twenty-four hours if he needed to, but now that he was forty-nine, he had to get up every three to four hours to stretch or his muscles would stiffen too much.

At one thirty-nine that afternoon, Luce picked up a news story on his smart phone about a warehouse robbery in South Boston involving Schedule Two narcotics, and it didn't surprise him when he matched the warehouse's GPS coordinates to where he had earlier tracked his target's van in South Boston.

Howlitz must've used that van to transport the drugs from the warehouse to another vehicle that he had waiting for him in Charlestown. Security guards claimed at least four men wearing ski masks were involved in the robbery. The news story didn't mention how much the stolen drugs were worth, or which Schedule Two narcotics were taken, but it did say that the stolen drugs were valued at a substantial amount, and Luce guessed that the drugs taken were oxycotin. Of course, it didn't matter what the drugs were, only how much money they could be sold for. Luce's palms itched as he thought about what would be a substantial amount. One million? Two million? More? He couldn't keep from thinking about how much money Howlitz might have with him when he returned back home.

For hours, Luce's mind raced with different scenarios regarding the robbery and Howlitz's role in it. He knew Howlitz would no longer have the drugs on him. He had already been gone too long for that. Most likely he had driven to another state so he could exchange the drugs for money, which left the big question: would he be returning home after splitting the money with the other members of the robbery, or would he be bringing all of it home with him? Luce's palms itched even more as he thought how it could be the latter.

While the news story didn't say how much the stolen drugs were worth, the word they had used, *substantial*, stuck in Luce's mind. If they were selling the drugs to a fence, which they probably were, they wouldn't get back the full amount. But even half or a third of a *substantial* amount could be more than enough for what he needed. Two hundred thousand dollars would probably be enough. More would be better, but two hundred thousand would allow him to disappear to some coastal village in Thailand or Vietnam where he could live out the rest of his life comfortably, and he knew he'd be able to do it in a way so that The Factory would never be able to find him. For months, he had been praying for this type of opportunity.

Luce no longer believed the story The Factory had fed him about who he killed. Maybe at first he did, but the sad sacks he assassinated couldn't possibly be insurgents. His gut told him that early on, and by the time he finished his eighth assignment he was convinced of it. The idea that he killed innocent people didn't much matter to him. If the government wanted the people dead, they had to have a reason for it, and while he didn't get any pleasure out of killing, he didn't lose sleep over it either. What stressed him out was knowing that the government would have to someday shut down The Factory, and when they did they'd have to scrub it clean completely, which would mean having to get rid of people like him. His was a job where when the pink slip came it would be delivered by two bullets to the back of his head, and then having his body dumped in the ocean or buried in a landfill. Understanding that kept him sleeping fitfully at night. But then came a potential way out.

While he waited for Howlitz, at times he'd start to panic, thinking his target might not be returning—that if the amount was substantial enough, Howlitz could be on the run at that very moment so he could cut out his partners. Whenever those thoughts seized him, Luce would breathe slowly and deeply until he could force a stillness in his mind. Just because that was what he would've done in Howlitz's situation didn't mean his target would do the same. Howlitz could be wired differently than him, or could be happy with his existence in the rundown neighborhood and crappy little house, or he could just be stupid.

Luce couldn't help making a celebratory fist when Howlitz arrived again, driving a late model Ford sedan into his garage at a few minutes before midnight. Soon, though, Luce found himself feeling too antsy to sit still and follow Factory protocol, which would be to wait until all the lights were off within the target's home for an hour before breaking in. He couldn't risk doing that. If Howlitz had brought all the money home with him, then there was the possibility that the other members of the robbery could show up at any moment for the split. Within five minutes of Howlitz returning home, Luce poured out the remaining water within the jugs down a bathroom drain, gathered up the food he still had and all the rest of his garbage and threw it into a large plastic bag, then slipped on a gray trench coat, and left the house. He had prepared ahead of time, and everything he needed for the job was already in the pockets of his trench coat. He left a gym bag that had the rest of his gear and the bag that he had filled with garbage by the side of the house, then circled around his target's property so he could enter the house through the back door.

He was good with a lock pick, and he barely had to break stride before he had the door open, which brought him into the kitchen. Howlitz was there also, his head stuck in the refrigerator as he gathered up food for a midnight snack. Luce had been quiet enough that Howlitz didn't hear him until a faint click sounded from the door being closed behind him. Howlitz froze for a moment, then looked over at Luce with his gaze first settling on the Beretta Nano 9mm that Luce held in his right hand that was pointed at him, then his gaze moved up to meet

Luce's eyes. Howlitz's eyes glazed then, a bitter smile twisting his lips as if he thought it was only a robbery and he knew who was behind it. Of course, the gun was just for show. Luce couldn't shoot him with the way The Factory had designated the hit, but Howlitz had no idea about that, and any thought of making a run for it died quickly with the way the open refrigerator door had him boxed in.

"I just want the money," Luce said. "There's no reason for you to take a nine millimeter slug to the stomach, is there?"

"I suppose not," Howlitz admitted grimly, still smiling as if this were only a bad joke.

"You're going to close the refrigerator slowly and then you're going to take me to where the money is."

"Okay, whatever." Howlitz hesitated, then added, "Look, I'm starving. I've been on the road nine hours straight. Seeing as how I'm going to be tied up for a while, how about being decent about this and letting me make a sandwich first before ripping me off? If you want, I'll make you one also."

"Uh uh. Close the door now while you still have teeth in your mouth. And don't say another word to me."

Howlitz made a shrugging gesture with his hands, then after putting the mustard, salami, and bread that he had taken out for his sandwich back into the refrigerator, he pushed the door closed and led Luce out of his kitchen and to his den. Luce saw the briefcase in the foyer that led to the garage before Howlitz bothered pointing it out, and he waved the gun at Howlitz, indicating for him to take a seat on a beaten up cloth recliner. Luce then took a cord from his coat pocket and ordered Howlitz to hold both arms straight back. Howlitz made a face thinking he was going to have his hands tied behind the chair, probably realizing that twisting his arms back like that for hours would do a number on his shoulders. He looked like he was going to complain about it, but Luce stopped him.

"You want to keep your teeth, don't you?" Luce said.

Reluctantly, Howlitz reached back with both hands as he was ordered. Luce pinned one of Howlitz's arms against the side of the chair with his hip, then jerked the other arm back. Howlitz screamed with pain as if Luce had dislocated his shoulder. Luce ignored it. Even if he had, it wouldn't change the medical examiner's finding of death by heart failure. The examiner would simply assume the dislocation happened somehow while Howlitz was suffering from his heart attack.

Before Luce had done that, he had slipped from his coat pocket the hypodermic needle filled with a fatal dose of digoxin, and while Howlitz screamed and tried to pull free, Luce stuck him behind the left ear with the hypodermic needle and injected its full contents into Howlitz's bloodstream. Seconds later, Howlitz's body jerked violently, and if Luce hadn't been pinning his arms, Howlitz would've fallen face first onto the floor. It continued for another few seconds before the spasms lessened, and after a few more seconds it was over. Luce let go of him, and Howlitz's body started to slump forward. Luce pushed him back and lifted the footrest so the body would be left in a reclined position and wouldn't tumble to the floor. He positioned Howlitz's arms so they would look more natural in death than in the more awkward way they had been pulled behind his body.

Luce then went to the briefcase, his palms itching like crazy as he opened it. It was filled with bundles of hundred dollar bills rubber banded together. He took out one of the bundles and his mouth went dry as he counted twenty bills, all hundreds. A quick estimate had somewhere between two hundred and fifty and three hundred bundles giving him at least half a million dollars, which would be more than enough to allow him to pull his disappearing act. His heart skipped several beats as he closed up the briefcase. He forced his eyes closed and took deep breaths until his heart slowed. Soon he felt himself calming down. He opened his eyes, picked up the briefcase, and walked through the house so he could go out the back way. He had found an inconspicuous spot several blocks from the neighborhood to park his car, and he had taken the precaution of replacing his license plates with ones he had stolen earlier from long-term airport parking.

Luce cut through his victim's backyard, then the next yard before remembering the gym bag and garbage that he had earlier left outside the neighboring home. His mind had been racing so much with thoughts of everything he needed to do before he could disappear into Southeast Asia that he had forgotten about it. He hesitated for only a moment before heading back for it. Now that he had a way out of The Factory, he couldn't afford any mistakes. Once he retrieved his gym bag and the other bag filled with not only garage, but plenty of DNA that could lead back to him, he moved quickly again to disappear into the night.

*

Luce had a forty-five minute drive back to the condo that he rented in Needham, an upper middleclass town west of Boston which turned out to be a perfect place for him to have moved to given that his neighbors kept a wide berth of him, with not one person approaching him in the four years that he had lived there. It was as if they smelled that he was different from them, and they kept their distance, allowing him to come and go as if he were invisible.

He had a hard time keeping himself from racing home, but he managed to maintain a speed within a few miles of the limit so as not to attract any late night police. As he approached Route 93, he took a small detour to Quincy, which was a large enough city for what he needed. Once in the center of town, he found an isolated spot behind a shopping center where he'd have some privacy, and after parking he opened the briefcase and flipped through all the bundles of money. He needed to make sure there weren't any tracking chips hidden within them. When he finished doing that, he filled up his gym bag with the money, then tossed the briefcase into a dumpster in case a tracking chip had been planted inside of the lining. Other than making sure the money was safe, he also knew exactly how much he had. Five hundred and fifty thousand dollars. For the rest of the ride home, he couldn't keep from grinning every time he thought about the money.

After he got home and found a safe place to store the money, he considered heading out to a nearby strip club with a few thousand dollars on him and flashing enough hundreds so he could bring home a nice piece of tail. It had been months since he'd been laid, or even wanted to get laid, and he was on such an exhilaration high that he wanted to celebrate properly. He quickly realized that would be a stupid thing to do. It was going to take him weeks before he'd be ready to do his disappearing act, and if he started throwing hundred dollar bills around now it could draw The Factory's attention, or even the police's. They could very well be looking for someone dropping hundreds at a strip club as a way to get a lead on the warehouse robbery. It wasn't like him to act stupid like that. He needed to settle down and get his thoughts under control.

Luce went to his refrigerator, grabbed a six-pack of Miller Lights, and cracked open one of them. As he sat on his sofa, he found himself staring at nothing in particular, an uneasiness settling into his gut. At first he couldn't quite figure out why, but after he had his second beer and his mind started functioning more normally, he understood all the mistakes he made.

The thought of all that money had made him temporarily stupid.

Even if they weren't insurgents he killed, The Factory could still have them under surveillance, and they could very well know about Howlitz's plans to rob that warehouse. Hell, that had to be why they marked him as a target. Luce needed to do a sweep of Howlitz's house and grounds and know whether there were any surveillance cameras or bugs that The Factory might've planted there. If there were, he was going to have to make a run for it soon, which would be close to suicide since it would only give him a small chance of escaping without The Factory being able to track him down. An even stupider mistake was not getting the names and addresses of the rest of the robbery team. It would've been tricky because of how Howlitz's death had to look, but there were still ways Luce could've extracted the information he needed. The others involved in the robbery wouldn't be able to find Luce, but that didn't matter. They still all needed to be eliminated. He couldn't allow any of them to get picked up by either the police or The Factory. If that happened, The Factory might find out about the five hundred and fifty thousand dollars, and if they did, they'd know that Luce took it.

Luce checked the time and saw it was twenty minutes past two. It would be hours, maybe even days, before the police found the body. He had time to do what he needed, which was to go back there and sweep the inside of the house for any surveillance equipment that The Factory might've planted, and also try to find out who else was involved in the robbery. If he couldn't find names and addresses in Howlitz's house, he'd have to set up surveillance again. It wouldn't be too long before the other crew members for the robbery would be checking up on their dead accomplice.

Luce gathered up what he needed and headed out again. As he drove, all giddiness from before over stumbling onto over half a million dollars was gone, his mind instead focused solely on what he needed to do. It was twenty past three by the time he had parked in a safe location and had made it back to Howlitz's address. As he crept toward the back of the house, he saw a flash of light through a window and understood that someone was inside with a flashlight. So one or more of the robbery crew were already there. It was too soon for him.

He crept over to a side window where the shades were only partially drawn. The room was dark, and from what he could make out he was looking into a small dining room. Whoever was in the house must've been in the den where the body was left. Luce moved to the front door and strained as he listened for voices within the house, and after a couple of minutes, he heard what he thought were two different voices, maybe three. He wished he could've opened the garage door, but he wouldn't be able to do that without alerting them. It was too bad. If he could've gotten into the garage, he'd be able to hear them better and know whether they were still in the den. He'd also know if they had brought a car into the garage, and if they did, he'd be able to plant a tracking chip on the undercarriage. What he really wished was that he could break in and kill all of them, but that would be as good as slicing his own throat with the way The Factory would react. Damn it! Once they got over the shock of finding Howlitz's body and the money gone, they'd be cleaning out any evidence of the robbery, as well as any ties to them, and then they'd be gone for good. Luce only had one way of playing it out and he edged away from the front door and then took off running, moving as fast as he could to get back to his car.

Perspiring badly and out of breath, he tossed the bag he'd been carrying onto the backseat, then got behind the wheel. Keeping his headlights off, he drove until he was five blocks from the entrance to the cul-de-sac and then parked under a heavily leafed oak tree that would shield his car from the moon and any overhead street lights. He caught a break with Howlitz's house being on a cul-de-sac. If the crew members he had overheard had brought their car into Howlitz's garage instead of doing what he had done, they'd be driving out of the cul-de-sac and giving him a chance to follow them. He sat back and waited and tried to stay calm, and twelve minutes later he was rewarded for his patience when a sedan pulled out of the cul-de-sac heading the opposite way with its lights off. If the car had driven towards him, it wouldn't have mattered. There were a few other cars parked on the street, and Luce would've lowered himself in the seat so he wouldn't be seen.

While still keeping his lights off, Luce followed the car,

making sure he kept enough distance between the two of them so he wouldn't be spotted or heard. After half a mile, the other car turned on its headlights, and as it passed under working streetlights, Luce was able to make out that there were two people in the backseat, which meant there was most likely another passenger up front. After a few more miles, the car stopped in front of a small cottage, the neighborhood similar to where Howlitz had lived. A heavyset man got out of the back and ambled his way to the front door. Luce watched as the car drove away and then as the man entered the cottage. He didn't need to follow the car anymore. All he needed was one to get the rest of them.

Once the man was inside the cottage, Luce turned his car around. He still needed to sweep Howlitz's home and property. If The Factory had set up any bugs or surveillance cameras, he wouldn't need to worry about these men. Eliminating them in that case would be pointless. What he'd have to worry about instead would be getting as far away as he could without leaving a trail. His face stiffened as he thought about that. He had to hope he'd be killing the men later, because with the resources The Factory had he didn't see how the other option would be possible, at least not without weeks of planning and having enough fake passports thrown around to make sure he was leaving only dead ends for any Factory operative to find.

CHAPTER 6

HENDRICK DROPPED WILLIS off after McCoy, and when Willis switched the lights on inside his rental cabin, he found Bowser lying on the bed, the dog's thick head resting on the pillow, one eye open, his tail cautiously thumping the mattress. Bowser showed a guilty look as he expected to be admonished for his transgression, but Willis decided the dog had earned a break after what he'd done earlier, so instead he sat on the edge of the bed and scratched Bowser behind his ear for half a minute, which made the dog's tail thump harder.

Willis got up and moved to the kitchen area where he sat by a small butcher block table, with Bowser, who after first stretching and yawning in an exaggerated manner, followed him. Once seated, Willis took a set of screwdrivers from his bag, found the right-sized one to use, and opened up the disposable cell phone that Hendrick gave him earlier. After he removed the GPS tracking chip planted inside and had the phone put back together, he walked back to the bedroom so he could pack up what he had into a duffel bag. He needed to find a new place to stay, somewhere that Hendrick and the other crew members didn't know about. Even if they weren't going to try anymore funny business, now that a Factory assassin was in the picture, he couldn't take the risk of one of them leading the assassin back to him. He had warned the others during the ride back that they should all find safe places to stay until it was over, but none of them appeared to take him seriously.

Once he had his duffel bag packed up, he wiped down all the doorknobs and the surfaces of the kitchen and bathroom with a cloth to remove any fingerprints, then moved to the front door where he whistled for Bowser. The bull terrier had stubbornly stayed in the kitchen. After letting out several angry pig grunts over not being fed the breakfast he had been expecting, the dog scampered over to him and followed him out of the cabin and into Willis's car, jumping onto the front passenger seat. Willis, before entering the car, used a bug detector to make sure the vehicle was clean. Once he was satisfied, he got in and headed to the same twenty-four hour diner in Quincy where Kate worked. It was ten minutes past four, which meant it was ten past three in Akron, Ohio where Big Ed Hanley lived. Willis knew Hanley wouldn't be happy if he called him then, but he did so anyways. After seven rings, Hanley answered, grunting out in a raspy smoker's voice made groggy from sleep, "Yeah?"

"We got problems," Willis said. "An uninvited guest showed up and ran off with the presents. I need your help if we're going to recover what was taken."

In a voice that had quickly become alert, Hanley told him he'd call right back. Three minutes later, Willis's cell phone rang. Hanley was on the other end using his latest disposable phone.

Every three days, Hanley changed the disposable cell phone he used. It was probably an unnecessary precaution to call back using it, but it wasn't worth taking a chance, no matter how remote, that the police or a government agency could be monitoring Hanley's cell phone communications. Even if they were, they'd have no idea who he was talking to, and Willis would've continued talking in code so they'd have nothing concrete from the conversation. Still, it made things easier.

Willis gave Hanley a quick overview as to what had happened without going into any detail regarding who he thought was responsible. He gave Hanley the names of the two Factory handlers he had gotten when he very loudly resigned months earlier from The Factory by killing his own handler after first interrogating him.

"Are those two guys the ones who ripped you off and killed Hendrick's man?"

"No, but they might lead us to who did."

"What do you mean *might*?" Hanley asked, brusquely.

"Just what I said. They might. There are no guarantees. But it's the only chance we have of getting our money back."

"You need to tell me more than this. Who's the guy you're looking for and why *might* these two lead you to him? And how'd the guy get tipped off about the money and where it was going to be?"

Willis had pulled into the diner's parking lot while talking to Hanley, and Bowser let out a few excited grunts on recognizing that they were in a place that cooked up bacon since he had grown to associate diners with bacon. There were only two other cars parked in the lot, both by the side of the building and neither were Kate's. The only person Willis could see through the front plate-glass window was a plump and bored-looking blonde waitress who sat in a booth reading a magazine. Willis parked his car and continued his conversation with Hanley.

"It's too long a story," he said. "There were no mistakes by any of us. No one tipped the killer off about the money. It was just dumb luck on his part that he stumbled on it. The two guys I'm asking about have no idea about the money, but they give us the only chance we have of finding the guy who has it."

"Yeah? Tell me why this is."

"Again, too long a story. What I need from you are addresses for those two names and a quiet place I can bring them to. We'll be doing all the heavy lifting here once you give me that."

Hanley didn't like what he was being told. His voice took on a more blunt edge as he told Willis that he wanted to know the odds of recovering the money if he got him those addresses. Willis thought about it, then told him it was probably fifty percent. He might've been somewhat optimistic with that number since he was told months earlier that there were eight handlers working in The Factory's Boston office, although there could now be only seven depending on whether or not they had replaced Barron. Even though he might only be grabbing twenty-five percent of the handlers, he still felt his fifty percent answer was reasonable as he was confident that if those two weren't responsible for handling Howlitz's killer, he'd be able to get from them the names of other supervisors in their office.

"Fifty percent don't sound too good," Hanley complained.

"It's better than zero percent, which is the odds of getting the money back if I don't get those addresses."

Bowser had been making pig grunts and soft whimpers ever since they arrived at the diner in his anticipation of the food that was waiting for him. At that moment, he let out a louder whimper, and that seemed to annoy the hell out of Hanley.

"Goddamn it, Willis, you brought that mutt with you on a job? That's not the way things are done!"

Hanley knew Willis's name because he was the one who Willis paid to set up both his cover identities—his criminal one, Burke, and his civilian identity, Connor.

"He's not a mutt," Willis said. "He's a purebred bull terrier, and I'm going to bring him wherever I damn well want. He might've saved my life earlier, so shut up about him and call me back when you have the information I need."

Willis disconnected the call and took Bowser into the diner. The blonde waitress working the graveyard shift first stared at Bowser, then gave Willis an annoyed put-upon look before telling him to sit where he wanted. Willis could tell that she wanted to make an issue over him bringing a dog into the diner, but decided in the end not to—that any tip out of him would be better than nothing. He didn't ask about Kate. She must've taken the night off after not sleeping much the night before.

Willis sat in one of the booths while Bowser lay down by his feet, his paws covering his nose, but his ears straight up as he knew bacon was close by. The waitress reluctantly put down her magazine and came over with a menu. Willis waved it off and told her he knew what he wanted.

"Maybe your friend would like to see it," she said with a smirk.

She was a very different type than Kate. At least fifteen years older than Kate, and she made it obvious that she didn't want to be working that night. There was a hardness to her flesh and not a drop of warmth in her eyes. Usually women melted on seeing Bowser, but not this one. When her eyes shifted to look at the bull terrier, her smirk only hardened.

"He doesn't need to see it either," Willis said. "Bring both of us a plate of scrambled eggs and bacon. Make his a double order of bacon. Coffee for me, and a bowl of water for him."

The waitress gave Willis one last dull put-upon look before walking away. When she returned five minutes later with coffee and a bowl of water, she left both on the table without uttering a word. She maintained her indifferent silence when she returned ten minutes later with two orders of scrambled eggs with bacon, with one order on a paper plate. Bowser was quickly sitting at attention and he gobbled up his food within seconds of Willis putting the plate on the floor, then sat staring intently at Willis while he ate at a more leisurely pace. When Willis finished with his food, he then lingered even more slowly over his coffee. Until Hanley called him back he had no better place to be.

CHAPTER 7

BUD MCCOY FELT too wired, too anxious, too frustrated, and overall, too pissed off to even consider sleeping. His leg hurt where Willis had hit him with a nightstick and his head still ached. He'd been buddies with Cam since fifth grade, just like he'd also been with Charlie and Jared, and he was pissed that Cam was killed, but even more so that their money was stolen. He was counting badly on that money. He owed people he couldn't afford to owe. Without that hundred and ten grand he'd been counting on, he was fucked.

He'd been sitting like a lump on an old beat-up cloth chair that he had in his small and equally beat-up looking living room, and he pushed himself off the chair and limped his way to the kitchen and stood in front of the fridge where he foraged through it, eventually pulling out a packet of bologna, a jar of mayonnaise and a loaf of stale Wonder bread. He stood for a long moment in front of the open fridge simmering in his anger before closing it and moving to the counter so he could make a sandwich. He didn't believe the bullshit story Burke fed them, and it pissed him off more than anything that Charlie had bought it so completely. That some shadowy government agency put a hit on Cam because he was collecting unemployment? He didn't know what game Burke was playing on them, or why he didn't kill them all off when he had the opportunity, but he knew in his gut that Burke had the money—or at least was working with someone who had it. He was going to have to convince Charlie and Jared of that, and then they were going to have to do what was necessary to get the truth out of Burke. Hopefully they'd get a chance to jump him when he didn't have that damn beast around.

McCoy shivered involuntarily as he thought about waking up with that dog's fangs bared as the animal stood on him growling as if he were going to rip McCoy's throat out. Damn animal was all muscle, jaws, and teeth. He almost crapped his pants back then, and thinking about it again only pissed him off even more.

He finished making his sandwich, and without even realizing it had wolfed down half of it before looking disgustedly at what was left. He had to quit eating angry the way he did. It was one of the reasons he was carrying an extra sixty pounds.

McCoy took what was left of the sandwich and a can of beer back to the chair he'd been sitting on earlier, and turned on the TV, keeping the volume low so he wouldn't wake Heather. She was a cute piece of ass and a true blonde both up and down. Curvy, with nice firm tits and a sweet face. Maybe not the sharpest knife in the drawer, but very cute, and most nights good in bed. He'd been seeing her for two months, and the two of them were interrupted earlier when Charlie called about what he found at Cam's.

His face folded into a frown and he took a halfhearted bite of his sandwich since he wasn't really hungry, and followed that up with an equally halfhearted swig from his beer. While he did that, he stared blankly at the TV and surfed through the cable channels, his mind drifting too much for him to pay much attention to what was on. When he came to a soft porn movie on one of the Cinemax channels, he left it on and thought more about Heather sleeping in his bed. After ten minutes of paying closer attention to the movie, he turned it off and went back to his darkened bedroom where he found Heather curled up on her side, snoring softly under the blanket. McCoy sat on the edge of the bed and took off his dungarees, stained tee shirt, and socks, leaving on only his boxers, then squeezed in next to Heather so that he was spooning her. He worked a hand under the nightshirt she was wearing so he could cup one of her large, firm tits, then pulled down enough of the blanket so he could kiss her back while he slid his other hand under her panties and between her legs.

She groaned as she woke up. "Honey," she croaked out in a tired voice, "it's too late for that. Baby's got to sleep."

McCoy kept up doing what he was doing. He had too much nervous energy and he needed a way to work it out of his system, and she'd do as well as anything he could think of. What he wanted to tell her was to quit her fucking complaining since it wasn't going to do her any good, and just roll over already, but instead he whispered to her sweetly, "Baby, you make me so hard being near you. Goddamn, you're a beautiful piece of ass."

He let go of her breast so he could guide her hand down and let her feel for herself how hard she had made him, although it was a lie. It was Cinemax's soft porn flick that did the trick, but it wouldn't do any good to tell Heather that. She continued to moan and complain, but before too long he could feel a wetness between her legs and soon after that she gave in.

About fucking time. He twisted over so he could reach into the night table drawer for a condom, and was too preoccupied doing that to notice that someone had slipped into the room, just as he'd been too preoccupied earlier to hear the soft scraping that the person had made when he picked the front door lock. At the very last moment, he caught a flash of movement out of the corner of his eye as the person stuck Heather with a hypodermic needle. He had an impression of the person being a man in his late forties. Thin, hard, and scary, and with a grayness to him. Before he could react, he was swallowed up by a way too loud zapping noise and his whole body seized up as if every muscle in his body were cramping. Simultaneously, it felt as if he was being smacked repeatedly in the back with a two by four. For that moment, he was completely paralyzed. Then there was another all too loud zapping noise and his world went black.

*

Martin Luce had injected the girl with etorphine hydrochloride, which was a powerful animal tranquilizer. It knocked her out instantly, and the dose he gave her would keep her unconscious for several hours. It was doubtful that she saw him, and if she did it would've only been a fleeting glance at best with little chance that she'd be able to identify him. He used a Taser on the guy. Twice, which knocked him out cold. After that, Luce left the bedroom and found an old sheet stored in a linen closet, which he used to drape over the cloth chair in the small living room that sat in front of the TV, then he went back to the bedroom, grabbed the unconscious guy underneath his arms, and pulled him off the bed.

Luce weighed a buck sixty, and while this guy was only about five feet eight, he had to weigh over two hundred and twenty pounds, and Luce was breathing heavily by the time he deposited the guy into the chair that he had ready for him. He rested for a moment to get his breathing more under control, then went back to work again, wrapping duct tape around the guy's chest, legs, and arms, securing him to the chair. After that, he searched the house more thoroughly. He didn't find an address book or any papers that could link the guy to the other members involved in the robbery, but he did find the guy's wallet, his car keys, and two cell phones—one an expensive smart phone, the other a cheap disposable. There were a record of outgoing and incoming phone calls, but there were no contact names or text messages left on either phone. If he could send the phones to The Factory's technology forensics lab, maybe they'd be able to get him the names of the other crew members, but since that wasn't possible, the phones weren't going to help him.

He stood for a moment, bleary-eyed, looking blankly at the guy he had secured to the chair, a tired sigh easing out of him as he did so. It had been over three days since he had slept more than a few minutes at a time. He just wanted to be done, get a good twelve-hour sleep, and then start planning for his disappearing act with the money he stole.

Luce headed to the kitchen and had some luck finding a Red Bull in the refrigerator. The caffeine rush from the drink helped. He then went back to the living room, took a pair of pliers from the bag he had brought, and used them to slowly twist the tip of the unconscious man's nose. After ten seconds, the man sputtered awake, his head jerking up, his eyes blinking wildly.

"Ow, ow, ow," McCoy yelled. "Goddamn it, that hurts!"

Luce released the pliers from McCoy's nose. "Not another word," he said.

McCoy's eyes were watering badly from the way his nose had been twisted. He turned his head enough so he could look at Luce, and his expression turned grim as he realized his situation. He kept his lips pressed tightly together, though, and obviously swallowed back what he wanted to say. Luce studied him for a long moment, then took McCoy's driver's license from his wallet.

"Donald McCoy," Luce said, reading the name on the license.

"My friends call me Bud," McCoy said.

Luce's eyes glazed as he stared at McCoy. Without a word, he grabbed hold of McCoy's right hand and used the pliers to begin to pull the nail off of his thumb. McCoy started to scream, but the look on Luce's face made him clamp his mouth shut. He was breathing raggedly as his thumbnail was ripped off, and although he glared at Luce with a burning fury, he kept himself from saying anything further.

"You make another smartass comment to me and all your nails go," Luce warned with cold detachment. "After that, if I need to hurt you I'll do so in ways you would never have imagined could cause so much pain. Do we understand each other?"

With his voice a little more than a grunt, McCoy forced out that he understood.

Luce hadn't found any hidden cameras or listening devices

when he had returned back to Howlitz's address to search the dead man's home and property. While he had done that, a thought had nagged at him. That maybe he'd been wrong about his targets. That they could've been part of a terrorist network after all, and that Howlitz and the others could've robbed that pharmaceutical warehouse as a way to fund the insurgency.

He asked McCoy to tell him about the insurgency, and a rush of adrenaline hit him as he saw the way McCoy reacted to the question. It was more than the way McCoy's skin paled to a sickly white, but that flicker of understanding that showed in his eyes. It was enough to tell Luce that he'd been wrong all along. That he actually had been killing terrorists. Luce realized then that it didn't much matter to him, but he was still amazed at how wrong he'd been.

"I'm not part of any insurgency," McCoy said, his voice ragged and strained, his eyes shifting from Luce.

"I warned you what would happen if you made any more smartass cracks." Luce stepped forward and forced the fingers of McCoy's right hand apart. Using the pliers, he grabbed hold of the nail of McCoy's index finger. "Lying to me will be so much worse."

"I'm not lying!" McCoy yelled out in a panic. He was trapped where he was with Luce having taped his arm against the chair's armrest, and Luce now using his weight to push down on his hand. He was so frantic he was close to babbling. "I know why you think I'm a terrorist! One of the guys on our crew used to be one of you! I swear to God. He told us about how one of you guys had to be behind killing Cam and stealing our money!"

Luce stepped away from his prisoner without yanking out

another fingernail. A coolness filled his head. He wasn't expecting that answer, but he didn't think the guy was lying. "What do you mean by that," he demanded.

McCoy had begun to hyperventilate, and it looked like he was having difficulty getting the words out. After a minute or so his breathing calmed enough for him to talk.

"He told us he worked for the same government agency, and that they told him he was killing terrorists. I thought he was bullshitting us."

The coolness in Luce's head intensified. He had gotten an announcement months ago about a half million dollar bounty that The Factory had put on some guy's head. He remembered at the time thinking that the guy must've worked for The Factory before performing his own disappearing act, and when he saw the guy's photo he knew the man had to have worked as an assassin, same as him. He couldn't remember the man's name, but he still had the announcement on his laptop.

"What's this guy's name?" Luce asked.

McCoy's expression turned glum. His breathing was now almost normal and some color had returned back to his cheeks, although his eyes were still buried deeply within grayish flesh. "Burke," he said,

The name wasn't familiar. Luce couldn't remember the name in the announcement, but he knew it wasn't Burke. That didn't mean anything, though. If he had quit The Factory he would be using an alias. He'd have to be if he wanted to stay alive.

"If your friend wasn't killing insurgents, then who'd he think he was killing?"

McCoy's expression turned even more glum. Grimacing badly, he said, "He's no friend of mine. Before this job I'd never seen him before. But he told us that the people he was being ordered to kill were just poor dumb saps who were unemployed. That's all. That the government is using all of you guys to fix the unemployment problem."

Luce couldn't help smiling. Not because he found anything amusing, but when he thought of the targets that had been assigned to him it made sense. *Those sonofabitches.* That was all he could think of when he realized that this Burke was right. That those sonofabitches were having him and all the rest of The Factory assassins killing only down-and-out unemployed slobs. He realized that that didn't matter to him either. He didn't really care who he killed. He wondered briefly how bad a guy that made him, and realized that he didn't care. In a month or so he'd be resettling to a remote costal village somewhere in Southeast Asia with enough money to live comfortably for the next fifty years if he had that much time left, and his killing days would be over soon enough.

Luce wished he had brought his laptop with him, but he'd left it in the trunk of his car, which was parked three blocks away. He'd like to get confirmation whether the other crew member, Burke, was the same man his Factory bosses had put a bounty on, especially since his prisoner was too terrified right then to do anything but tell him the truth. But even without confirmation, he was sure it was the same man, which meant there was another half million dollars that he'd be able to get his hands on. The coolness in his head grew worse, almost like ice was being stuffed into his eye sockets, and he soon found himself feeling overly anxious. At first he didn't understand the reason for it, but after a minute or so he did. His situation had just gotten all that more urgent. If Burke was who Luce believed he

DAVE ZELTSERMAN

was, then Burke knew all about The Factory and could very well stir things up with them to try to get back the money. That was what Luce would do if he was in Burke's place, and he saw half a dozen different ways that it could lead to The Factory finding out about the money he stole. He had a moment of panic. It was as if he had been swimming blindly in the ocean and suddenly realized he had gone out too far and was now going to drown. The moment passed.

Luce went back to the kitchen and sat down at the table so he could more calmly think things out, and it kept coming back to the same thing. He had to take care of the rest of the robbery crew as quickly as possible, especially this Burke—an hour ago wouldn't have been soon enough. He checked the time. It was a few minutes past five. He was going to have a lot to do before he could start hunting down those other men.

He went back to McCoy and asked him for the names and addresses for the rest of the robbery crew. The deadness in his eyes and the coldness of his tone were enough to let McCoy know he wasn't someone to be fucked with right then. In a defeated voice, McCoy gave him three names and addresses. Luce wrote it all down, and then asked his prisoner again and got the same information, McCoy's expression showing how he was betraying his fellow criminals. Still Luce told him that he had the license plate of the Malibu sedan that McCoy and the rest of them were in earlier.

"I followed the car when all of you drove away from your dead friend's house. I watched them drop you off first, and I saw that there were three others in the car, so it's good for you that you gave me three names. When I get to my laptop, I'm going to be checking that license plate's registration with the names you gave me and there better be a match."

Luce was lying. He didn't bother getting the license plate of the Malibu. It wouldn't have done him any good since he wouldn't be able to get the registration information without alerting his boss at The Factory. There was little chance, though, that his prisoner would know he was lying.

"The Malibu had a stolen plate on it," McCoy insisted. "So the registration's not going to match."

There was no shiftiness in his prisoner's demeanor, just anger. Luce decided McCoy was telling him the truth, and he left again for the kitchen. Once there, he rummaged through drawers until he found a butcher's knife, which he brought with him to the bedroom. It was going to be his first killing that wasn't sanctioned by either the army or The Factory, but when he was done he found that he didn't feel any different about this one. While he didn't get any enjoyment or satisfaction from it, stabbing the girl to death while she lay unconscious didn't matter to him either. He brought the bloody knife to the living room making sure blood dripped onto the carpet as he did so, and when McCoy saw it he squeezed his eyes shut.

"It's not your time yet," Luce said, and instead of stabbing McCoy also, he forced McCoy to grip the knife handle in his right hand so he'd get a solid set of prints on it, then forced the knife out of his hand and onto the floor. Luce had been wearing gloves ever since he had entered the house so he didn't have to worry about his own prints. He needed to put McCoy out again, and he had only brought one dose of etorphine hydrochloride with him, so he used the Taser on McCoy. Twice.

CHAPTER 8

AROUND FIVE THIRTY, truckers and other early commuters started trickling into the diner. During all that, Willis and Bowser maintained their vigil. At six o'clock, the sour blonde waitress was replaced by a gray-haired grandmotherly type. By then, the diner had gotten more crowded with the counter space taken up and most of the booths occupied. The new waitress gave both Willis and Bowser a tentative smile and asked if he needed anything more or whether she could bring him his check, which meant she'd been filled in about him camping out at the booth since twenty past four.

"Sure," Willis said. "I'll have another refill of coffee and a slice of apple pie if you've got any. Bring a slice also for the dog."

She hesitated, her smile growing weaker. She was a stout woman with plump arms and thick legs, her gray hair pulled up into a steel wool-type ball.

"Dear, I'm afraid it's against health code violations for your dog to be here. Maybe it might be best for you to settle the bill?"

"Not yet," Willis said, and he looked away from her. Five minutes later, she came over with a coffee pot and two slices of apple pie. Eight minutes after that Hanley called back.

"It was damn harder getting that information than I would've thought," Hanley said gruffly, his voice showing that he still held some resentment for Willis telling him to shut up earlier. "And it cost you some money. Two grand, which I'm not getting a dime of."

"Okay."

Hanley gave him the addresses of the two Factory super-visors, and the address of a home in Winthrop he could use. "The place is scheduled to be torn down for new construc-tion, but that ain't happening for another two weeks, and it's only eight miles from one of those guy's homes, the one with the Somerville address. I was promised this house is isolated enough where you'll have all the privacy you need."

"Is that it?"

"Yeah, that's it. You can settle up on these costs next time you see me. And don't worry about those two guys. Do what-ever you need. If they disappear, it won't get back to me or you from asking about them. The guy I bought the information from is solid."

Hanley disconnected the call on his end. Willis waved over the waitress and settled the check, then left the diner with Bowser following close behind. Once he was back in his car, he called Charlie Hendrick's disposable cell phone using the dis-posable he'd been given. When Hendrick answered, Willis gave him the name and address of The Factory supervisor he wanted

Hendrick to abduct, and the address to take him to once he had him.

"Take your buddies Gannier and McCoy with you," Willis said. "The three of you figure out how to grab him quietly. I'm heading off now to grab the other guy, and I'll meet all of you at that Winthrop address. We need to all move now and see if we can get those two men before they head off to work. If we miss them we won't have another chance until later tonight."

"Okay. Jared's with me now and the two of us are ready to roll. I'll give Bud a call. Are you sure you don't need one of us to help you with your guy?"

"Yeah, I'm sure. Just don't screw this up. If we don't nab them this morning, we've got to wait until tonight. If you make a play for him and your man escapes, it will get tougher as there will be more security next time."

"Don't sweat it. If it's possible for us to take him, we'll do it."

Willis had given Hendrick the one living in Somerville. His target had a Waltham address. He knew he was cutting it close. Maybe by seven o'clock he'd be in position to try for an abduction, and he just had to hope his man wouldn't be leaving for work any earlier than that. Willis knew where the Boston office was located—he'd been there once before when he abducted his handler; a deranged fanatic named Tom Barron who truly believed he was saving the country with what The Factory was doing—and he knew there wasn't any way of gaining access to the building without a Factory badge. So it was either grab these two men while they were at home or wait until much later and lose valuable hours. Ten minutes after he'd ended his call with Hendrick, his cell phone rang again as Hendrick was calling him back.

"There's a problem with Bud," Hendrick said, his voice hollow and tinny as if he were stunned and couldn't quite believe what had happened. "He wasn't answering his cell so I swung over there with Jared." His voice dropped off for a moment, then, "It's bad. Bud's gone and his girlfriend's on the bed stabbed to death. It wasn't Bud who did it. No way he did that, not Bud. But whoever it was made it bloody." Another hesitation, then, "It's got to be the guy we're hunting."

Willis grimaced, as he could see then what must've happened. "He must've followed us from Howlitz's house to where we dropped off McCoy."

There was more silence from Hendrick, then with a desperation edging into his voice, he asked, "Why'd he go after Bud? He doesn't know about you. He doesn't know we know who he works for and can track him down. So why'd he have to go after Bud like this?"

"He's cleaning up loose ends. He's afraid if anyone involved in the robbery gets picked up by the police, his Factory bosses might find out that Howlitz was involved also and start thinking that their man took the robbery money after finishing up with the hit, which they wouldn't like. Where are you now?"

"In the car heading to Somerville. Jared's with me." There was more hesitation, then, "The bastard left the knife in the middle of the living room. I'm sure it was left as a frame and has Bud's prints on it. I took it with me so I can dump it. I'm hoping Bud's still alive, and fuck, I need to get back there later and get rid of the body and clean up in case Bud ends up surviving this. I just hope that fucker doesn't send the police over there before I can do that." More silence, then, "I've never done anything like that before, and I'm assuming you have. I could use the help. I'll pay you."

"We'll work something out. Are you okay to grab your guy? You sound shook up."

"I'll be okay." Hendrick's voice dropped lower. "I never expected this shit to come down on us. Bud and Cam have been buddies of mine and Jared since fifth grade. I want this fucker badly. When we catch up to him and get our money back, I want to spend a long time with him before I kill him. Someplace quiet where I can spend days with him."

The last was said with a forced bravado, and it had Willis almost deciding then to cut his losses, but he had seen how well Hendrick and the rest of his team had performed during the robbery, and the steel that Hendrick had shown then, especially when he was sizing Willis up trying to decide whether he could get away with killing him. Hendrick had taken a shock to the system and Willis had to hope he'd get it together soon. He hated the idea of giving up on the hundred and ten thousand dollars he was owed. More, since it was going to be either a three-way or four-way split.

Willis said, "Just remember, we know he's chasing us, he doesn't know we're chasing him."

"Yeah, okay, I don't need any fucking pep talks. I'll be fine. So will Jared. You do your job and we'll do ours."

Hendrick disconnected the call from his end. Willis smiled thinly over hearing that touch of steel once again in Hendrick's voice. He just had to hope it would stay there.

CHAPTER 9

FOR THE NEXT two hours, Luce was kept busy. First, he needed to use McCoy's car to drive back to where he had left his own car so he could transport his unconscious prisoner from one car trunk to the other. Then, while McCoy was still out cold he drove to the small ocean-front cottage that he'd been given as Burke's address while at the same time arranging to have McCoy's car picked up and disposed of in a way so that there would be nothing left to be found. He needed to do that outside of The Factory, but he knew someone, who, for a reasonable fee, would pick up the car within the hour and by noon have it chopped up for scrap metal and parts.

When Luce was a mile away from Burke's address, he pulled over and brought up Google Earth on his laptop so he could figure out his approach to the cottage. Nothing was any good. There was no cover. However he tried approaching the cottage he'd be out in the open, so he'd have to try going in fast through the front door and try to catch Burke by surprise if he was there. The one break he caught was since it was off-season the other cottages were probably empty so there wouldn't be any neighbors around to see him busting his way in. Luce pulled back onto the road and continued on. Five minutes later, he pulled into the driveway of a cottage four addresses away from Burke's. He attached a silencer to a 38-caliber pistol that he earlier had kept in his trunk, and then was out of his car moving swiftly to where he was hoping Burke would be.

He felt a tightening in his chest as he ran crouched over to keep his body as low as he could. Burke was the one he was anxious to eliminate. He'd be the most dangerous for several reasons—he'd be the toughest of them to kill after his Factory training and the one who could cause him the most problems with The Factory. The other two would be fairly routine, especially if they were anything like their friend who he had bound and gagged in his trunk, or their other buddy he killed earlier.

When he got within fifty feet of the cottage, he saw that the blinds for a side window were partially up. Instead of kicking down the front door as he had planned, he instead made his way to the window. The cottage looked empty and there was no sound from inside. He stayed crouched there for three minutes without seeing or hearing anything. There no longer seemed any reason for a quick entrance. Instead of busting down the front door, he used a lock pick and moved swiftly through the rooms of the cottage. If Burke had ever been there, he had since packed up. Luce spotted drops of blood on the floor in several places and in the front hallway the plaster was cracked as if someone had thrown a bowling ball into it. He also found the wall damaged in the back of the cottage.

Luce had to rush things. He couldn't risk the police stumbling onto McCoy stored away in his car trunk. Even though the man was bound and gagged, he'd still be able to bang against the inside of the trunk. Luce would come back later after he had McCoy stored away someplace safe and private, and then more thoroughly search the cottage for anything Burke might've left behind.

When he returned to his car, he headed to Plymouth, which was twenty-three miles south of where he was. His previous assignment before Howlitz had his target living in Plymouth and he had access to an empty house a few doors away from his target that he used for surveillance. The house should still be empty and he planned to put McCoy on ice there. Things would be easier if he could simply kill him and be done with him, but he needed to keep him alive for the time being. While Luce believed his prisoner had been truthful with the address he gave for Burke, he wasn't so sure about the other two. It was obvious that McCoy had a closer relationship with those two, and he could've been trying to protect them. If that turned out to be the case, Luce would do what was necessary to get the information out of him. Luce might also need to use McCoy to lure the others, the way you hunt a tiger with a staked goat. In any case, he needed to store McCoy someplace safe until he was ready to deal with him. When the time was right, he'd have to make sure McCoy disappeared completely. He couldn't allow for someone inside The Factory to get wind of McCoy's death—as well as any of the others he was going to be killing— that person might end up connecting them to Howlitz and get suspicious about why they were being killed, and Luce wasn't going to let that happen. At least not until he took off to parts unknown.

While the house Luce drove to was going to be empty, it

wasn't completely safe for him to use it. With McCoy in the trunk, Luce was going to have to drive into the attached garage, and it was possible a neighbor might see him. The house was set back on the property and had a dense set of trees bordering the neighbor to its right, but he'd still be exposed to several houses if anyone was watching. Most likely if anyone saw him, they'd think he was from the bank that foreclosed on the house, and wouldn't bother interfering. He'd just have to take his chances. If the police were called, he'd deal with them.

It was a quarter to seven when Luce approached the street the house was on. It was a more middleclass neighborhood than where most of his targets had lived. While the houses were all small capes or modest colonials, the area was less seedy, less rundown. Luce felt exposed as he pulled into the house's driveway and used a Factory-issued gizmo to open the automatic garage door. While the house had been foreclosed on, the bank kept the electricity on. Luce wondered whether The Factory was responsible for the bank doing that. He also wondered about the assortment of devices The Factory had given him. The one he had used was supposed to be able to override any commercial security system as well as open a standard garage door, and so far it had worked like a charm whenever Luce had needed to use it. The Factory could've built the device by hacking the security systems, but most likely they were handed special codes by the companies that built them—codes that The Factory must've insisted on. Luce pulled into the garage and used the gizmo to lower the garage door.

Luce exited the car. As he expected, McCoy was awake. His prisoner lay on his side with his stubby arms behind his back, his wrists taped together, his knees almost to his chest, with his ankles also taped together. A wadded up piece of newspaper had been stuffed in his mouth and then duct tape was used to keep his mouth closed. McCoy looked up at him with a mix of fear and rage, with maybe rage having the upper hand, his eyes both watery and burning bright. Luce ignored it. It was just business and if the guy wanted to take it personally, that was his problem.

Luce grabbed McCoy under his armpits and pulled him out of the trunk, letting him fall onto the floor. The body hit the cement with a dull thud, the gag blocking any grunts of pain.

Luce left him there and went to unlock the door to the house, then came back and grabbed McCoy by his feet and dragged him through the door and into a small room that had once been a den, but was now empty of all furniture. The only reminder of what the room had once been was ugly orange shag carpeting. Luce went back to his car for his laptop and brought it into the house. Once he found the memo that had been sent about the man with a half a million dollar bounty on him, he showed the picture of the man to McCoy and asked if that was Burke. He didn't bother pulling the tape off and taking the wadded up newspaper out of McCoy's mouth. From the shift in McCoy's eyes, he knew the man in the photo. McCoy nodded in a defeated way, not that Luce needed to see that.

The man in the picture was named Dan Willis, or at least that was the name The Factory used. Luce recognized the man's eyes. The same cold dead eyes he saw every time he looked in a mirror or accidentally caught his reflection. There was no doubt the man had been a Factory assassin. The memo had been sent over four months ago. Instead of Willis running to a remote part of the world like he should've, the damn fool had hung around after deserting The Factory to commit armed robberies. It was a miracle the guy was still alive. Luce remembered hearing about a Factory supervisor in the Boston office who had disappeared around the same time the memo was sent. What was his name? Barry? Barron? Something like that. He wondered if the two were connected. Probably. He put his laptop down, grabbed hold of McCoy's feet again and dragged him to a coat closet that was just big enough to fit McCoy's bulk. He closed the closet door on him. It would be fine leaving him there. He'd be out of sight if anyone looked through a window, and he sure as hell wasn't going anywhere.

Luce got into his car and drove out of the garage, then parked two blocks away and sat idling, waiting to see if anyone had called the police. After fifteen minutes, he decided it was safe and drove off. He'd be passing by Willis's rented beachfront cottage to get to either of the other addresses McCoy gave him, so he decided to make a short detour back to the cottage. It was seven thirty when he entered it again. He gave the place a thorough search, but found nothing useful. No receipts, no papers, nothing. He looked over the dried blood drops on the floor and the two places where the walls were damaged. There had to have been an altercation there. The plaster in one place was caved in as if someone had been swung head first into it.

It wasn't hard for Luce to imagine what must've happened, and he had little doubt that Willis and the rest of the crew, after their misunderstanding, were now trying to hunt down the Factory hit man who stole their money. But how they could possibly do that, especially given that Willis would be taken out immediately if he tried approaching The Factory office downtown? The bounty offered was for his death, not for taking him alive.

The more Luce thought about the situation, the more anxious he got. It didn't matter that Willis had no way of tracking him down, he could still cause problems for Luce with his Factory bosses, and Luce's chest tightened as he thought of all the ways Willis could accomplish that.

His thoughts were interrupted by the sounds of footsteps on the front porch. Luce pushed apart slats on the closed blinds of one of the front windows. A woman holding a box with two coffees and a bag of donuts. She was a redhead in her early thirties. Thin, cute, and wearing a pair of worn jeans and an even more worn-looking suede jacket. She had an almost tragic smile, as if she was unsure of the reception she would be receiving, but also showing a sad hopefulness. If Luce wasn't such an utter sociopath, he knew that look on her face would've touched him. It also would've bothered him what was going to be happening to her. But since he was a pure sociopath through and through, he was fine with it all.

CHAPTER 10

A T SEVEN FORTY three, Willis sat silently on the cement floor behind an older model Honda Accord. The Factory supervisor he was going to be abducting was named Allen Patterson. Willis had arrived at the Waltham house thirty-five minutes earlier, and had spent the first four minutes scouting the grounds before breaking in.

The house was a modest beige-colored colonial with a recently added attached two-car garage. A quick look through a side window showed an older model Honda Accord and a shiny new minivan, as well as evidence of young kids. Fortunately, they didn't have a dog. If possible, Willis wanted to take Patterson without involving his wife or kids, and if a dog was in the picture that wouldn't have been possible.

Willis was able to gain access to the house through a side window that led to a small laundry room. A children's cartoon of some sort was blasting on a TV in the kitchen, and that drowned out any noises Willis might've made. Moving quietly through the house, he was able to get a look at Patterson, his wife, and their two young children. Patterson was in his early forties, his wife in her late thirties, their two girls no older than five and three. Patterson sat at the kitchen table reading the newspaper as he drank coffee and chewed slowly on a Danish pastry. His wife was dressed conservatively in a skirt and blouse and rushed around the kitchen putting away dishes. The two girls sat mesmerized by whatever they were watching. Bowls of cereal were laid out in front of them and they each had spoons gripped tightly in their chubby hands, but neither was eating. If Willis didn't know better the scene would've been one of a typical middleclass family: the balding and out-of-shape white-collar husband, the harried working mom who probably would've been pretty a few years earlier but was now putting on weight and mostly just looked tired, and their two young children. But it wasn't anything typical. Not with the husband spending his days supervising the killing of unemployed men and women. Willis slipped away to the garage.

He'd have to wait and see whose job it was to drop the kids off at daycare. He'd rather that it was the wife's, because if Patterson was taking the girls, Willis would have to grab them also, maybe the wife, too. He tried to just breathe slowly and blank his mind as he waited for Patterson, and not think about those valuable minutes that were ticking away. When he heard the door to the garage open, he moved into a crouching position. The wife had the two little girls with her, and she loaded them into the minivan. A minute later, she got behind the wheel and pulled the van out of the garage. As she did that, Willis moved to the front of the Accord so that he wouldn't be seen by the wife or girls or anyone else while the garage was open. When the garage door closed, he moved again, this time to the side of the door that led into the house. Three minutes later the door opened, and as Patterson stepped into the garage, Willis put him in a chokehold. Patterson flailed away uselessly for nine seconds before dropping into unconsciousness. Willis lowered him to the floor, searched his pockets, and pulled out Patterson's car keys and wallet. He checked Patterson's driver's license to make sure he had the right guy—the last thing Willis wanted was a fuckup where he grabbed the wrong man. After that, he went through Patterson's briefcase which gave him plenty of reassurance that he had grabbed a trusted Factory employee. He found Patterson's Factory badge inside the briefcase. While the badge could be used to gain access to the Boston Factory office, it also contained an embedded tracking chip. Willis left the badge on the garage floor, then after using duct tape and a rag to bind and gag Patterson, he moved the unconscious man into the Honda's trunk. While Patterson had a good amount of flab around his middle, he was tall with long, bony legs and had a pronounced Adam's apple showing in his thin neck. He was dressed conservatively in a blue suit, button-down white shirt, and black oxfords. It took a little bit of work, and Willis had to empty out the contents of Honda's trunk first, but he was able to position Patterson inside the trunk so that he could close it. He had found a safe place to park a mile away, and would transfer Patterson to his car's trunk there. Willis had stolen plates on his car, which he would be replacing, so it wouldn't matter in the remote event that someone stumbled upon his car and paid attention to his license plate number. Nor would it make any difference whether the police or The Factory found Patterson's Honda in that same location.

*

Patterson had woken up by the time Willis opened the Honda's trunk to move Patterson to his own car. At first, Patterson glared hotly at him, but then something clicked as he recognized Willis, probably from a Factory memo. His eyes opened wide and became liquid, and the fear that rushed over him was palpable. Willis didn't bother saying anything. Once he had Patterson moved to his car trunk, he headed off to Winthrop.

Traffic moved sluggishly, at times coming to a standstill, and what should've been a forty-minute drive took Willis over an hour, but he was pleased with what he saw when he arrived at the address Hanley had given him. An old, dilapidated Victorian set far back from the road, and as it turned out, with a separate brick garage in the back so that Willis's car would be well hidden. Hendrick's Malibu was already parked in one of the bays and Willis pulled into the other one. They had agreed to call each other only if they ran into problems. Willis's disposable cell phone rang. It was Hendrick.

"No problems on my end," Hendrick said, his voice unnaturally tight. "I want to make sure you're the one who just pulled up in back. I can't get a good view from the window here."

"Yeah, it's me."

"Yeah, okay. Jared and I have been sitting around playing with our dicks the last hour and a half," Hendrick complained, his voice turning whiny and surly. "What the fuck took you so long?"

Willis ignored the question. "I'm going to bring Patterson in through the back door. I don't want him seeing your guy," he said.

"He won't," Hendrick said. "And fuck you. It's almost nine

o'clock. You were supposed to be here an hour ago. I want to know why the holdup—"

Willis disconnected the call. He got out of his car and, with Bowser following closely behind, walked around to the back of his car and opened his trunk to find Patterson crying softly, his sobs muffled by his gag. Willis had planned to flip the man onto his shoulder and carry him into the house, but he didn't want Patterson's snot and tears staining his clothes. He got Hendrick on the cell phone again and asked him whether he or Gannier could come outside and give him a hand with his man. Hendrick hung up without saying anything, but a minute later Gannier came out the back door carrying a crumpled sheet under his arm. As he approached, Willis could see that his nose and jaw were bruised. Gannier nodded to him, then looked into the trunk, his lips pulling into a tight smile as he did so.

"Fucking pussy," he swore under his breath.

Willis grabbed Patterson under the arms and dragged him halfway out of the trunk before Gannier tossed the sheet over him and grabbed him by his feet, then the two of them hustled Patterson to the house and through a back door, which put them in the kitchen. Bowser scooted into the house behind them. Hendrick wasn't there.

"Where do you have the others?" Willis asked.

Gannier smiled thinly over Willis asking about *the others* as a way to keep Patterson clueless as to how many Factory supervisors they had grabbed. Since Patterson had a sheet draped over his head, he couldn't see the smile.

"We got *them* upstairs."

Willis nodded to a door that was off the kitchen and led to the basement, and they carried Patterson down the steps.

While the house still held some furniture covered with sheets, the electricity had been cut off and there was no heat. It was a cool October morning, and the basement was a good deal colder than it was outside, at least by ten degrees. Or maybe it just felt that way because of how dank and musty it was, and how little sunlight penetrated the dirt-encrusted casement windows.

They dropped Patterson on the floor and headed back upstairs. Bowser stayed behind to sniff at the sheet that covered Patterson. When he started to push his nose under it, Willis whistled for him and the bull terrier turned and scurried up the steps after him. Once they were out of the basement with the door closed behind them, Willis asked Gannier where Hendrick was.

Gannier rolled his eyes, grimaced. "He's upstairs sulking. I know it doesn't make any sense, and I'm sure he knows it also, but he's gotten it in his head that it's your fault these spooks killed Cam, and maybe Bud, too. You know, with you once working for them."

"You're right. It doesn't make any sense."

"I know. But you need to remember all of us have been tight since fifth grade, and what happened to Cam and Bud hit me and Charlie hard. But he'll be all right. He just needs a little more time to process than I did. In my case, the thought of some cocksucker out there doing what he did to Cam and Bud and walking away with our money was all I needed to get me to focus properly. Charlie will come around, too."

It confirmed what Willis had picked up in Hendrick's tone, but he still didn't like what he was hearing. It was going to be hard enough tracking down The Factory hit man who had stolen their money without having to deal with irrational behavior from Hendrick. It would be so easy for Willis to just get in his car and drive back to Ohio, and maybe he would've done that if it wasn't for his recent close call in Florida. He needed his share of the money and the new face it would buy him.

"Either of you try questioning Finder yet?" Willis asked.

Elliot Finder was the name of the other Factory supervisor. Gannier shook his head. "You told us not to, so we didn't. We dumped him in a bedroom upstairs and left him alone."

"You made sure you didn't bring him here with his Factory badge?"

"What do you think? We did just as you asked."

"Was he carrying a briefcase with him when you jumped him?"

Gannier nodded. "Yeah, he was. His spook badge was in it." His eyes glazed and his tone shifted and took on a more cautious note as if he thought Willis might not be happy with what he was about to tell him. "We left it behind. We didn't know what else might've had tracking chips hidden in it."

Willis couldn't blame them for that, but it was unfortunate. He still needed to go back to his car for Patterson's briefcase so he could search through it, and it would've been good to have had Finder's also, but it was his fault for not prepping them better. He nodded towards the bruises on Gannier's face. "Finder do that?" he asked.

"Yeah, he was feistier than we expected. We had to bust him up somewhat, but he's conscious and can talk. You ready to question them?"

"In ten minutes," Willis said.

CHAPTER 11

WILLIS SEARCHED THROUGH Patterson's briefcase and found budget reports and department forecasts that showed the Boston office was falling short in meeting their quarterly murder goals. Also in the briefcase were profiles of upcoming targets and other assorted interoffice memos, but nothing that helped in naming the hit man assigned to Howlitz, or whether Patterson was the one supervising the killing. While Willis came up empty in that regard, he did find a memo with the name of The Factory's Northeast regional manager and the address for the New York office, which he planned to make use of when the current business was over and he could focus on his war against The Factory. He also found a small device the size of a smart phone, which he knew from experience was used to track Factory employees by inputting their badge numbers. Hendrick and Gannier hung around while Willis went through the briefcase's contents, Gannier standing relaxed with a smart-alecky grin, Hendrick seething.

"You're wasting our time here," Hendrick complained, his

voice coming out in an explosive burst, his eyes shining brightly with violence. Like Gannier, he showed signs of Finder's feistiness. In his case, he had scratch marks along his right cheek and some swelling under his eye. "We've had our guy on ice here almost two hours while you've been dicking around."

Willis folded up the two memos he planned on using in the future, and tucked them into an inside jacket pocket. He also pocketed the employee tracking device, then dumped the rest of Patterson's papers back into the briefcase. He didn't bother explaining to Hendrick that he had spent less than ten minutes going through the contents of the briefcase as he had promised Gannier. There was no point in doing so. The guy was all set to go off the same as if someone had touched an exposed nerve.

"I'll question Patterson first, then Finder," Willis said.

Hendrick made a disgusted face. "I could've beaten the truth out of both of them by now. Chrissakes, I could've been working Finder over for the last two hours, and I would've had him begging to tell us everything he knows."

"You don't understand their mentality. You would've gotten nothing out of them. If you want to join me with Patterson, fine. But stay away from Finder until I'm ready to deal with him."

Willis ordered Bowser to stay where he was. The bull terrier, who'd been laying by Willis's feet, let out an angry pig grunt, but didn't move from the floor as Willis headed toward the basement door with Hendrick and Gannier tagging along. Earlier, when Hendrick saw that Willis had brought Bowser to the house, he gave Willis an earful about it until Willis ordered him to shut up. Since then, Hendrick acted as if the dog wasn't there.

Patterson still had the sheet covering him, and had tried wiggling like a snake across the basement floor, but hadn't gotten far. Maybe six feet from where he'd been left. Possibly he was trying to find something sharp to cut the tape binding his wrists. Or it could've been simply panic that drove him into action whether it made sense or not. Whichever it was, Willis didn't care. He pulled the sheet off Patterson and saw that the man was sweating badly even in the dank coldness of the basement, his face dripping with it. While there wasn't much light, there was enough for Patterson to recognize Willis, and he shrunk into himself at the sight of him. Willis crouched low so he was just about sitting on his heels. After he dried off Patterson's face with the sheet, he removed the gag, then grabbed Patterson by his jaw so he could force The Factory supervisor to face him.

"You know who I am," Willis said.

While it wasn't said as a question, Patterson still nodded bleakly, his eyes red-rimmed and teary.

"Tell me who you think I am."

"You used to be employed by us," Patterson said, his face puckering up as if he was fighting to keep from bawling. "You killed your supervisor. Tom Barron."

"And you know how many others I killed because of your outfit, right? Let me remind you. Twenty-five. All innocent people. I'm reminding you of that so there's no misunderstanding on your part on what I'm willing to do. Just so you know, I could've taken your wife and two girls also, but I waited so I could take you alone. If you give me the slightest provocation, I'll bring them here."

Patterson lost his fight and burst out sobbing. "Please," he pleaded, "I was lied to also. I didn't know who we were really killing until six months ago, and I don't believe in what we're doing any more than you did. I needed a job and got sucked in the same as you. I hate being a part of it. I swear. If I could've quit, I would've. But I can't. Not with a wife and my girls. You have to know that!"

Willis had no sympathy for him. He guessed that Patterson was lying, at least about when he found out that the people they were killing were the unemployed and not terrorists. Management, even at the lowest levels, had to know that. Willis didn't bother saying the obvious. That even if Patterson was telling him the truth, once he discovered what The Factory was up to he had a moral obligation to do something about it. In Willis's case, he had no evidence that he could've taken to the media, but Patterson would've had access to countless files and other hard evidence that could've been used to bring what The Factory was doing to light. By simply continuing on with his job the last six months, he was no different than all the Nazis who after World War II tried claiming they were simply following orders.

Willis waited until Patterson brought his sobbing under control before telling him that there was a chance he'd be able to go back to his family. "I didn't bring you here to kill you. One of your hit men murdered an associate of mine and stole a large amount of money that belonged to us. All we want is our money back. If you supervised this assignment and you give us the name of the hit man involved, we'll let you walk away from here once we get our money back."

Patterson gave Willis a dubious look. "You'd just let me walk out of here?"

"Why not? All we want is our money. Besides, you wouldn't be able to tell your Factory bosses what happened. If you did, and even if they believed you when you left out the part of how you betrayed one of your hit men, they still wouldn't be able to trust you and they'd have you eliminated."

He accepted what Willis told him. "What if the assignment wasn't one of mine and I don't know who the field agent is?"

Willis shrugged. "Then you're not seeing your family again. Our friend who was killed was named Cam Howlitz. Do you know who was assigned?"

Patterson nodded, a wave of relief relaxing his facial muscles. "That was one of mine," he said. "The agent's name is Martin Luce."

Willis gave him a hard look trying to decide whether he was lying or not, but couldn't tell. "When was the hit done?" he asked.

"I don't know. Luce hadn't reported it yet."

"How was the hit designated?"

Patterson smiled at that. "Natural causes."

"Where did the hit take place?"

"I don't know." Thin lines grooved Patterson's forehead as he concentrated to remember something. "The target lived in Scituate," he said at last, nodding. "Given the designation, I'm assuming the assignment was carried out in the target's residence."

Willis straightened up, his knees creaking as he did so. "What's Luce's address?" he asked.

"I don't know. I'd have to access Factory files for that."

"What's his phone number?"

"I don't have that memorized either."

"How come you didn't have a cell phone on you?"

"I left it at the office. I guess I didn't want any of my field agents calling me last night."

"You're not being very helpful to us in tracking down Luce."

"I'm sorry. I don't what else I can tell you."

Willis pulled his .40-caliber pistol from his waistband. "You almost could've walked out of here," he said. He flicked the safety off and pointed the muzzle of the gun at Patterson.

"No, no, no!" Patterson screamed. "Look in my briefcase! I have a device you can use to locate Luce! It can track any employee from their badge!"

Patterson looked as if he were about to pass out, and his screaming so vehemently left his voice hoarse. Willis shoved the gun back in his waistband leaving it hidden by his jacket. He took the tracking device from his pocket and powered it on. He had done it earlier, but the screen needed a badge number before proceeding.

"What's Luce's badge number?"

"You don't need it. Press two, six and nine simultaneously for three seconds."

Willis did as he was told, and the screen changed to show a list of names. He scrolled through it and counted twenty-two names. He then went back to where he had seen Luce's name. When he selected it, the screen gave him an address in Scituate. He showed the address to Hendrick and Gannier, but neither of them recognized it.

"If you get your money back, you're going to let me live?" Patterson asked, his voice shaky.

Willis nodded. He lowered himself again into a crouch so

he could force the gag back in Patterson's mouth. Once that was done he straightened up, and with a tilt of his head, signaled for Hendrick and Gannier to follow him up the basement steps. After they were out of the basement and had the door closed behind them, Gannier offered that he couldn't tell whether the guy was lying or not.

"He could just be playing for time," Gannier said. "You know, throwing us one of his goons and hoping that we get caught or killed. Or that someone stumbles on him while we're off on our goose chase."

"That's not it," Hendrick stated, his jaw muscles tightening. "He knew where Cam lived and how he was killed. The guy he gave us, Luce, is the fucker we're after."

"Maybe," Gannier said. "I don't know. It just seemed too easy getting him to spill his guts." Then to Willis, "Burke, I thought these guys were supposed to be tough, hardened muthafuckas. This guy was a pussy. What's going on? Is he on the level or is he playing us?"

Willis scratched his jaw as he considered it, then shook his head. "It was mostly a performance," he said. "He wants to live, and he doesn't care if we kill this Luce character. But Luce is still probably who we're after."

"He has to be the guy. Especially with him being in Scituate now," Hendrick insisted.

Willis shrugged. He thought it was likely, but he wasn't entirely convinced. It was just too easy getting Patterson to tell what he knew. It was also possible that Luce was on another assignment in Scituate and had nothing to do with Howlitz, McCoy, and their money, because it didn't make sense for him to be there otherwise. If the GPS address had him outside of either Hendrick's or Gannier's house, then it would've made perfect sense, but not if he was at an address those two didn't recognize. So maybe Patterson was on the level, or maybe he was simply playing out the cards he was dealt the best he could.

Willis told Hendrick he was going to talk to Finder, which caused the other man's face to redden and his jaw muscles tightened to where his skin looked like it might rip.

"We haven't wasted enough time yet?" Hendrick demanded.

"I'll be talking to him for no more than five minutes," Willis said, rubbing his knuckles impatiently. It had gotten tiresome to deal with Hendrick, and every minute he spent with him made him question whether it was worth going after the money if the guy was going to act like that. "Which will be a lot less than what we'll be wasting if Patterson gave us the wrong man."

Bowser had started to push himself to his feet, and Willis ordered him to lay back down, which the dog did after letting out a few angry grunts in protest. Hendrick opened his mouth as if he were going to continue arguing the point about spending time interrogating Finder. Willis ignored him and headed up the stairs. While he did that, he called Hanley and gave him Martin Luce's name and asked for an address. Hanley told him he'd call him back.

Willis found Elliot Finder in what used to be a young girl's bedroom given the posters that were still hung on the wall. Finder was on the short side, stocky. His ankles were taped together, and he was left sitting on the floor barefoot with his arms behind his back and his wrists tied together and bound to a radiator pipe. Only stubble remained of his reddish hair as he had shaved it close to the scalp revealing a bullet-shaped head.

Hendrick and Gannier had shoved his socks in his mouth to gag him. Both of his eyes were badly swollen, his nose looked like a lump of raw hamburger meat and the area around his mouth was a bloody mess. Still, he sneered at Willis and maintained his sneer even after Willis detected a glint of recognition in Finder's eyes.

Willis reached down and grabbed Finder's jaw tightly enough to make the man wince, and pulled the socks out of his mouth. The Factory supervisor spat out blood and continued to sneer at Willis.

"Look who's here," Finder forced out, his voice hoarse and cracking. "A goddamn traitor. Too bad we haven't killed you yet, but we will."

Willis was amazed. From Finder's reaction, he believed that The Factory was killing terrorists. Patterson must've told the truth about being misled on who they were killing. It didn't seem possible that The Factory high command could keep their supervisors in the dark like that, especially given that Willis's ex-supervisor, Tom Barron, knew all about what was really going on, but it seemed that that was what was happening.

"You haven't connected the dots yet on who you're really killing? I could let you die thinking you're a hero, but fuck that. Tom Barron knew that you weren't killing terrorists, but just out-of-work slobs, and that The Factory's real mission is to get the unemployment rate down to something manageable."

A flicker of doubt showed in Finder's eyes as maybe at that moment he was connecting the dots on his victims. He spat out more blood, then told Willis he was lying.

"No, I'm afraid not."

Willis lowered himself and pushed his fist against Finder's

throat, modulating the pressure so that he wouldn't kill him right away, but he used enough pressure so that Finder knew he'd be dead within a minute. Finder wanted to keep sneering, but he couldn't. There was too much confusion and doubt mixing in his eyes. He probably wanted to know the truth about who he'd been arranging to have killed. Maybe he didn't want to die not knowing.

"Unfortunately for you, we took another Factory supervisor. Allen Patterson. I'm guessing you know him?" Willis didn't wait for an answer. "It doesn't matter whether you do or not. He told us what we needed to know. That one of his men killed Cam Howlitz. So Patterson gets to live and you get to die."

"He's lying," Finder forced out, his voice barely a gurgle, his face purple.

Willis released the pressure. It took Finder a minute before he was able to regain his breath enough to talk.

"Howlitz was one of mine," he claimed.

"How was his death designated?"

Finder made a face. "Natural causes."

"Where did Howlitz live?"

Finder's face scrunched up more to show how ridiculous he found the question. "I handle over twenty assignments each week. I don't memorize each of the cases. But Howlitz lived somewhere on the South Shore."

"Who did you assign to Howlitz?"

Finder hesitated a moment before asking Willis why it was important to him to know.

"Because whoever it was stole a lot of money of ours, and we want it back. You've got five seconds to tell me who you assigned before I decide you're full of shit."

Finder tried to meet Willis's stare, but his blood-red eyes weakened and he looked away. "If I tell you, I get to live and Patterson dies?"

"If we get our money back from the guy you give us, yeah."

"Jeremy Dunson," Finder said, his voice a cracked whisper.

"What's his badge number?"

Finder shook his head. "I don't have it memorized, but he lives in Revere. You're a smart guy, right? It shouldn't be too hard for you to track him down."

Hendrick had taken Finder's cell phone when they grabbed him. He powered it on and showed Willis a call log that had Dunson's cell phone number. Indecision weakened Hendrick's expression, as if he weren't so sure anymore whether Luce was their guy. Willis forced Finder's mouth open, and shoved his socks back in to gag him. Willis then led Hendrick and Gannier out of the room. As they walked down the staircase to the first floor, Willis called Hanley and told him they needed Dunson's home address also. Hanley sounded annoyed that he was being asked for more information, but told Willis he'd call him back when he had the address, and that he was still waiting to hear about Luce's address. Hanley paused, then added, "This business just keeps spreading. That's four names now. Four guys you got to take care of."

"Maybe not," Willis said. "If our guy stashed the money where he lives, we might not have to do anything with these two."

"Yeah? And how likely is that?"

"Likely. Doubtful that our guy would've had time yet to stash it anyplace else."

Willis disconnected the call and turned to Hendrick and

Gannier. "Either of those two could be who we're after," Willis said. "Or it could be someone else entirely. It's possible these Factory supervisors are briefed on all the targets within their office, not just the ones they're responsible for. So it could be a different hit man and supervisor."

"Patterson knew Cam lived in Scituate. Finder could've guessed the South Shore because of my accent and Jared's," Hendrick said without much conviction.

"Possibly, or maybe he remembered the briefing better." Willis breathed in deeply and let the air out slowly as he shook his head. "The one break we have is our guy is probably too busy looking for us to find a better place to stash the money. Once we get those addresses, we'll break in and see if the money's there. If not, we'll have to grab both of them and see what they can tell us."

"What if it's neither of those two guys?" Gannier asked. "What if it's like you said earlier, that it could be a different supervisor involved?"

Willis's eyes dulled as he scratched his jaw. "Then we have a decision to make," he said. "We either walk away from the money or we squeeze out of Patterson and Finder names of other supervisors in the Boston office. It will be tougher to grab any more of them after grabbing these two, but not impossible. But it's premature to worry about that now." Willis whistled for Bowser who had been laying on the floor watching Willis intently. The dog pushed himself to his feet and scampered over to Willis.

"I'll take Luce," Willis said. "If I don't hear back from Hanley in time, I'll be able to track Luce down as long as he keeps his badge with him and try to intercept him. You two head off to Revere. When I hear back from Hanley, I'll call you with an address."

Hendrick gave Bowser a disgusted look. "You're taking the dog with you?" he asked.

"I'm not leaving him here," Willis said.

Willis turned from them and left the house with Bowser staying close to his side.

CHAPTER 12

MCCOY SAT IN the darkened closet sweating profusely. He'd been struggling for almost two hours to maneuver his arms past his ass as if his arms were a jump rope that he was trying to slide underneath himself. When he was in high school he could've done it. Back then he was eighty pounds lighter and as thin as a bean pole. He was also a star on the wrestling team, and had a good deal of strength and flexibility. Even though he had put on all that added weight since then and appeared stocky with thick stubby arms, he was still deceptively athletic and somewhat limber. If he had just a little bit larger opening he would've been able to do it already, but with the way that psycho had taped his wrists together there just wasn't that much space.

The fucking psycho. Unless he was dead, McCoy knew that psycho could be back any minute. Maybe someone killed him. Maybe that was why he hadn't come back yet. McCoy hoped so. He'd given Luce Burke's address, and McCoy liked Burke's chances, especially with his dog there to alert him when that psycho got anywhere near his rental cottage. But that would only be if Burke was still hanging around there, which McCoy didn't think was likely. If Burke didn't get him, maybe one of the others would. McCoy didn't give him Charlie or Jared's addresses. Instead, he gave him addresses for two cops that McCoy had been holding a grudge against since he was eighteen. Both of the cops were tough bastards, both would have a shot against Luce. And if Luce took out both of them instead, at least McCoy would get a little satisfaction knowing that.

He had to take a break. He'd been taking a lot of them lately, but he couldn't help it. He'd been trying to stretch and lengthen his shoulder muscles, and two hours of that left him feeling as if nails had been hammered into his shoulder blades. It wasn't just his shoulders. His thigh and calf muscles were cramping, and his arms also hurt like hell. Because of all that, his thumb that that psycho had ripped the nail from barely bothered him.

McCoy took a dozen deep, slow breaths as he concentrated on loosening his muscles and ignoring the pain wracking him. He tried to numb out his mind and not pay any attention to the pain. He took one last deep breath and forced himself to stretch his shoulder muscles to their limit, and goddamn, his arms moved past his ass so that he had his hands under his thighs. He rolled onto his back and worked his legs and feet through his arms until his bound wrists were in front of his chest. He burst out laughing. That goddamned psycho fucked up. If he hadn't underestimated McCoy, he would've tied him up better, but he fucked up.

With his hands now in front of him, McCoy worked the duct tape from his ankles. He spent a minute trying to rub out the cramps in his legs, and then hobbled to his feet. For a minute or so, he stood unsteadily, barely able to keep his balance. Once he felt like he could move, he opened the closet door and walked out of there.

He squinted against the sunlight until his eyes better adjusted, and then searched through the house for something he could use to cut the tape binding his wrists, but found nothing. The house had been emptied out, and he searched futilely through each room and then the basement, and found nothing. He went back upstairs and used his elbow to break a window in a bedroom in the back of the house. When, or if, that psycho returned, it was doubtful that he'd notice the broken window, at least not unless he circled the house. McCoy used the jagged edge of the broken glass to cut through enough of the duct tape so he could free his hands. He cut the front of his right wrist pretty good in the process, but not enough to kill him.

*

Luce spent longer with the woman than he had planned. Until he finally broke her, she stubbornly refused to give up anything about the man who Luce knew had to be Willis. Early on, she tried lying repeatedly to protect him. They were clumsy lies, although to be fair, even a good liar would've had trouble fooling Luce. He was just too paranoid to be lied to. As his interrogation seemingly stalled, he grew anxious to end things with her so he could go after the other two men McCoy had given him, and it didn't help matters that she passed out on him several times and how difficult it was to bring her back to consciousness when that happened. Whether it was due to lack of sleep or his excitement over finding all that money or a combination of the two, he'd been making too many mistakes over the last nine hours, and he had to keep reminding himself not to be rash. Burke or Willis or Connor, which was the name the woman had been given, he was the one who posed the biggest threat to him. Luce had an opportunity to extract potentially useful information, and he couldn't throw it away because he was too impatient. So he forced himself to stay methodical, knowing that if he did so, he'd find Willis and the other two men. And eventually he broke her. When that happened, he knew everything she told him was the truth.

It turned out she didn't know all that much. She'd only met Willis the night before. But Luce then knew the name of the diner where she worked. Possibly Willis would return there looking for her. He also knew that Willis had a white bull terrier with him, which could prove useful. The rest of what he got out of her was suspect. There was little doubt that she believed it, but Willis must've been stringing her along about what he did for a living, telling her that he bought and managed storage properties, although there might've been something there about Willis being from Akron, Ohio. Luce had learned long ago that there was usually a grain of truth in most lies.

After he finished up with her, he cleaned up and headed to one of the other addresses McCoy had given him. It was in Scituate, the same town where Howlitz and McCoy both had lived, and the address was for Hugh Simon. According to McCoy, Simon was the top man in their crew.

Luce arrived at the small Cape Cod style home at ten minutes to nine. The house didn't have a garage, and the driveway was empty, but parked out front was a late model Buick, not the Chevy Malibu that Luce had seen all of them drive away in from Howlitz's house. That didn't mean anything. The Malibu could've belonged to the other guy McCoy gave up. And the Buick could've been parked there by a neighbor. Still, it showed how sloppy Luce had been. He should've had McCoy tell him what cars Simon, and the other guy, Gerrity, drove. If he could've accessed Factory resources, he'd have everything he needed about Simon: photos, car registration, arrest records, and other assorted background information. But since he had to do this without The Factory's knowledge, he had no choice but to go in blind.

Luce slowed down enough to get a good look at the house, then drove past it. The curtains were drawn, and he didn't see anything that gave him any help. He continued on to the street behind the house so he could get a look at the back of it. If he tried going through Simon's front door, he'd be exposed. A small copse of trees separated the two properties and blocked him from getting a good look at Simon's house. Those same trees, though, would provide enough privacy so he'd be able to break in without being seen.

He pulled over to try to think it through, and felt a tightness in his chest as he did so. The house could be empty for all he knew, or it could just be Simon in there. If it was just him, there would be no problem, at least if he was the same sort as Howlitz and McCoy. But it was possible that Willis could be there. Maybe Willis and the other two could all be there together strategizing over their next move. The thought of that possibility unnerved Luce. Another thought also nagged at him. That McCoy was fucking with him, and Hugh Simon had no involvement with the robbery. While McCoy gave up Willis's address, that could've been only because he didn't care about him. Of course, that fat slob would've also been hoping that Willis would be the one to kill him instead of the other way around. At the time, Luce believed McCoy was giving up not only Willis but his two friends—that he was too afraid to do otherwise, but now he wasn't so sure.

Luce sat paralyzed for several minutes as he tried to sort it all out. Simon, or whoever lived in that house, could be one of the men Luce was after, or could not be. Luce had no way of knowing. There wasn't any place to set up surveillance, and even if there was, he had no time for that.

He had to make a decision, and make it fast. He could ask neighbors about the man who lived there and try to get a feel for whether Simon was who he was after. Or, he could just break in, and if there was someone home, interrogate and kill the person. Possibly he'd be killing an innocent—someone McCoy set him up to kill. The more Luce thought about it, the more the neighborhood felt wrong to him. Both McCoy and Howlitz had lived on far seedier streets, this street and the one Simon lived on were better kept up, and had a more family-oriented feel to them. But Luce decided it didn't matter. If he ended up killing an innocent man inside that house, it wouldn't much matter to him. For now, he just needed to do whatever was necessary. Once he eliminated the rest of the robbery crew, he could plan his great escape from The Factory and the killings would stop soon enough. Not that that even mattered to him.

He found a place to park a quarter of a mile away, then rummaged through his trunk for what he needed. He put on a jacket and cap that identified him as working for the electric company, attached a silencer to his 9mm Beretta, which he shoved into his waistband, and added to his jacket pockets a Taser, two fully loaded eight-round clips, and a lock pick. He then packed up a small bag with other items he might need, grabbed a clipboard that held a dozen or so generic forms clipped to it so it would look more authentic that he worked for the electric company, and started moving in a light jog back to the street that ran behind Simon's.

When he got to the house directly behind Simon's, he casually walked to the side of it as if he were there to read the electric meter, then drifted to the back of the house as if he were studying something of importance. He continued drifting back until he slipped past the trees separating the two properties and made his way quickly to the back of Simon's house. Once there, he dropped his clipboard and bag onto the ground, then took his Beretta in his left hand while using his right for the lock pick. The lock on the back door opened easily. Luce dropped the lock pick back in his pocket, switched gun hands, and held the Beretta straight out in front of him. He swung the door open and waited several seconds. Nothing happened. If Willis was there with his bull terrier, the dog would've smelled him already and would've been waiting to charge him. The tension that had been building up in his chest released. With his free hand, Luce picked up his clipboard and bag and brought them into the house, then dropped them onto the floor by the door.

He moved quickly through the house to the front door. He needed to make sure there wasn't a keypad for an alarm system. If there was, and the alarm had been set, he'd use his Factory gizmo to disable it. There was no keypad in sight. Luce relaxed more then and walked back to the small living room he had raced through. It felt wrong. It had a homey, pleasant feel, completely unlike what he found in McCoy's and Howlitz's homes. It didn't seem likely that this could be the home of a lowlife thief unless he still lived with his mom. Luce spotted the first photo then. A police officer in full uniform surrounded by his wife and three kids. He saw more photos scattered about the room, all with a mix of the cop, his wife, and one or more kids. The pictures were taken at different times over at least a fifteen-year period given the varying ages of the participants. If this was Hugh Simon, not only was he a cop, but he had to be in his late forties. A hard smile etched Luce's face as he accepted that McCoy not only sent him to someone unrelated to the robbery, but to a cop's home.

He heard a gasp. Standing fifteen feet to the left of him was the same woman from the photos. She had one hand raised to her mouth as if she were going to bite down on a knuckle, her other hand was grasping her chest as if she were afraid she might have a heart attack at any minute. Luce guessed she was in her mid-forties, although she might've looked older than she really was given her fright. It was a shame she had to walk in on him right then. Another thirty seconds and he would've been leaving the same way he had come in without having to harm her.

"My husband's a police officer," she said in a gasping, shaky voice. "Get out of here now or I'll call him!"

Luce sighed. She had gotten too good a look at him. Without any hesitation or bothering to say a word, he raised his Beretta and shot her once in the forehead. She hit the floor hard. There was no doubt it was a kill shot. He didn't have to check whether she was still alive. He walked to the back of the house and was opening the bag that he had brought when his cell phone vibrated. He frowned at the cell phone as he saw the Caller Id indicating the call was from *Homeland Protection*. That was the actual name of the government agency that he worked for—The Factory was only a nickname. In the past, when his handler called, the Caller Id would show up simply as *Pat*, which was the only name Luce had for him. It was the first time it showed as *Homeland Protection*.

Luce's heartbeat began racing as he realized that if they were tracking his GPS coordinates they'd know his address, which meant they'd later know he killed this woman. It was yet another fuckup on his part. He knew there was a chance that he'd be killing an innocent person, and he should've left his badge in his car or someplace further away. Somehow he kept his voice under control as he answered the phone.

"Luce," a man's voice said in a heavy drone, "let me introduce myself. My name is Wally. Your supervisor, Pat, works for me. We have an incident we need you to investigate. This will take priority over your current assignment."

"Okay," Luce forced out. He hadn't reported in yet that he had completed his assignment with Howlitz. If they were tracking his GPS coordinates, they were probably only paying attention to the fact that he was in Scituate, which would make sense to them since Howlitz lived there. It was very possible they'd never make the connection between those coordinates and the woman's murder.

"We need you to go to an address that I'll be texting you," Wally said. He hesitated as his voice made a breaking-up croaking-type noise, kind of like what a door with severely rusty hinges might make. Then, "I don't know what you'll find there. The house might be empty, or possibly you might find someone incapacitated or dead. You need to locate and recover the

Homeland Protection badge for Allen Patterson. You also need to clean out any work files that he may have in his home and bring them directly to our Boston office, and you are not to look at them in any detail. You will be questioned under a polygraph later about this, and there will be severe consequences if we find that you have disobeyed this order." There was another slow breaking-up croaking noise, then, "If Patterson's body is there, and it appears that he has died violently, you will need to clean the area and dispose of him according to protocol."

"What's going on?" Luce asked.

There was a pause, then, "What I have told you is all you need to know for now," Wally said, abruptly, as if taken aback by the question.

Luce knew it was a mistake pushing it, but he couldn't help himself. There was something going on, something he needed to understand.

"Patterson is *Pat*, my handler, isn't he?" Luce asked. "That's why you're calling me instead of him."

There was a dead quiet over the connection for several seconds, then, "Do what you're being told, and don't ask any further questions. Report once you're at the address."

The call was disconnected from Wally's end. A text message came shortly afterwards with a Waltham address, and a phone number for Luce to call once he investigated the address.

Luce felt a numbness spreading through his head, almost as if he had a killer MSG headache. Somewhat mechanically, he searched his bag for a blond wig, fake mustache, and matching goatee. After he put them on, he pulled his cap low to his eyes and slipped on a pair of dark sunglasses. He put the Beretta and

Taser away in the bag, closed it, and left the house holding the bag and clipboard in one hand.

He knew there was more going on than what Wally had told him. His Factory bosses suspected Allen Patterson—his handler—had met with a violent death, and Luce couldn't help thinking the timing of it with what he was going through wasn't a coincidence. It had to be related, but his mind was too foggy to figure out how. When he was halfway across Simon's backyard, it clicked and the obvious struck him. He panicked badly then, but he forced himself to stay under control. When he crossed into the other property, he put on the same act as before, stopping at the meter so he could pretend to be reading it, then moving at a normal pace away from the house. He waited until he was a block away before he started running to his car.

Willis must've grabbed Patterson, and he knew enough to leave Patterson's badge behind. And he did that because he was trying to find out which field agent had been assigned to terminate Howlitz. Luce guessed Willis must've grabbed other supervisors also. There was something more going on—Luce picked that up from Wally's voice, and that must've been it. Factory supervisors were being grabbed. And that was why there was such an urgency to send Luce to check out Patterson's home. And that was why Luce was panicking. If Willis was able to get Patterson to talk, he'd have Luce's name and address, and he'd be heading straight to Luce's apartment for the five hundred and fifty grand. While Luce had hidden the money in his apartment, he didn't hide it well enough. He didn't know that he needed to.

Now it was a race.

And if Willis beat him to his apartment, all of it would've been for nothing.

Worse, Luce had been rushing things, possibly making more mistakes than he had realized. That would've been okay if he had the money and could disappear in the next two to three weeks. But if the money was gone, one of those mistakes might end up leading The Factory to what he had been up to. Which would leave him a dead man.

CHAPTER 13

WILLIS WAS STUCK in traffic on the Mass Pike. Cars were stopped for the most part, maybe spurting forward by as much as a dozen yards every half minute or so before slamming on their brakes. There could've been an accident further up the turnpike. Or it could've been construction. Or something else entirely. It didn't matter. There was nothing he could do about it except watch the small handheld GPS tracking device and see that Luce was speeding up Route 95 North at an average speed of seventy-two miles per hour. Willis had originally hoped to intersect with Luce in Quincy, but Luce had driven past that intersection point twenty minutes earlier.

Bowser sat on the passenger seat next to him. The dog yawned in such an extreme fashion that his jaw seemed to unhinge enough where he could have swallowed a small piglet. Once his yawn was completed, he let out a short whine to show that he was anxious for the car to get moving. Bowser loved riding in a speeding car, but hated sitting in traffic. Willis reached over and scratched him under the ear.

"I know the feeling, buddy," he said.

His cell phone rang. It was Hanley calling to give him the addresses of the two Factory hit men that Willis had asked for.

"You're getting off cheap with these two," Hanley said, gruffly. "It only cost me five hundred dollars. We'll settle later."

Willis had him text him the addresses. When he saw a Needham address for Luce, it was what he expected. The GPS tracker had been showing that Luce had been stopped at that same address for the last seven minutes.

Willis called Hendrick to give him Dunson's address, which was for an apartment in Revere. After that, he found a seventies music station, and sat back and relaxed to Creedance Clearwater's *Have You Ever Seen the Rain* as he waited for the traffic jam to break up. There was no reason to get anxious or impatient. Unless Hendrick and Gannier found the money in Dunson's apartment, sooner or later he'd catch up to Luce.

*

Luce found the money still hidden in his rented condo. He should've felt relieved by it, but he didn't. His handler, Patterson, had been either killed or kidnapped. Other Factory handlers probably also. It was turning into a mess. The Factory would soon be engaged in a full-scale investigation as to who was involved, and that meant it would be a race soon to see who would get to Willis first—Luce or them. There was also the fact that if Patterson talked, Willis would know who he was and where he lived, and that sonofabitch would be coming after him soon. As far as Luce was concerned there was no *if*. Even though he'd only known Patterson through their phone calls, the man impressed Luce as weak. Given the opportunity to try to save his life, he'd talk in a heartbeat.

Luce decided his best course of action would be to wait for Willis to try breaking into his apartment, and ambush him then. He was thinking through places nearby where he could set up surveillance when his cell phone rang. The Caller Id showed *Homeland Protection*. Luce answered the call and Wally asked him why he was at his home instead of at the address that had been texted to him.

"I had to stop off here to pick up some tools," Luce said.

"You've been in your apartment for fourteen minutes. I'm assuming by now you've gathered up whatever you might need, and that you'll be leaving within the minute."

They were keeping tabs on him. Goddammit!

"Not quite," Luce said, mostly keeping his voice a dull monotone, but he let some of his irritation show. "I haven't eaten in twenty hours. I'll be leaving in five minutes after I pack a lunch."

"I don't believe you appreciate the seriousness of this—"

Luce hung up on him. The phone rang with Caller Id showing *Homeland Protection*. He turned the phone off. Wally and the other Factory bosses had to be nervous. Setting up surveillance outside of his condo was out of the question. Not with them tracking his movements. But he had five minutes, and he had a good idea of how to use the time.

Luce kept a stash of weapons and explosives, including hand grenades, hidden in a false wall in his bedroom. He cleaned all of it out of the hidden compartment, packed it into a duffel bag, and then went to work taking the back panel off of his dresser. Once that was done, he rigged a grenade up so if the bottom drawer of the dresser was pulled open, it would detonate. After reattaching the back of the dresser, he pushed it against the wall. He checked his watch. Six minutes. Wally would just have to stew over that extra minute.

Luce slung the duffel bag over his shoulder and left his apartment. If Willis broke into his apartment, he wouldn't expect to find the money in that bottom dresser drawer—he'd expect instead to find it in a hidden compartment in one of the walls—but he'd check the drawer anyway to be complete. The Factory would figure that Willis had gotten names of field agents from Patterson, and that he was out to kill as many field agents as he could and was in the process of booby trapping Luce's apartment when the grenade went off prematurely. The police wouldn't be a problem either. The man broke into his apartment, and the police would have no reason to believe that the grenade wasn't Willis's, especially with the additional urging from The Factory. With some luck, not only would that happen, but Luce might be able to wrangle out of The Factory the five hundred grand bounty that they had put on Willis's head.

Luce packed the duffel bag into the trunk, then got in the car and headed to the address in Waltham that Wally had given him.

CHAPTER 14

ONCE BURKE CALLED them, it took Hendrick and Gannier seven minutes to drive from a coffee shop in the center of Revere to the address that they were given for Jeremy Dunson. If Burke had the right information, Dunson lived in an ugly five-story brick apartment building that was stuck between similar eyesores on a depressingly rundown city block. Rusted out and badly dented cars lined both sides of the street, and the sidewalks were littered with broken glass and garbage. Hendrick parked his Malibu in a lot for one of the neighboring buildings. He and Gannier left the car and walked casually to the building where Dunson lived, and continued on to the back of it. Gannier carried a large gym bag that clanked as he walked.

They had little trouble as they made their way through the building's back entrance, and then up the back staircase to the fifth floor. They knocked on the door of Dunson's neighbor. A shriveled, white-haired woman of around eighty answered, and Hendrick moved fast as he covered her mouth with his hand to keep her from screaming. He moved her further into her apartment and Gannier slipped in behind him and closed the door. Hendrick asked the old lady whether she'd be more comfortable tied her up on an easy chair that she had in her living room or on her bed. She indicated that she'd prefer the easy chair, so Hendrick helped her over to it. Once she was seated, he wrapped her ankles and wrists together with duct tape, and placed a piece of it across her mouth. Her face was small enough that the tape also covered her wrinkled chin.

"I'm sorry about doing this," Hendrick told her. "But I can't allow you to leave here now or make any noise. Don't worry. We won't be robbing or hurting you. And what the hell. I'll leave you forty bucks for your trouble."

When the old lady had first opened the door, she wore thick glasses which Hendrick took from her. There was little chance she'd be able to later pick them out from photos or provide the police a useful description. He took two twenty dollar bills from his wallet and held them close to her face so she could see that he was giving her forty dollars, and once she appeared to recognize what the bills were he folded them into her hand. She shrugged, indicating that it was okay as far as she was concerned. Gannier smiled thinly as he watched, amused.

He whispered to Hendrick, "I always suspected that you had a soft spot in there somewhere."

Hendrick whispered back, "That old lady could be my grandma for fucksake."

They found two water glasses in the kitchen and brought them out to the living room and held them up against the wall that separated Dunson's apartment from the old lady's. They stood quietly then listening as each of them pressed an ear against the bottom of a glass. After twenty minutes Gannier shook his head and whispered to Hendrick that the apartment was empty.

"It has to be," he said, whispering.

"Yeah," Hendrick agreed.

They moved away from the wall. Gannier rummaged through the old lady's pocketbook looking for her apartment key. Once he had it, he compared it with a set of lock picks that he had brought and found one that was a decent match. Satisfied, he put her key back in her pocketbook, and headed toward the door, picking up the gym bag that he had left on the floor. Hendrick stopped to tell the old lady that they would be calling the police in no more than thirty minutes and someone would be helping her soon.

"You've gone soft, you know that?" Gannier said in a whisper.

"Shut the fuck up," Hendrick whispered back.

Gannier led the way to Dunson's apartment door while Hendrick kept watch. Using the lock pick that he had chosen earlier, he had the door opened within thirty seconds. They then moved fast to get inside of Dunson's apartment.

The apartment seemed more like a hotel room than a place someone lived. There were no books or photos or any sort of personal touches. The living room was bare bones with a chair, end table, and TV. The bedroom had a king-sized bed, a dresser for clothing, and a laptop computer on a small computer stand with a matching chair. The closets were neatly arranged with what seemed like a minimal amount of clothing for a man living there. They searched the closets and dresser drawers first, then Gannier unzipped the large gym bag and pulled out two crowbars. He handed one to Hendrick and kept the other for himself.

First, they flipped over the mattress on the bed, and using a knife, Hendrick cut it open but found nothing unusual inside of it. They separated then with Hendrick taking the bedroom while Gannier searched the living room, both of them looking for hidden compartments. Gannier found one first, whispering loudly enough for Hendrick to hear him say that it held files and other papers, but no money. A few minutes later, Hendrick found a false wall behind the bed, and using the crowbar, he opened it up and found a stash of guns, ammunition, and an assortment of explosives. He was examining what looked like a stun grenade when a glint of reflected light from something small and silver caught his eye. It was partly buried in the wall. If he wasn't standing where he was, he never would've seen it. He dug it out with a knife. The object was the size of a quarter, about three times as thick. Frowning, Hendrick gave it a closer look and realized what it was. He brought it out of the bedroom so he could hold it up and show it to Gannier, who was busy tapping along the wall looking for other hidden compartments.

Gannier's eyes and nose scrunched up to show his annoyance for a few seconds until he realized what the object was. Then his expression deadened. "We should get out of here," he said.

Hendrick nodded. He needed five minutes so he could pack up the guns and explosives he found, and he told Gannier to head out first. "Find a place where you can watch for him, and call me if he shows up."

Gannier gave Hendrick a quick nod and moved fast to the apartment door. When he opened it, there was a muffled *puff* noise. A good amount of brain matter, blood, and gore exploded from the back of Gannier's skull. Hendrick stood frozen for a brief second, but before his friend's body crumpled to the floor, he was moving fast toward the bedroom. He heard another muffled *puff* noise, and felt something whiz by his cheek.

CHAPTER 15

BUD MCCOY DIDN'T know how long he had been waiting for that psychopath to return, but it must've been at least an hour. When he first escaped from the closet, the idea of surprising Luce when he returned seemed like his best bet given that he had no idea where he was and that he was left wearing only his boxer shorts. More than that, he badly wanted to kill Luce with his bare hands, but he was no longer sure that that psycho would be returning. It had been at least three hours since he was brought here, and if Luce was coming back he should've done so by now. Maybe Burke killed him, although the more McCoy thought about it, it didn't seem likely. Not that Burke wouldn't have it in him to do it—he was bigger and every bit as tough and mean, maybe more so. But if Burke had gotten his hands on Luce, he would've forced out of him what he had done to McCoy, and either Burke or Charlie would've come by already to rescue him. No, if Luce was dead, it wouldn't be because of Burke. Maybe Simon killed him. Or if not him, Gerrity. And if it was one of those two cops, McCoy would like to think that whichever one of them it was also ended up dead in the process.

McCoy hadn't had anything to do with either of those cops for over eight years, but he still kept tabs on them, and at times he'd find himself slipping into daydreams about what he'd do to them if given the opportunity, although until he gave their names to Luce it was likely that he never would've done anything. But he hated those two pricks with a passion and was glad to be able to send Luce after them. He blamed both of them for the wrong turn his life took. Simon more than Gerrity, but Gerrity was to blame also.

Back when he was in high school, he might've been a little wild, and it might not have been the best idea to hang around with Charlie, Cam, and Jared as much as he did, but he had a very different future mapped out than his friends. They were juvenile delinquent potheads while he was a jock—both a star wrestler and starting second baseman on the varsity baseball team. So while he stayed good friends with the three of them, and might've joined them on a few of their vandalism excursions, he kept away when they did their home break-ins and burglaries. He had an athletic scholarship for college, and he wasn't about to fuck that up. The problem was that fascist cop, Simon. The sonofabitch had it in his thick cement skull that McCoy was involved in that burglary shit, and whenever he hassled Charlie and the others, he'd always end up focusing the most on McCoy.

It was two weeks before graduation when Simon and his asshole partner, Gerrity, fucked him royally. The night it happened, McCoy was driving home at one o'clock at night after hanging with Charlie and the others in Charlie's parent's basement. All they did that night was smoke a little weed and watch DVDs of John Carpenter's *The Thing* and *They Live*. Harmless shit for them, and McCoy didn't think much when Simon pulled up to the left of him in his police cruiser. He might've noticed Simon giving him the stink eye, but fuck him. He hadn't done anything that night other than a little weed, or really any night, so he didn't think anything about it until Simon steered into his lane and sideswiped his car.

The collision scared the shit out of him. He wasn't expecting it, and although he had been keeping his speed at thirty, he lost control of his car and drove into a lamppost. What happened next was pretty much a blur. He remembered getting out of his car and seeing that his '82 Mustang looked totaled, the front of the car crumpled and driver's side bashed in. Maybe he mouthed off to Simon in his shock and rage—he couldn't say for sure, but that fucking cop was soon smacking him with his nightstick. Within seconds he was on his back on the asphalt road trying to cover up and protect himself. Before he blacked out, he knew that Gerrity had joined in and both cops were beating the hell out of him with their nightsticks.

When he woke up next, he was in the hospital with a fractured skull, broken jaw, four broken ribs, and a broken left wrist. He was pretty much out of it as they kept him doped up on painkillers, but when his court-appointed lawyer visited him he learned he was under arrest. Simon and Gerrity claimed in their police report and later affidavits that McCoy was the one who drove into them, and that after the crash he physically attacked them and that they responded only with the required force to subdue him. There were no witnesses, so it was McCoy's word against the two cops. With his lawyer's urging, he took a plea against the long list of charges that were filed against him, the most serious of which was assault on a police officer with a deadly weapon, with the deadly weapon being his Mustang. So instead of going to college, he did nine months at MCI Concord. When he got out, he was twenty pounds heavier, his scholarship had been taken away, and his admission to college had been revoked. With not much else to do, he joined Charlie and his crew, who had moved on from home burglaries to armed robberies.

McCoy found himself choking with rage once more, which happened every time he let himself think about what happened that night all those years ago. He forced himself to take deep breaths until he began to calm down. He couldn't afford to waste time filled with rage. He had a decision to make. Whether to stay put and wait for Luce or to get out of the house. It was more that he wasn't sure any longer whether Luce would come back. When he had first escaped from the closet, he felt confident that he could take Luce by himself, but he wasn't so sure about that anymore. His thumb with the missing nail hurt like hell, his wrist was still bleeding, the cold had left his muscles stiff and aching, and overall, he felt a lot weaker than he did an hour ago.

He rubbed a thick hand across his eyes, trying to wipe the exhaustion from them. It was possible the police hadn't found out about Heather yet. If he could get a hold of Charlie, then Charlie and Jared could either pick him up, or join him in laying in wait for Luce. Charlie could also arrange to get Heather's body out of his house. He might still escape the mess Luce had stuck him in.

In an attempt to conserve his strength, McCoy had been

sitting on the carpeted floor while waiting for Luce's return. He pushed himself to his feet and peered out the front window while keeping himself as hidden from view as he could. The neighboring houses were all newer colonials, all with small but well-kept yards. It would be simple if he could just knock on a door and ask someone to call the police, but that was impossible with the way Luce had left Heather. The police wouldn't believe his story, not with the murder knife that Luce had left in the living room covered with McCoy's fingerprints. While the police would have no reasonable way to explain how he ended up where he did with the injuries he had, they'd still make sure he went down for Heather's murder.

From where McCoy was standing, he could see three of the houses that were across the street. If one of them was empty and he could break in without a neighbor calling the police, then he'd be able to phone Charlie. It was a better bet than waiting where he was any longer. Luce had to be dead. If he wasn't, he'd be back already. Every minute McCoy wasted trying to decide what to do was another minute where the cops could stumble on Heather's body. He had no idea how Luce had left things. Maybe the bastard had left his curtains wide open so the mailman or someone could look in and see the bloody knife laying right there by his easy chair. A resolve hardened McCoy's features. He walked up the stairs to the second floor and then moved from window to window so he could look out at more houses in the neighborhood and figure out which would be his best bet.

After ten minutes, McCoy made his decision.

CHAPTER 16

WILLIS HAD FINALLY broken free of traffic. It took almost an hour for him to travel to the next exit so he could get off of the Mass Pike and drive the back roads through Boston. During that time, he followed Luce on the GPS tracking device, and saw that after The Factory hit man left his apartment, he went directly to Patterson's home in Waltham.

Willis's lips twisted into a thin, grim smile on seeing that. Luce would've gotten McCoy to tell him about Willis, so when Luce's bosses called him to investigate Patterson, he figured out that Willis was grabbing Factory supervisors so he could find the assassin assigned to kill Cam Howlitz. Which was why Luce made the trip to his apartment. He knew Willis would be breaking in there looking for the money.

Willis continued tracking Luce after he left Patterson's home. The Factory hit man was traveling south toward Cape Cod, and Willis had hoped to intercept him in Quincy, but Luce turned out to have about a fifteen minute head start on him. That was okay. Luce might know that Willis had learned his name and home address, but most likely it hadn't occurred to him that Willis would be tracking him by his Factory badge. Luce was probably heading someplace where he thought it would be safe to hide the money until he had the rest of the robbery crew eliminated. Willis liked the idea of tracking him to wherever that place was, especially if it was someplace quiet and private.

His disposable cell phone rang. Hendrick was calling. His voice sounded odd as he told Willis that Dunson wasn't the one they were after. Willis was distracted as he was busy following Luce's GPS coordinates. He mumbled something to Hendrick about how he had tried calling him earlier to tell him that it looked like Luce was their guy and not Dunson, but that Hendrick didn't answer his phone.

There was a pause from Hendrick, then, "When did you try calling?"

Again distracted, Willis looked away from the tracking device to glance at the dashboard clock. "Thirty-four minutes ago," he said.

"I had the phone turned off. I was busy and didn't want to be disturbed. Thirty-four minutes ago? It wouldn't have helped me any then to get your call. But I bet you thought I was dead."

Willis frowned. He didn't want to waste time with any sort of conversation. He also didn't like the way Hendrick's voice sounded or what he was saying. The steel that he'd seen in Hendrick while they were pulling off the warehouse robbery was gone. He wondered whether the guy was having a mental breakdown. He also wondered if it would be a liability involving him any further.

"I thought it was possible," Willis said. "I also thought that maybe you were out of cell phone range. Or you that you had a good reason for not answering."

"Fair enough." Another pause. "What makes you think Luce is the guy we want?"

Still frowning, Willis explained it to him, and after Hendrick appeared to digest what Willis told him, he conceded that it made sense. "I can guarantee you it wasn't Dunson." He paused again. His voice had dropped to a whisper when he added, "Jared and I searched his apartment. We found hidden compartments and opened them, and there wasn't any money. There was other stuff. Like weapons, and records he was keeping, but no money. And he didn't hide it any place else. I know that because I spent enough time doing things to him to make him talk, and once I got him talking, he told me everything. He had nothing to do with Cam or our money."

Willis didn't much care what happened to Dunson, but he wanted a clearer picture of what had happened since he was still trying to make up his mind whether it was worth having Hendrick join him in going after Luce. "I told you to make sure his apartment was empty before you went in," he said.

"We did. But he came home while we were there." Another pause, then, "The fucker had his apartment wired with spy cameras. These little quarter-sized devices that fed a cell phone app he had. Because of that he knew we were in his apartment." Another pause, and when he continued his voice sounded as if he were fighting to keep from crying, or maybe laughing, Willis wasn't sure which. "He killed Jared. I'd be dead now also but I got lucky."

"You left Dunson dead?" Willis asked.

"Yeah, he's dead. It's funny, I tell you that he killed Jared, and that's all you've got to say?"

Willis's frown grew more severe over the nonsense that Hendrick was telling him. The guy didn't sound stable, but five hundred and fifty grand was at stake and he knew Luce wasn't going to be a pushover. "It's a tough break," he conceded. "Look, I'm going after Luce now. You can either join me or not. But if your head's not in it, stay away. You'll get your cut regardless."

Hendrick laughed bitterly at that. "You're going to decide what my cut's going to be?"

Willis didn't bother going over the obvious. That Hendrick wasn't calling the shots, and the split was going to be either a third each if McCoy was still alive, or an even fifty-fifty if they were the only two left. But Willis could wait until they had the money back before he reminded Hendrick.

"Forget it," Willis said. "Are you up to helping me or not?"

"Fuck you. Just tell me where he is."

"He's on Route 3 driving south to Cape Cod. Right now he's entering Plymouth. Where are you?"

Hendrick's voice cracked as he told Willis that he was just getting into Quincy, which put him about five minutes behind Willis.

"Keep this line open," Willis said. "I'll fill you in with where he's going. The odds are good he's got the money with him."

"I want more than the money," Hendrick said, his voice trembling slightly. "I want time alone with him."

"You can have all the time you want." According to the GPS tracker, Luce had pulled off Route 3 and was driving along a residential street in Plymouth. He told Hendrick, and then focused his attention back on where Luce was going.

*

Hendrick once more replayed the scene in his mind of the back of Jared's head exploding, and once more flinched because of it. He wished he could stop thinking about it. It certainly wasn't doing him any good to keep running those images through his head. There was nothing he could do to change that Jared was dead, and it was just his dumb luck that he was the one still alive.

His knuckles showed bone-white as he tightened his grip on the wheel, his shoulders hunched. A muscle along his left eye began twitching which made him wink involuntarily. By all accounts he should be dead. Dunson fired two shots at him from less than fifteen feet away, both bullets flying close enough to his face that he felt their heat. What saved him was he was still holding the stun grenade he had picked up earlier, and he had enough presence of mind to pull the pin and toss it over his shoulder. It turned out the grenade was a dud, but Dunson didn't know that. He also didn't recognize it as a stun grenade, which was reasonable since he had plenty of fragmentation grenades also in his hidden arms cache, and he must've thought the grenade was one of those with the way he dove over the sofa for protection. The Factory hit man didn't land quite right and ended up knocking his head against the hardwood floor, the impact jarring the gun out of his hand. Hendrick saw it out of the corner of his eye, and he turned in his tracks and dove after Dunson.

The blow to the head didn't knock the hit man out, but

it dazed him, and it was a good thing it did. As it was, the man nearly fought Hendrick to a standstill with the two men grappling on the floor, both breathing hard as they tried to do severe damage to the other, but neither of them saying a word, neither of them wanting to make any noise that could bring a passerby from the hallway into the room. So they fought like that until Hendrick was able to jab his forearm into Dunson's throat, which left the hit man momentarily helpless and gasping for air. Hendrick then climbed on top of Dunson, grabbed the man by his ears, and slammed his head into the floor enough times to knock him out.

The door to the apartment had been left open. Dunson had been in too much of a hurry to shoot Jared and go after Hendrick to bother closing the door. Fortunately, no one had walked by. Hendrick got up, looked out into an empty hallway, closed the door shut, then searched through Dunson's bedroom until he found the necessary material to gag The Factory hit man and used the duct tape to bind him. After he had the man properly prepared, he dragged him into the bathroom and pushed Dunson's face into the toilet bowl until the man sputtered awake.

Hendrick did things to Dunson that he would never want done to himself. Really awful grisly things, and it turned out to be surprisingly effective for someone who was supposed to be as hardened as the Factory hit man. Hendrick could tell from the panic that danced wildly in the man's eyes that he would've talked much earlier if Hendrick let him. But Hendrick kept it going for a full half hour before he took the gag out of the man's mouth. And when Dunson babbled his answers to Hendrick's questions, he knew the man was telling him the truth. He also found that it didn't bother him at all the things he did to Dunson. In fact, he would've been happy spending much more time with him, but he knew that Dunson had nothing to do with the money or Cam, so he needed to go after the other one, the one that Burke was chasing. He dragged Dunson back to the toilet and drowned him in it.

The effort of fighting, torturing, and killing The Factory hit man had left Hendrick's muscles limp and rubbery, like he barely had the strength to do anything. He took his leather gloves off so he could wash his face. The cold water helped invigorate him somewhat. His stomach, though, felt like a bottomless pit, and he felt if he didn't eat something he'd pass out. He made his way to the galley kitchen off to the side of the living room, and foraged through the refrigerator. There wasn't much there that he could eat quickly other than olive loaf, which he found unappetizing. *Reason enough to have killed the sonofabitch*, he thought as he chewed on one of the slices of processed bologna and pimento-stuffed green olives. As he ate more of the slices, he stared at Jared's dead body and all the gore and blood and brain matter that was left splattered on the floor and on the wall. He was going to have to get rid of Jared's body. Even if the police failed to connect Jared to him, he knew The Factory wouldn't miss that connection. He didn't have time to clean the place, and even if he did, it was doubtful that he'd be able to scrub the floor and wall of all of Jared's DNA. So the police and The Factory would know someone else was killed here. He'd just have to hope that Jared's DNA wasn't on record in any law enforcement database. He didn't think it was. At least Jared never said anything to him about it.

He found two blankets that he used to wrap up Jared. It

was obvious that a body was inside them, but it didn't matter. He wrapped duct tape around both ends and the middle, then went back to Dunson's bedroom and the dead man's hidden arms cache. He used the gym bag that Jared had brought and filled it up with guns, ammunition, and explosives. It wouldn't help the police or anyone else by ditching the crowbars there. There were no prints on them and no way of tracking them back to him, so he didn't bother leaving space in the gym bag for them.

When he went back to the living room, he noticed the two bullet holes in the wall between Dunson's apartment and the old woman's. With the fucked up way the day had gone she'd probably been hit by one of the stray bullets. Hendrick thought for a moment about checking on her, but he didn't have time, and besides, if she'd been hit, what was he going to do? He checked that the hallway was empty, and then with the gym bag slung over his shoulder he dragged Jared into the hallway and to the back stairwell. Once there, he proceeded to drag Jared's body down the five flights of stairs. It went fast and wrapping him in the blankets made it easier to move him. When he got to the bottom of the staircase, he left Jared by the door and then sprinted to where he had left his car. At least it was still where he had parked it. With everything else that had happened it wouldn't have surprised him if it had been towed.

After he drove his car to the back of Dunson's building, he loaded Jared's body into the trunk. It was tough squeezing him into the available space, but with some effort he was able to get the corpse in there and the trunk closed. It didn't appear as if anyone saw him getting the body out of Dunson's apartment and into his car, and presumably no one had walked in or out of the back of the building during the four minutes it took him to retrieve his car. At least he caught a break that way, otherwise the police would've been there also. If the police had shown up, Hendrick had enough weapons and explosives to have made it a slaughter.

Hendrick had never killed anyone before. As he drove out of Revere and toward Scituate, he had the thought that before he'd join Burke to chase after the other hit man he'd first drop Jared at his home so that his friend's body could be discovered and that Jared's mom would be able to hold a funeral for him. Of course she'd be distressed knowing her son had been shot to death, but a funeral would be better than never knowing what happened to him. For stretches, Hendrick's mind would blank out before he'd snap back to attention. By the time he approached Quincy, he realized he badly wanted to do more killings that day, especially killing the sonofabitch responsible for all this. Not just with what happened to Jared, but to Cam and Bud. He decided he could wait on returning Jared's body to his home until after he caught up with that other hit man, Luce. That was when he called Burke.

After he got off the call with Burke, he hit the gas harder, pushing his Malibu to ninety and then a hundred. He had ground he needed to catch up. If anyone was going to put a bullet in Luce's head, it was going to be him, and not Burke, but only after he had time to do worse things to Luce than he did to Dunson. He tightened his grip on the wheel as he darted in and out to pass cars. A grim smile hardened his lips. If any cop tried pulling him over, it would be that cop's rotten luck.

CHAPTER 17

MCCOY CHOSE TO break into the house directly behind the one he was in. From looking out the windows, both front and back, he couldn't tell whether any of these houses were empty, but at least with the house he picked it would be less likely that a neighbor would see him running outside wearing only his boxer shorts. So he left through the back door of the house which Luce had brought him to, and keeping low, he ran to the wooden fence separating the two properties, climbed it, and ran to the back door of the house he picked. Using his elbow, he broke a pane of glass, then reached inside so he could unlock the door. He prayed silently that he wouldn't hear a security alarm go off. He didn't, and he entered the house.

At least they had the heat on. He was shivering badly after spending hours in that other house with no heat and no clothes. He grabbed a man's coat from the closet and put it on to help him warm up, then made a quick search of the house. It was a small, boxy colonial. On the first floor: a modest kitchen, living room, and dining room, and upstairs, three bedrooms. No one was home, but there were also no landline phones. Of all his crappy luck he had to pick a house where the owners decided to go with only cell phones! Fuck it. He had no choice in the matter. He'd get something to eat, because he was fucking starving, then he'd find some clothes to put on and break into another house.

He couldn't fucking believe it as he searched through the refrigerator and found only yogurt, fruits, vegetables, and salad shit. He took out some of the bowls half-filled with leftovers and wrinkled his nose with distaste over what he smelled. Only fucking health nuts could eat the shit they had in there. There was nothing edible for him in the freezer either—no steaks or hotdogs or anything else he could defrost, just leftovers from vegetarian hell. Stuff that made his stomach queasy just thinking about it. The only things he found with any meat were jars of baby food that were supposed to be chicken and gravy. It was nasty stuff, but at least it would tide him over until he broke into the next house and found some real food. He was on his fourth jar of the shit when it occurred to him that baby food usually meant stay-at-home moms. Fuck. He was so crazy with hunger before that he ignored the empty bedroom that had been made up into a nursery.

He went back upstairs and found her hiding in the closet inside the master bedroom. She was in her early thirties with short, blonde hair and on the scrawny side. Her complexion was ghastly white and her eyes were liquid with fear as she stared at him. She held a baby in her arms that she was trying to keep quiet. McCoy saw that she was also holding a cell phone in one of her hands.

"I called the police," she told him, defiantly.

"How long ago?"

She didn't answer him. Instead, she looked away, cringing, as if she were trying to shrink her body so that she couldn't be seen.

"Goddamn it!" he near exploded. "When did you fucking call them!"

"When I heard you break the glass in the door."

She burst out crying. McCoy's head was spinning. The cops had to be on their way. He went to the window and looked out toward the front of the house, and sure enough he spotted a police cruiser driving toward the address. His only chance was to go out the back and make a run for it. He went back to where the woman was hiding in the closet.

"Give me the phone," he said, trying to keep his voice calm.

She looked dumbly at him, but acted as if the words didn't register. Her sobbing became something hysterical.

"Give me the fucking phone before I beat you to death with your own kid," he growled at her with every intention of doing what he had just threatened. Her color paled even more as his words registered, and she threw the phone out of the closet, but not to him. It skidded along the floor and under the bed. She then used her slight body in an attempt to shield her child from McCoy.

He could've killed her at that moment he was so angry. The fucking bitch! She couldn't just hand him the fucking phone? But the sound of tires squealing to a stop outside knocked him out of his murderous fury. He moved fast and nearly flipped the bed over in his attempt to push it aside so he could grab the cell phone. He peeked out a window that faced the front of the house, then he was racing out of the room, down the stairs, and out the back door. He was nearly across the yard and only ten yards or so from jumping the fence, when a cop yelled at him to stop. Even though he had his back turned to the man, he would've known from the tone that it was a cop even if he hadn't seen a police cruiser pull into the driveway thirty seconds earlier.

He almost kept going. He might've made it if he did. But the cop barking at him to stop slowed him down enough where it would've been impossible to get his momentum back, and once that happened he wouldn't have had a chance of outrunning the cop. With his shoulders slumping, he stumbled to a complete stop. He forced a half-hearted smile and turned slowly to face the cop.

"I know this doesn't look good, officer," he started, which he knew was the understatement of the year. How could it look good with him running out of a strange house wearing only a coat and boxers in cold mid-October weather with bare legs and feet. "But it's not like it looks. I swear."

The cop was about his age and was staring wild-eyed at him, his service revolver pointing at McCoy's chest as he held it out in front of him with both hands, the muscles visibly straining as he gripped the gun. He looked scared, as if he never imagined himself being in this situation. "What did you do to the woman living here?" he asked, his voice shaking.

"I swear, I didn't do anything to her," McCoy said, talking fast so he could get it all out while the cop was still struggling over what to do next. "She's fine. Look, I'm a victim here. Some psycho nutbag kidnapped me, brought me out here, and tortured me. I don't even know what town I was taken to—"

"Shut up," the cop ordered, his composure returning. The fear in his eyes faded as they narrowed to slits. He glanced at McCoy's bare legs and then were back meeting McCoy's eyes. "Just shut up and lower yourself onto your stomach. I don't want to hear what you have to say."

McCoy did as he was told. The cop's eyes had become little more than dead ice, and McCoy knew the cop would shoot him dead if given any excuse. That in his mind McCoy was nothing but a pervert who broke into the house so he could rape the woman living there. While he lay facedown on his stomach, the cop jerked both his arms behind his back to cuff him. The cop hesitated on seeing the bloody mess making up the front of McCoy's right wrist.

"I told you I was kidnapped," McCoy grunted out, his face pushed partially into the dead grass. "The fucker who did it wrapped my wrists with duct tape and I had to break a window so I could cut the tape loose using the broken glass. That's how my wrist got cut up. You got to listen to me—"

"I told you to shut up. I don't want to hear what you have to say."

The cuffs were slapped on and tightened to where they bit painfully into McCoy's damaged wrist, and he was jerked to his feet. As the cop ordered him to walk toward the front of the house, McCoy tried again, desperation edging his voice.

"Forget my wrist," he said. "Look at my thumb. The fucker pulled the nail off with a pair of pliers. If you look in the house behind this one, you'll find evidence that I was brought there. You'll see the torn duct tape that I was able to get off my wrists and ankles. Other stuff, too."

The cop slowed down a step, as if he were maybe starting to think that McCoy wasn't completely full of shit.

"Why'd you break into this house?"

"I was scared out of my mind," McCoy said, trying his hardest to sound sincere. "I didn't know when that psycho was coming back to torture me more, or worse, so when I was able to free myself I came running over here. No one answered when I knocked on the door. I broke in only so I could call the police, but they didn't have any phones in there—"

They had walked past the side of the house and were on the front yard, maybe twenty feet from where the police cruiser was parked, and another cop interrupted them by walking out of the front door of the house and yelling over to the cop with McCoy that the residents inside were scared but okay. That cop was older. In his fifties, thick body and barrel-chested. His face a square block that looked even ruddier and beefier with how red his ears and neck were and how short his hair had been cut. He fixed hard angry eyes on McCoy and added, "This perv broke in to rape the woman living here, but didn't have time because she called the police. This guy's a real perv, Stan, with some sicko baby food fetish."

McCoy could feel the change in the cop who had cuffed him and was taking him to the car, and it chilled him. He had no chance anymore of changing the guy's mind. He was going to be arrested, and they'd find Heather stabbed to death in his bed, and assume he was a rapist who killed one woman and tried to rape and kill another. The fact that it made no sense for him to be in this town, wherever the fuck he was, wouldn't matter. Nor would it matter that his thumbnail had been ripped off. By the time he was able to convince anyone to search the house he'd been taken to, it would be cleaned up, either by Luce, if he was still alive, or that fucked up agency he worked for. It was over for him.

A car pulled up to the house and a wire-thin man in his late forties got out of it. The older cop yelled at him to move on, but the man flashed a badge and waved him over. McCoy stood blinking, not quite believing what he was seeing. It was that sonofabitch psycho, Luce, and whatever he was saying, the cop seemed to be eating it up. He could hear snatches of their conversation. That McCoy was a serial rapist and killer that the FBI had been after and that he had killed a young woman earlier in Scituate, with the cop saying that he had almost struck again in their town. He wasn't quite sure, but it looked like Luce was showing the cop photos, probably of Heather's body. More stuff was said, and then Luce and the cop shook hands, with the cop saying something about him needing to make a call, but it shouldn't be an issue. McCoy realized then what was going on. That Luce was pretending to be FBI and that the cops were going to be handing him over to Luce.

"That's the psycho who kidnapped and tortured me!" McCoy forced out, pleading.

"Just shut the fuck up," the cop behind him ordered.

McCoy stared dumbfounded at Luce while The Factory hit man smiled sadly back at him the way you would any other sex-crazed pervert. Panic seized McCoy so tightly that he could barely breathe. But that didn't last long. Soon the panic was taken over by an intense rage. It might be over for him, but he was going to kill that sonofabitch before he breathed his last. He might have his hands cuffed behind his back, but he still had enough skill from his wrestling days where he should be able to knock Luce to the ground and stomp hard enough on the bastard's throat to do the job. And with the older cop sitting in his police cruiser busy making a call, that was as good a time as any.

In a swift, fluid motion, McCoy swept his right leg behind him in a counterclockwise motion so that his thigh was pressed behind the younger cop's leg. In a split second, he lowered and twisted his body and pushed upward into the cop, striking him hard in the chest with his shoulder. The blow sent the cop tumbling backward over McCoy's leg. It took him another second to right himself, and then he charged Luce with the intent of ramming The Factory hit man in the jaw with the top of his forehead. That other second where he righted himself cost him his chance, because the cop who had been in the car making a call must've been able to get a shot off. A bullet struck McCoy in the back and tore through his heart. A half a second more and he would've had Luce, but as it was he was dead before he hit the ground.

CHAPTER 18

WILLIS FIRST TRACKED Luce to an address in Plymouth that turned out to be for a gas station. As Willis drove past the location, it was doubtful Luce had stopped there to hide the money—most likely he needed to fill up, and possibly also wanted to grab some food. The nine minutes that Luce had spent there allowed Willis to catch up and watch as The Factory hit man drove out of a one-car garage at the second address Willis tracked him to—a single-family house that looked abandoned, probably one that Luce had been given to use as surveillance for one of his hits. It would be risky to use that house to stash five hundred and fifty thousand dollars, but then again, if there was a good hiding place inside, Luce would've had plenty of time to find it.

Willis had parked at a corner where the street intersected with the one running perpendicular to it, and he used a newspaper to shield himself from view. Luce, though, had barely pulled out of the driveway when he brought the car abruptly to the curb and got out of it. He took several steps in the direction of the house's backyard as if he had heard something, then jumped back into his car and drove past Willis. He took a left at the intersection and drove down the street behind the one he was just on and came to a stop halfway down this other street. Willis got out of his car, and using the house on the corner to hide behind, watched the scene unfold. After McCoy was shot in the back, the older cop who had fired his weapon knelt by the body and felt for a pulse. Several seconds later, he stood up and shook his head. Willis got back to his car and drove off then, pulling into a strip mall parking lot three miles away. Hendrick had heard the gun shot over the cell phone connection that Willis had kept open, and insisted on knowing what happened. Willis told him that McCoy had been shot.

"Did that fucker Luce do it?" Hendrick demanded, his voice cracking.

"No, a cop shot him. Your buddy was making a run for Luce."

"Is… is there a chance Bud's still alive?"

"No chance."

Hendrick got quiet after that.

Willis didn't say it, but he was relieved that cop shot McCoy. There was little doubt McCoy charged Luce to kill him, and from the stunned look on Luce's face and the way he froze, McCoy just might've succeeded. If he had, Luce's car would've been impounded and the money would've been found, because it still had to be in his car. Luce hadn't gone to that house to stash the money. He went there because he thought he had McCoy on ice. Somehow McCoy escaped, but that fat slob had to get himself picked up and killed by the police.

Willis wondered about the badge Luce flashed the police

officer. Maybe it was his Homeland Protection badge, or maybe The Factory had changed their protocol and was now issuing fake FBI badges to their hit men. Whichever it was, Luce's Factory bosses weren't going to be happy hearing about it. The first rule they drummed into Willis's head when he was in training was to keep a low profile and never talk to any law enforcement unless you had absolutely no other choice. But then again, if Luce was planning to flee with the money some-time over the next several weeks, then it wouldn't hurt him to take the chance he did.

Five minutes after McCoy was shot dead, the GPS tracker showed that Luce was on the move again. Most likely the cops were only too happy to lose their sole witness to how they bungled their arrest and had to shoot an unarmed and hand-cuffed prisoner. While Luce couldn't have gotten a good look at Willis with the way he had hidden behind the newspaper, he made sure to give The Factory hit man enough of a head start so that Luce wouldn't spot his car for a second time. For the next hour and a half, Willis followed Luce through south-ern Massachusetts and into Rhode Island and then to the small town of East Greenwich. The trail led Willis onto a single-lane dirt road bordered on both sides by tall sea grass. He knew that things were coming to an end. That this was where Luce was planning to stash the money.

Luce had come to a stop a mile up the dirt road from where Willis was, and had been there for the last ten minutes. Willis's plan was to drive within a half mile of Luce's location, and then proceed on foot to finish things. This changed when Bowser sat upright in his seat, growling in a severely agitated way. If Willis hadn't reacted by pulling the car off the road into the sea grass to his right while slamming on the brakes and spinning the car around, he would've been killed. A split second before the attack came, he threw himself across the passenger seat and forced the bull terrier down also. The hand grenade that exploded where he would've been driving without Bowser's warning still threw the back end of his car several inches up into the air. The barrage of bullets from the AK-47 that followed blew out the back window and back tires.

Willis held onto Bowser's collar while he flung the passenger door open. The dog strained against his collar wanting badly to go after their attacker, but Willis pointed straight into the sea grass and ordered the dog to go there. Bowser didn't like it and let loose several angry pig grunts, but Willis held onto the collar while pointing straight ahead and ordering the bull terrier to 'go', and when he let go of the collar, Bowser reluctantly followed his command and scampered away into the tall grass to safety. Willis had crawled out of the car when he heard another grenade hit the driver's door. He flung himself away from the car, landing behind a rock just as the grenade went off. He was pinned where he was. Little more than dead meat.

*

Back in Plymouth, Luce had spotted the white bull terrier lying in the passenger seat of the car parked on the corner. If it wasn't that he had heard a cop yelling at McCoy, he would've stopped and fired several rounds at the man behind the wheel acting as if he was reading the newspaper. He knew who the man was and he realized then how the man had tracked him there. When Willis had grabbed Patterson, that weak-kneed traitorous sonofabitch boss of his must've shown Willis how to track Luce by his badge. First things first. He had to stop McCoy from being taken into police custody, and the cop bought the story he gave him. If he hadn't, Luce would've executed both of the police offers at the scene before putting a bullet in McCoy's head. But the cop accepted what he told him and was willing to call Wally for further confirmation, and Luce knew The Factory higher up would support him. He hadn't quite figured out what story he'd give Wally afterward, but it would be something along the line of McCoy being behind Patterson's abduction, and that would buy him enough time to arrange for his disappearing act.

He had to admit, McCoy surprised him twice that day. First, escaping from that house, second, the way he broke free from that cop and charged him with murderous intent. Luce's reaction time sucked. He stood frozen like a deer in the headlights as McCoy charged him, and McCoy might've been successful if that other police officer hadn't shot him in the heart. It was a hell of a lucky shot, but it did the trick, and the whole incident showed that it was time for Luce to get out of the game.

With McCoy dead, he could focus on Willis, which would require little more than luring him to an isolated spot and ambushing him. And so he drove to this desolate coastal area in the middle of nowhere in Rhode Island. After turning down a dirt road, he bounced along the road for another seven miles before hiding his car in the four-foot high sea grass, and then running down the road a mile so he could wait for Willis.

The first grenade should've finished Willis off, but for whatever reason the guy drove off the road and spun the car around. Luce had hidden himself well enough in the grass that that shouldn't have happened, but it did. It didn't matter. After two grenades and plenty of automatic rifle fire, he now had Willis pinned behind a rock, and the next grenade should be it. Hell, Luce could use all his remaining grenades and it wouldn't matter. Once he took off to Southeast Asia with his newly acquired retirement money, he wouldn't be needing any of them.

Luce took another grenade from his bag and pulled the pin. Before he could throw it at Willis, his right knee exploded. The pain was excruciating and he dropped to ground, and only after letting out a loud scream did he realize that someone else had shot him and that he had dropped a live grenade into the bag with his others. He reached in for it just as the grenade went off, and he saw his hand fly away from him like a missile. The first explosion triggered a much larger one that lifted him off the ground. When he landed, he noticed with some curiosity that his legs were missing completely, blown off from his waist. This curiosity didn't last long as he first went into shock, and then bled out seconds later.

*

"Shit!"

After the gunshot and explosions, it didn't surprise Willis to hear Hendrick's voice. He yelled out, asking whether Luce was dead.

"Yeah, the fucker's dead. Goddamn it! I wanted him alive!"

Willis got up and saw Hendrick standing twenty feet away, staring at the ground with a look of disappointment and anger. Hendrick looked over at him. "I shot the asshole in the knee. Fuck! Fuck! Fuck! He must've dropped a live grenade into a bag of other grenades," Hendrick said, disgusted.

Willis joined him and saw that Hendrick was staring at the

little that was left of Luce. "We need to find his legs," Willis said. "It will be easier if we have his car keys."

They found his legs about thirty feet from where the rest of his body landed, but there were no car keys in his pockets. Willis went back to his car and got the GPS tracking device, which was still intact and operational. Ten minutes later they found where Luce had hidden his car. His Factory badge was left on the dashboard and his keys were in the ignition. They found three hundred thousand dollars inside the trunk.

"He must've split up the money as a precaution in case he couldn't go back to his car," Willis said. "The rest could be hidden anywhere between here and where he ambushed me." He paused for a moment thinking about it, then halfheartedly added, "We could look for it, but I don't think we'll find it. I also don't think we should stick around after all the gunshots and explosions."

Hendrick looked extremely pissed off with how tightly his jaw muscles were clenched, but he didn't argue, nor did he say a word when Willis split the money fifty fifty between them.

"My car's ruined," Willis said. "I'm going to take this one. Get in. I'll give you a ride back to where you left yours."

"This has to be worth at least ten grand," Hendrick forced out, his voice strained to where it was barely a whisper.

The car couldn't have been worth more than seven thousand, but Willis didn't argue. He counted out five grand to Hendrick then turned to head to the driver's door. He had only taken two steps when he heard a loud thud behind him. When he turned, he saw Hendrick and Bowser struggling on the ground, with the bull terrier's jaws locked on Hendrick's right arm. A 9mm Glock was gripped within Hendrick's right hand, and he was fighting to get that pointed at Bowser. Willis stomped down on Hendrick's hand until he let go of the Glock. Willis then picked up the gun.

"It's your fault my buddies are all dead! It's all your fault!"

A craziness shined in Hendrick's eyes as he stared defiantly at Willis. The accusation was ridiculous. Luce would've done what he did whether or not Willis was part of the robbery. Maybe Hendrick believed what he said, or maybe he was just using it as an excuse to explain trying to double-cross Willis so that he could grab all the money. Whichever it was, Willis didn't care. He ordered Bowser to let go of Hendrick's arm, and after the dog relented and did as he was ordered, Willis shot Hendrick twice in the middle of the forehead. He collected Hendrick's share of the money, wiped the Glock of any prints, then got in Luce's car while letting Bowser jump onto the passenger seat.

He drove back to his wrecked car, and after transferring to Luce's car his duffel bag and other belongings, including a stack of stolen license plates, he wiped his wrecked car clean of prints, changed Luce's license plate with one of his stolen ones, and left Luce's Factory badge lying on what remained of the hit man's corpse.

If anyone had heard the gunfire or explosions, they either didn't call the police or they sent them to the wrong location, because Willis was able to drive down the dirt road and out of Rhode Island without incident.

CHAPTER 19

W HEN WILLIS RETURNED to the house in Winthrop where he was keeping the two Factory supervisors, he first went up to where they had left Elliot Finder, and without saying a word, shot the man dead using his thirty-eight with an attached silencer. He then went down to the basement. Patterson lifted his head from the floor and gave him a hopeful smile.

"Were you able to get back your money?" he asked.

"Not all of it."

Willis used the same thirty-eight to end Patterson's life.

Earlier, when he was driving to Winthrop, he had called Hanley to fill him in on how much money he was able to recover and what had happened to the rest of the crew.

"How many of them did you kill?" Hanley asked.

The question annoyed Willis. "Only Hendrick, and that was because he tried killing me first."

"Why'd he do that?"

Willis ignored the question. "Your cut of ten percent is going to be thirty grand. That's all you need to worry about. And I'll be paying you your other charges. What we talked about before about me buying a new face, I have the money now, so I need to get this done sooner than later. Arrange it with your guy, okay? Sometime next week?"

Hanley told him he'd take care of it and hung up.

It wasn't until Willis was leaving Winthrop that he thought of that cute waitress he had slept with and how he wanted to spend some more days with her. The Factory would be on high alert after what had just happened, but that didn't matter as far as Willis was concerned. He had already gone over Luce's car with a bug detector and there was nothing planted on it. Still, he'd use some of the three hundred grand to buy himself a used car and ditch Luce's, and as long as he was careful they'd have no way of tracking him down, so he wouldn't be putting himself at any additional risk if he stayed in the area for another three or four days. A slight grin twisted up his lips as he thought about Kate's slightly upturned nose and her infectious smile and how comfortable he felt with her. A call from Hanley knocked him out of his daydreaming. Willis felt a deadness settling in his stomach when Hanley demanded to know whether he had butchered that very same waitress.

"What are you talking about?" he demanded.

"What do you think I'm talking about?" Hanley asked, exasperated. "It's all over the news about you butchering this girl. They found her all chopped up in a house you had rented, and they got a drawing of you and that you're traveling with a white bull terrier. Goddamn it, Willis, are you some sort of sicko who gets off on doing shit like that to young girls?"

Willis's mind raced as he thought about what must've

happened. "Kate went back to that house while Luce was watching for me," he said. "It had to be that. Luce did this."

"Luce is the same guy who ripped all of you off? The one you left dead in a swamp in Rhode Island?"

"Yeah."

"Well, it fucks you just the same. The new face can't wait anymore. I got it set up for tomorrow."

"Okay."

Hanley gave him an address in Akron, Ohio that Willis needed to be at by ten o'clock the following morning and what the cost was going to be. "You need to lay low as much as you can. They're out there looking for you. And you need to get rid of that dog. Not just dump it, but put a bullet in its head. Every second you're out there driving with that dog is another second the cops might pull you over. And you can't leave that dog alive to identify you later. These fucking dogs and their sense of smell, you know? It won't matter whether you got a new face or not, the dog will still pick you out of a lineup."

"Alright."

"I mean it, Willis. You owe me over thirty grand. You want to take chances and act stupid, that's your problem, but not until you pay me what you owe me."

"I said alright."

"You'll kill that dog?"

"What did I say?"

Willis disconnected the call. He looked over at Bowser, who was laying on the passenger seat with his nose buried under his paws. Instead of pulling over so he could force the dog out of the car, Willis kept driving. When he could, he got onto the Mass Pike and headed toward New York.

He was taking a chance with toll booth operators, but he was betting that they hadn't seen the news yet, and it appeared his bet paid off when three and a half hours later he double-parked in front of an apartment building in Queens. Three weeks earlier, an eighteen year-girl who lived in the building took care of Bowser for a day, and the two of them seemed nuts about each other. Bowser, on recognizing the building started making excited pig grunt noises while his tail beat rapidly against the seat. Willis took him out of the car and rung the apartment for where the girl lived. When she answered the door, she kept the door open no more than three inches. Bowser became more excited on seeing her than if she had been a hundred and five pounds of bacon. The girl, though, gave Willis a fearful and timid glance, and looked like she was trying to decide whether to scream or slam the door shut.

"Whatever you saw on the news isn't true," Willis said. "I had nothing to do with that woman. But I need to find a new home for this dog. Someone who'll take good care of him. Are you willing?"

She nodded and opened the door enough to let Bowser in, and then pushed it shut.

Willis stood awkwardly for a moment as he considered opening the door so he could tell the girl how much Bowser liked bacon. But he didn't. Instead, he turned and walked down the stoop. He felt a strangeness in his chest as he walked to his car. Whatever crack to his heart Bowser had opened up was scabbing over quickly, and Willis needed some time to adjust to it. Three hours into his drive to Ohio, he realized he felt nothing, and he was okay with it.

I'd like to thank all these generous folks whose kickstarter donations allowed The Interloper to be published:

DIAMOND LEVEL ($50+)

Mary Blumenthal	Jessica Boar	Allen Luedeking
Jeff Michaels	Mike Sockol	Steve Taschereau

GOLD LEVEL ($25+)

Vinod Bhardwaj	Max Cage	Jamey Calhoun
Ron Clinton	Bobby Craig	Benjamin Del Cid
Terrie Farley Moran	Christopher Irvin	Jean-Pierre Jacquet
David Kanell	Kyle Lybeck	Mark Nevins
Danny O'Dell	Patrick Ohl	Derek Pandolfo
Laura Pzena	Carol W. Rachels	David Rachels
John Radosta	Trent A. Reynolds	Clint Salisbury
Scott Schnackenberg	Frank Solensky	Mark Sullivan
Paul Tremblay	Dan VanderKooi	

SILVER LEVEL ($10+)

Jack Green	David Honeybone	Dan Luft

CPSIA information can be obtained
at www.ICGtesting.com
Printed in the USA
LVHW091536130619
621125LV00001B/87/P